Celeste stared at the diagram on the napkin. The reality of the threat conveyed by the word "mutant" became all too clear... Celeste had been talking about an Eke virus mutant like it was just another biological variant. But of course it wasn't...

Her mind was now racing down the path of the worst possible scenario. What if Phillipson was in such a hurry to tie up the Fukuda deal because he planned to release the mutant virus in order to make money from Bazuran?

PRINCIPAL INVESTIGATION
A Scientific Mystery

"A stunning new talent... great insights into how the hottest science is done... B. B. Jordan is a dazzler!"
—Jon A. Jackson, author of *Dead Folks: A Detective Sergeant Mulheisen Novel*

"*Principal Investigation* is a wonderful biomystery. The characters are lively and humorous. The gripping plot, centered on the immune system, rings true. I could not put the book down once I started reading it."
—Lubert Stryer, M.D., Professor of Neurobiology, Stanford Medical School

MORE MYSTERIES FROM THE
BERKLEY PUBLISHING GROUP...

PRINCIPAL
Investigation

B.B. JORDAN

BERKLEY PRIME CRIME, NEW YORK

PRINCIPAL INVESTIGATION

A Berkley Prime Crime Book / published by arrangement with the author

PRINTING HISTORY
Berkley Prime Crime edition / November 1997

All rights reserved.
Copyright © 1997 by B.B. Jordan
This book may not be reproduced in whole or in part,
by mimeograph or any other means, without permission.
For information address: The Berkley Publishing Group, a member of
Penguin Putnam Inc.,
200 Madison Avenue, New York, NY 10016

The Putnam Berkley World Wide Web site address is
http://www.berkley.com

ISBN: 0-425-16090-4

Berkley Prime Crime Books are published
by The Berkley Publishing Group, a member of Penguin Putnam Inc.,
200 Madison Avenue, New York, NY 10016.
The name BERKLEY PRIME CRIME and the BERKLEY PRIME CRIME
design are trademarks belonging to Berkley Publishing Corporation.

PRINTED IN THE UNITED STATES OF AMERICA

10 9 8 7 6 5 4 3 2 1

To my parents

I am deeply grateful to my alliterative and literary support team, including my partner PP, my writing mentor JJ and my agent CC, for their faith, tolerance and tutelage. I would also like to thank N. Rosenstein for her editorial advice, T. Jones, L. Herman and M. Herman for their comments on the first version of the manuscript, M. Lemonick for his comments and introduction to C. Cannell, R. Steinman for his encouragement to begin, the staff at the Teller Wildlife Refuge for a nurturing place to write, and my colleagues from Takeda Chemical Industries Ltd. for introducing me to Japan.

PRINCIPAL
Investigation

Simon Phillipson stared at the tiny luminescent patches infiltrating the slime covering the bottom half of a plastic petri dish. He had a gut feeling that this was it. In two hours, he would know for sure. By then the virus should have invaded and destroyed most of the tissue culture cells that were providing its food and temporary lodging. Then there would be enough virus for DNA analysis, the final confirmation that he had actually succeeded. So far everything had gone like clockwork. From long experience in the laboratory, he knew that when things go like clockwork, it's a sure sign of being on the right track.

If Phillipson's instinct was correct, he had finally achieved success in what he had come to think of as his life's work. This particular series of experiments had been building steadily toward tonight's result for the past six months. But really he had been working for this goal ever since he left his postdoctoral training, almost fifteen years earlier, through the lean times in academia and finally, where he had at last found a home, in biotechnology.

Phillipson couldn't help feeling the rush of the power he would wield when the outcome was certain. He would never have to worry about money again—not grant money, not investment money, not personal expenses. And in the bargain, he would have his revenge. At last he would expunge his humiliating experience in that bloody woman's laboratory, and wipe the slate clean. The timing was brilliant, too. Her reputation was already on shaky ground with the pending government investigation. And once his new results were revealed, proving the Stanley theory wrong, the woman would be dust both scientifically and ethically. This anticipated satisfaction gave him a tremor of pleasure that was very like sexual arousal.

Phillipson carefully replaced the stack of petri dishes on the incubator shelf. He then washed his hands thoroughly with surgical soap and entered his office, through the back entrance from his adjacent personal laboratory. Walking directly to the liquor cabinet, he poured himself a celebratory shot of Macallan.

Savoring the glow from his first sip, Phillipson sat down on the leather sofabed and looked about him with satisfaction at the expensive office decor. His assessing eye rested on one of the native Brazilian woodcuts that had inspired the earth tone color scheme. The raw sexual energy of the images never failed to excite him. Their design was sufficiently geometric that the viewer had to look carefully to interpret what was depicted. Phillipson derived considerable amusement from watching a visitor suddenly realize what the figures in the woodcut were doing and react in embarrassment.

Stimulated by contemplation of the woodcut and the feeling of sexual anticipation he had experienced in the laboratory, Phillipson felt the need for some kind of release. During the day, he would have arranged for some "confidential consultation" with one of his usual squeezes among the female employees. But he knew no one was around. He had already checked the night log. Well, no one was around but that insipid-looking security guard.

It had annoyed Phillipson, when he signed in, that his valuable trade secrets were under the protection of a moonlighting university student. But, short of female companionship, maybe he could coax some intellectual conversation from the chap and at least pass the time while the virus incubated. Let him earn his salary. He picked up the bottle of Macallan and a second glass and headed downstairs for the guard desk.

The student didn't even look up as Phillipson approached the reception desk. Phillipson noticed with distaste that this so-called security guard was not only not in uniform, but also it looked like he had slept in his clothes. The desk was covered with library books, bristling with yellow Post-Its. Totally absorbed, the student was picking at a blemish among his scraggly facial hairs. With the other hand he was highlighting an open paperback book with a yellow marker pen.

Phillipson slammed the whiskey bottle down on the desk. The student jumped, and the blemish became a glistening spot.

"What if I were an intruder, young man?" asked Phillipson.

"You couldn't be," said the student. "Uh, sir," he added uneasily. "I can see if anyone comes in." The student gestured to the front entrance.

"Did it ever occur to you that an intruder might not waltz through the front entrance?" asked Phillipson.

"Well, there isn't any other way to get in after hours," whined the student.

"I suppose that's true, young man, if one were an intruder relying on legal means for gaining entry." Phillipson found this naïveté incredible. "Do you have any idea what goes on here?" he asked.

"Uh, no, sir. Not me. I'm an English major. Deconstructionist analysis of Shakespeare." The student indicated the scholarly mess spread out in front of him.

"And where do you carry out these literary pursuits?"

"On the Farm, sir. Stanford."

"Well, my Shakespearean scholar, join me in a little drink and I'll tell you about an institution of higher learning that far more deserves to be called the Farm." Phillipson poured two half tumblers of the Macallan and shoved one toward the student. Then he pulled over one of the lobby chairs. Sitting down with a sigh, Phillipson took a deep gulp from his own tumbler before he began. "My first and last academic job was at a place called Alberta College. Ever hear of it?"

"Uh, no, sir," said the student. "But not many places are into the kind of approach I'm taking to old Will, here."

"Don't try to flatter me," said Phillipson. "There's no reason anyone should ever have heard of Alberta College. It's basically a finishing school for the offspring of Canadian oil magnates and cattle barons. There wasn't a single student there who wouldn't rather have been shagging a sheep. In fact, I should never have heard of the place either, if I hadn't been screwed royally by an equally backward institution."

"Sir?" asked the student.

"Harvard," said Phillipson. "Harvard University. You'd think the professors at Harvard would know when a good opportunity was staring them in the face. But evidently not. Not my experience at all.''

''Harvard?'' said the student, genuinely puzzled. ''I thought you were British.''

''Very clever. Must be the accent,'' smirked Phillipson. ''Of course I'm British. Well, British-born, that is. Grew up in Brazil. Diplomatic family and all that. Spent a lot of time in the Amazon, one way or another. Returned to Oxford, of course. Graduate and postgraduate.''

''Neat,'' said the student.

''Well, it was rather,'' said Phillipson. He refilled his empty whiskey glass. The student had barely touched his. ''I was the first person to do a chemical analysis of toxins used by the Amazonian shamans. Those chaps really know what they're working with—light-years ahead of Western medicine. Got my D.Phil.—Ph.D. to you—on the strength of that work. Then went to Harvard to test whether the toxins might have antiviral medicinal properties.''

The student was trying to digest what Phillipson was saying so he could make an intelligent comment. In his limited experience, scientists were always getting excited about some totally obscure thing, and frankly it bored him. But the unnerving manner of this scientist made him feign interest. On the surface Phillipson looked like a British aristocrat. The student supposed that most women would find him attractive, perhaps even handsome. There was something, though—perhaps his prematurely gray hair or the hardness of his eyes—that produced an unpleasant chill.

Phillipson continued, ''Jane Stanley's lab at Harvard Med was supposed to be the best virology lab in the world, the perfect place for testing my brilliant idea. What a disappointment. Not only was the lab full of incompetents, but even she couldn't see success when it was staring her in the face. Well, she'll regret it now."

The student looked completely lost.

"You see," said Phillipson, "something that's poisonous to humans in a high dose might be more poisonous to viruses at a low, so-called sublethal dose, that doesn't have a bad effect on humans. In fact, I've just proven it. And that means, of course, that Virotox is going to make a fortune."

"I'm not sure I like the idea of making money off medicine that people need," ventured the student.

"Young man, you know nothing," said Phillipson. "I dedicated my first academic job to the single purpose of demonstrating the antiviral effects of the toxin Bazuran. When I wasn't lecturing to an unappreciative group of cowhands and well-diggers, I was slaving night and day in the laboratory, supported only by contract work for the Alberta Oil Company. None of the public funding agencies I tried— and believe me, I tried—supported the project. A combination of bad-mouthing from the Harvard group and working in a Canadian backwater made me untouchable. Would that make you philanthropic?"

"No, I guess not," said the student.

"No, you bloody well wouldn't be. I wasted some of the most creative years of my life in slavery to the academic research system, trying to squeeze money from intellectual snobs. Now I'm going to do research my way and fund it myself."

The student's discomfort grew. "Uh, which virus can you cure?"

"It's called Eke virus. Happen to listen to the evening news?"

"Yeah, isn't that the one where they just had to quarantine a whole village in Brazil?"

"That's right."

"I thought there was already a drug that cures that virus."

"Correct," said Phillipson. "There's a drug that cures the normal form, but what if the virus mutates to become resistant to the drug? Then you need a second drug. Heard of mutation, have you?"

"I've seen the film *Outbreak*. You know, where the virus mutates really fast to a worse form," said the student. "I went 'specially 'cause of my job here."

"Well, let me put it this way. I've developed an insurance drug that will eradicate the virus even if it mutates and becomes resistant to the one that's currently used to control infection."

"Well, I guess it's a good thing you already found a cure, in case mutation happens," said the student.

"Oh, it will certainly happen. You've seen *Outbreak*," said Phillipson with assurance. "Now you'll appreciate having worked here." He stood and picked up his glass and the bottle of whiskey. "Enjoy the rest of your Macallan. I've got to get back to my experiment."

Though an English scholar is not necessarily a grammarian, the student thought he detected a past participle and wondered if he had just been fired.

Back in the laboratory, Phillipson assembled the materials he would need for analysis of the virus DNA. His undergraduate practice of returning to the laboratory after the pubs closed had trained him well, and he worked comfortably even after several drinks. He was actually better at routine laboratory manipulations that would otherwise have made him impatient. Exactly two hours after he had shut the virus cultures in the incubator, he removed them for inspection. They had multiplied to the necessary numbers, on schedule, possibly slightly faster than anticipated. This accelerated growth rate was precisely what Phillipson had been working toward. Now it was just a matter of confirming that it was the mutant virus that was exhibiting these growth properties. Phillipson was completely confident that analysis of the virus DNA would reveal his success. He smiled to himself as he opened the lid of the petri dish on the top of the stack of cultures and got to work.

ONE

Hot Water

Mongolian deities were not usually the focus of Celeste Braun's attention. But she was having trouble focusing her attention on anything at this point in the ten-hour flight to Japan. Celeste looked more closely at the colorful tapestry reproduced in the DeYoung Museum catalog. In the center was a faceless but clearly female figure astride a horselike beast. Although not entirely enlightening, the caption enhanced the impact of the image. ''Palden Lhamo is the only woman among the Eight Guardians of the Law. Her face is traditionally invisible, but she is recognizable by her attributes. The eye on the haunch of the mule, which bears her across the sea of blood, is a mark from an arrow shot by Lhamo's husband from a former life. The skin bag, hanging from the mule's trappings, is full of diseases for germ warfare against enemies of religion. The germs in the bag are the excess ones left over from the time when Lhamo tried, out of compassion, to swallow the world's diseases.''

No wonder the image appealed to Celeste. Here was a strong female deity, one who had survived male indignities and wielded the power of the microbial world, yet had compassion. Perhaps this was what a world panicked by AIDS and the Ebola virus needed.

Celeste was procrastinating. Looking through the catalog from the Mongolian art exhibition was a break from working on a grant proposal. This was her third trip to Japan, and the novelty of crossing the Pacific had long since paled. At least, Celeste mused, she hadn't accepted the assistant professor position at Harvard. The trip from Boston would have been five hours longer. In fact, her decision to join the faculty at Bay Area University instead, had generally proved to be a good one, though it had been agonizing to make. Jane Stanley, her Ph.D. adviser, had really wanted her to return to the department as a colleague. And her parents, suspicious of anywhere west of Philadelphia, couldn't believe she would give up the prestige of being a Harvard professor. But the molecular biology faculty that had put BAU on the map had a stronger pull for Celeste. And besides, BAU had only recently left the state university system to become private, so tenure decisions would be less capricious than in the notorious Harvard environment.

Anyway, the fact that Celeste was physically separated from Jane hadn't made much difference. Jane was still the person to whom Celeste turned for professional advice, and Celeste was still Jane's finger on the pulse of the younger scientific world. And this new Japan connection for Celeste had unexpectedly strengthened the link between them.

Two years earlier, Fukuda Pharmaceuticals had sponsored Celeste's lecture about her work on virus assembly at a conference in Hokkaido. She would never forget the look of dismay when they first met her. Later, when she got to know Toshimi better, he confirmed that they had been expecting a man. Evidently the famous elephant couple Babar and Celeste were not part of the literature for Japanese children. The initial shock was soon overcome when Toshimi, now vice president for all of Fukuda's research operations, discovered the coincidence of their both having spent time in Jane's lab. However, Celeste attributed the permanent cementing of her bond with Toshimi to the hot springs outing that also took place on that maiden voyage.

Celeste had been completely unaware of the protocol of Japanese hospitality and caused quite a stir when she mentioned to one of her hosts that she planned to take the train to visit the hot springs at Noboribetsu Onsen during the "free" afternoon. The obligatory excursion party that immediately got organized filled two cars with all the necessary participants. Upon arrival they discovered that male and female nude bathing at the hot springs was barely segregated in adjacent, fully exposed pools. The way Toshimi described it after inspecting the facilities was, "Entrance separate. Baths not. Towels very, very small!" After some embarrassed hesitation, the group decided instead to hike around the sulphur springs. As they left the entrance to the bathhouse, Toshimi promised, "Next time we take bath together." Now this threat of further intimacy had become an established joke between them. Toshimi's parting words to Celeste were always the same. "Next time we take bath together." She looked forward to seeing him again.

Celeste closed the museum catalog and hit the "return" button on her Powerbook to continue work on the grant proposal. Before she could even think about tenure, she needed to keep her laboratory funding solvent. She moved the cursor to check that she had remembered to set up the "header" for the top of each page of the grant application. Outlined in the rectangular box that appeared were the words "Principal Investigator: Celeste Braun, Ph.D." It had often occurred to Celeste that the "P.I." title sounded far more romantic and exciting than merely the designation for the head of a research project funded by the National Institutes of Health.

"Experimental Design and Methods," she typed. This was the last section, and would be the most carefully scrutinized by the review committee.

The computer flashed a "low power" warning.

"Damn," said Celeste out loud. Having exhausted the last of her spare batteries, it was either video entertainment or catching up on paperwork. She had long since finished the mystery novel she'd brought aboard. Doubtfully, Celeste glanced up at the videoscreen.

Figures dressed in yellow space suits were rushing around in blurry half darkness. These biohazard outfits were now a familiar sight, thanks to *The Hot Zone* and associated media hype on emerging viruses. Celeste assumed the video was yet another fictionalized version of these thinly disguised horror stories and, with irritation, felt driven to pull out the work from her briefcase. She was fed up by this fascination with deadly disease. There was never any rational discussion of what it takes for an epidemic to flourish, and besides, there was always the fairly blatant implication that science was falling short. Scientists were generally portrayed as fooling around with obscure research and not really concentrating on developing cures. No one ever pointed out that if we didn't have fundamental knowledge of biological systems, we couldn't even begin to control them.

Celeste determinedly opened the folder on the top of the

pile in front of her, but her eyes were unavoidably drawn to the screen above. The jerky cinematography invaded the door of a mud hut and made its way to a cot in the dark interior, where the body of an emaciated child lay. The camera lingered on this sight, displaying the oozing sores of his disease in uncompromising detail. Celeste was disgusted. Abruptly the image in the hut disappeared and was replaced by a scientific diagram next to a photograph taken from an electron microscope, with the label "EKE VIRUS" underneath. And suddenly Celeste realized that this was no fictional film, but the actual news.

She fumbled hurriedly in the seat pocket in front of her to retrieve the headphones, but before she could plug them in, the screen was filled with the title of the next media byte, "*Spotlight on Health.*" The title faded to a woman sitting at a newscaster's desk in a sterile broadcasting room, with two large screens located strategically on either side of her.

"Good afternoon, and welcome to *Spotlight on Health.* I'm Diane DiMaggio, and today we're going to discuss the issues surrounding yesterday's frightening outbreak of Eke virus in Bahia, Brazil." To Celeste's eye, the look of concern on Ms. DiMaggio's face was about as authentic as the texture and color of her stiff blond hair. "We'll first be speaking with Dr. Jane Stanley, professor of microbiology at Harvard Medical School. Dr. Stanley's laboratory developed the only known treatment for Eke virus. Then we have a surprise special guest from Washington, to discuss some of the national and international implications."

Oh, my, thought Celeste. This must be what the phone message from Jane was about. Celeste had listened to her phone messages too late last night to return them. This morning she had been so busy getting ready to leave that she decided to wait to call Jane until after she arrived in Japan.

In front of her, Jane's familiar face had materialized on the screen to the left of Diane DiMaggio's desk.

"Good afternoon, Dr. Stanley. Thank you for joining us from the Boston studio."

"Good afternoon, Diane. I'm glad to be back on your program."

Diane DiMaggio smiled politely. She had a predatory look on her face.

"We've just heard about the current outbreak of Eke virus near Bahia, on the northeastern coast of Brazil. Could you tell us why it's so critical for the World Health Organization to get there as soon as possible?"

"Well, first of all, Diane, only one in twenty children who are infected with Eke virus survives. Eke virus is only marginally less lethal in adults. The most serious concern, of course, is that the virus is highly contagious and is spread rapidly through airborne saliva. If it were to escape to the urban population, an epidemic would result."

"I understand that outbreaks of Eke virus can be completely controlled by the drug Protex, so are now extremely rare. If Protex is such a good drug, why hasn't Eke virus been entirely wiped out—like, say, the eradication of smallpox?"

"Well, Protex doesn't prevent Eke virus infection. However, once someone is infected, Protex can stop multiplication of the virus and consequently prevent transmission. If Protex is given soon enough, immunity to the virus will develop and the infected person recovers. The problem is that Eke virus, like many viruses, exists in another animal host. In this case, pigs can harbor the virus as a chronic low-grade infection. If humans eat the undercooked meat of an infected pig, Eke virus enters the human system, where it grows more rapidly and becomes lethal.''

''Can you tell us how the WHO will get the disease under control?''

''Once Protex is taken by everyone in the village, the infection will cease to spread and those in the early stages of infection will recover. As long as all the infected pigs are slaughtered and none of the infected villagers leaves the quarantined area, an epidemic can be prevented.''

''Your laboratory developed Protex when you were at the National Institutes of Health. Could you tell us something about the history of the drug?''

''The initial experiments in my lab were carried out in 1962 by Dr. Toshimi Matsumoto, when he was a visiting fellow. When he returned to Japan, he and I collaborated on development of the drug in its final form. It was a joint project between commercial laboratories at Health, Inc., in the United States and Fukuda Pharmaceuticals in Japan, where Dr. Matsumoto is now vice president for research.''

''But am I correct in saying that Protex is now the exclusive product of Fukuda Pharmaceuticals?''

''Yes, that is correct. Once the domestic pig population in the United States was completely cured of Eke virus and outbreaks were only confined to the Third World, Health, Inc., was no longer interested in marketing Protex and sold out to Fukuda.''

''Didn't the fact that Protex was developed with U.S. government funding have any influence or restriction over its commercial rights?''

''Not insofar as we could interest any United States companies to continue to produce it. In fact, we are fortunate that Fukuda has maintained an interest in producing Protex because it's still needed when Eke virus occasionally reinfects the human population, as we have seen in Bahia. At the time Health, Inc., sold out, we worked many hours with the United States Office of Technology Transfer to sort out the details of the commercial rights to Protex. Although that was at least twenty-five years ago now, some of the profits still go back into funds allocated to the National Institutes of Health.''

''Thank you for your point of view, Dr. Stanley,'' said Diane DiMaggio, emphasizing the word ''your.'' She paused for dramatic effect. ''I'm sure our viewers will not be surprised to hear that the congressional Committee on Scientific Integrity has uncovered another side to this Protex story. The chair of that committee, Senator Teresita Jiminez, has graciously taken time out of her busy schedule to join us from our Washington studio to discuss their findings.''

An attractive Hispanic woman in her late thirties appeared on the screen to the right of Diane DiMaggio's desk. Her elegant femininity made Jane, with her short-cropped gray hair and wire-rim glasses, look ferociously schoolmarmish. Until that moment Celeste had been impressed by the air of confident authority that Jane had exuded. Now she wished Jane looked a little softer, like she really was underneath.

''Good afternoon, Senator,'' said Diane DiMaggio. ''Thank you for joining us and for choosing *Spotlight on Health* to make your disclosure.''

''Good afternoon, Diane,'' and with a nod in the direction of Jane's screen, ''Dr. Stanley.''

Celeste knew this woman Jiminez was trouble. Her election had been an ironic consequence of the ''Clarence Thomas backlash'' a few years earlier. In spite of her ultraconservatism, she narrowly defeated the male Democratic incumbent, taking advantage of a sexual harassment accusation from his former aide, which had, in fact, been withdrawn. The rapacious look on Diane DiMaggio's face heightened Celeste's worry. Jane looked visibly tense.

The senator continued, "What I am about to say will certainly not be news to Dr. Stanley, and I regret that the case has proceeded to the point where we are obliged to bring it to the public arena."

"Perhaps you could fill in some background on the CSI and your goals for our viewers," Diane prompted.

"Oh, excuse me, Diane. The makeup crew distracted me and I missed how much introduction you had given." After a brief girlish giggle, the senator continued with a now-it's-time-to-be-serious-even-though-I'm-a-woman tone of voice. "The Committee on Scientific Integrity has been investigating the financial returns of a number of so-called miracle drugs that were discovered during the early sixties, through a United States government-sponsored drug development program. The only one of these drugs that still turns a profit is the drug Protex. When we looked into it, we found that most of this profit was actually going to the Japanese and that the American public was getting almost nothing, in spite of the fact that we invested in its development. We have therefore initiated a full-scale investigation into the legitimacy of the proceedings that occurred at the time of technology transfer."

The tension in Jane's face looked like it was about to erupt into fury as Diane DiMaggio asked, "Would you like to respond to this accusation, Dr. Stanley?"

"Ms. DiMaggio," said Jane, "I would like to point out that I am not being accused of anything at present. You have simply been told by the senator that the CSI is initiating an investigation into the technology transfer procedures that were followed when Protex was first commercialized. As far as I'm concerned, this investigation is a waste of taxpayers' money. I've already mentioned that there could have been no violation of the rules set out by the Office of Technology Transfer, as they worked closely with us throughout the transfer process.''

"But Dr. Stanley,'' said Ms. DiMaggio, "you did tell us a few minutes ago that the only profits from Protex that come back to this country are in the form of nominal research funds to the NIH. Perhaps the senator could give us some idea of those figures.''

"According to our sources at the CSI, Diane, the amount of money coming back to the United States is only a few percent of the profit that Fukuda Pharmaceuticals makes from selling Protex. Surely for their tax contributions to government-funded research programs the American public deserves more than a few hundred thousand dollars into the pockets of scientists.''

"As I have explained to you in private, Senator, and am now being forced unexpectedly to explain in public,'' began Jane, "there are a number of issues here that you and the CSI are not considering in perspective. . . .''

"Thank you, Dr. Stanley,'' said Diane DiMaggio. "I think you have already explained your point of view, and we certainly wish you luck at the hearings. As the senator's time has been limited, I would like to give her the last word before we wind up the program.''

"Thank you, Diane,'' said the senator. "I think I have explained the essence of the investigation. We on the CSI feel that it is high time that those who receive government money for research are made accountable to the government. I sincerely thank you for bringing our mission to the attention of the viewers of *Spotlight on Health*.''

"Thank you, Senator, and Dr. Stanley, for joining us. It is unfortunate for all of us that these matters of life and death have come down to commercial disputes. We can only hope that the WHO gets to Bahia in time to prevent major disaster in the form of an Eke virus epidemic. This is Diane DiMaggio, signing off for *Spotlight on Health*."

The previous afternoon, when the show was recorded live, Diane DiMaggio had to wait a few seconds with a neutral smile frozen in place before the "On the Air" light switched off. Then she scooted her chair back from the newscaster's desk with a self-congratulatory whoop. Who says you couldn't make your career at Washington parties anymore? Just last week she had met that gorgeous man. What was his name? Phil or something, and he had introduced her to Senator Jiminez. It was all smooth sailing from there. And now her reputation would be up there with Mac-Neil-Lehrer. She'd love to thank him in person, and hoped he'd get in touch like he promised, next time he was in New York.

If Celeste had been in the *Spotlight on Health* studio, she would probably now be in jail for assault. As it was, she was confined by her seat belt to fume helplessly.

Celeste could not make any sense out of what she had just seen. It certainly wasn't Jane's fault if the American private sector had lost interest in Protex once it was only needed in the Third World. Besides, Jane Stanley was the least likely person to be guilty of a lapse in scientific integrity. At Harvard, Jane had established the very first committee for overseeing conflicts of interest between industrial consulting by faculty and the academic training program. She was also particularly strict in her own lab. Just before Celeste joined her group, Jane had asked someone to leave under suspicion of fraud, a painful incident that no one ever discussed. Celeste wondered what motivation the Committee on Scientific Integrity had for the attack on Jane Stanley. Perhaps it was just that she was an educated and outspoken liberal woman.

Celeste's righteous indignation shortly gave way to a wave of guilt. Jane must have kept the CSI business from her because she had believed in her own integrity and didn't think the investigation would go anywhere. For a woman who had overcome so many social prejudices, Jane still, amazingly, expected people to behave rationally. Celeste wished she had given her more moral support recently. She should have been calling Jane regularly since the memorial service for Roger six months ago. Jane had been philosophical about the death of her former mentor and devoted husband, but she had undoubtedly been tremendously lonely. And her loneliness must have been accentuated by this unanticipated battle so late in her career.

In Celeste's eyes, Jane and Roger had been a model professional couple. He had encouraged Jane to abandon their joint medical practice and pursue a career in academic research, unheard of for a woman at the time. Jane had in turn established a valuable link between Roger's clinical expertise in tropical medicine and the diagnostic and therapeutic applications of molecular biology. Their mutual professional respect enabled them to maintain a loving and supportive relationship throughout their careers. Celeste had admired their relationship and, if the truth be told, rather envied them since she had yet to experience anything similar. In her exhaustion and frustration, Celeste's thoughts began to drift to some of her own less-than-satisfactory experiences. Finally, she fell into an uneasy doze that was eventually broken by the flashing of the seatbelt sign and announcements in preparation for landing at Narita International Airport.

TWO

Mature Student

The afternoon that Celeste left for Japan, the landscaping job at General Roberts' home in Pacific Heights was finally finished. John Macmillan, known as Mac to his friends and employers, wiped the sweat from his face and resettled his baseball cap on his head. He had learned the value of a visored hat during his days in Vietnam. Although the jungle experience was almost twenty-five years behind him, it was never far from his conscious thoughts and often resurfaced, particularly on hot days. Fortunately, in San Francisco such days were rare. Looking across the city, Mac could see that the BAU hospital complex was already shrouded in a thick blanket of fog. Within an hour, the plants he had just bedded would likewise be bathed in cloud, and his work for General Roberts would be complete.

The only person who would be disappointed was Elaine Roberts, the latest in a long string of frustrated matrons to whom Mac provided additional services besides gardening.

By now, the pattern was totally predictable. Within the first day or two after starting a job, Mac would be invited indoors for a glass of iced tea or a cold beer. This was usually late in the afternoon, long after the woman of the house had helped herself from the liquor cabinet but long before the workaholic husband might appear. It would start with a polite discussion of the garden, continue with a polite discovery of Mac's divorce, usually prefaced by the question of whether he had kids, proceed with a sometimes tearful description of her own business-induced "widowhood," and would end in the sack. Mac knew he was good value in bed. He had been well trained by his ex-wife, Martha. Martha had little tolerance for and certainly derived no pleasure from what she called "wham-bam" sex.

A number of San Francisco society women faced life with renewed self-confidence after their gardens had been landscaped. Mac, for the most part, felt he was making a useful contribution to the city's subculture. The tricky aspect, of course, was establishing emotional independence by the end of a job. A few years earlier, after trouble with a particularly clinging consul's wife, Mac had developed a fairly effective extrication strategy based on Martha's advice. It was time to apply it to Mrs. Roberts.

Mac gathered up the last few gardening implements and added them to the pile in the back of his pickup. As an afterthought, he removed his cap and tossed it onto the pile. He wasn't sure if he was stalling for time or preparing to make a quick getaway. Checking his reflection in the passenger-side window, Mac ran his fingers through his hair and smoothed his mustache. Then he squared his shoulders and walked toward the house.

Mrs. Roberts answered the door. She was wearing a loose, ivory silk top over brown velour leggings. From the undulation underneath, it was obvious she had left off her bra. Mac never failed to be impressed by the luscious shapes of these fiftysomething women. He had seen the fashion magazines and mailings from beauty spas that were piled high on his lovers' bedside tables and understood that they demanded a heavy financial investment. But as far as he was concerned, it was worth every penny, or more likely, every hundred-dollar bill.

"Oh, Mac! I wasn't sure it was you," said Mrs. Roberts.

"Well," said Mac, raising his eyebrows appreciatively, "I'd like to know who you *were* expecting."

"Oh, you know what I mean, you tease. You don't normally ring the bell."

Mac looked serious. It was this lost-youth look that captured most of his women in the first place. "Listen, Elaine. I'm here to deliver the bill. I mean, I've finished the garden." He blushed as he realized the implication.

"I knew it would happen eventually," she said, her voice harder than when she had greeted him. "I just wasn't quite ready for it today." She gestured at her ripe, inviting body.

"Oh, Elaine," said Mac. He stepped across the threshold and drew her toward him. He gently caressed her, enjoying the texture of the cool silk and the soft velour around her hips, which felt like balm to his rough gardener's hands.

"You've made me wet just by touching me," she said into his embrace. "What will I do without you?"

"I'll tell you exactly what you'll do, ma'am," said Mac. He pulled her into the huge living room and sat down on the gold brocade sofa, drawing her onto his lap. The feel of her body on his made it difficult to control his own body parts, but he had a lecture to give.

"First of all, you'll stop messing around with guys like me and pick on someone more classy."

"I don't 'mess around with guys.' Just with one guy. You. And you seem fine to me."

"Look, Elaine. I may be fine in bed, but I'm not fine for you anywhere else. I don't know how to play golf, and I sure don't know which fork to use."

"I don't care about stuff like that," she said with a pout.

"But you do," said Mac. "I'd embarrass you in a flash, and then you'd get bored with me. Besides, all guys are the same once they get their pants off."

"No, they're not. That's the whole point."

"Well, they are really. It might just take a little instructing. I'll show you what I mean. First, let's think of some guy you always see at parties that you wish you could—"

"Fuck."

"Okay, fuck."

"All right. How about my husband?"

"Well, he'll do," said Mac a little dubiously. "But let's practice on someone else."

"Okay, Harvey Moss."

"You didn't have to think long about that."

"Hey, no fair."

"Now what does Mr. Moss do?"

"He's our investment adviser."

"Okay. So get this Moss guy to come over for some private counseling. Tell him you want to do some investing on the side. Make some money to buy a present for your husband, or something. Then all you have to do is wear that getup and the rest'll be a piece of cake."

"Well, what if he doesn't get it? Or worse, what if he jumps on me and just sticks it in?"

"Don't you realize you can call the shots? Men love to be bossed around in bed. Ask him to rub a crick in your back or something. Then take his hand and put it on your breast.''

''Like this?''

''Mmmm. Like that.'' Mac could feel her nipple harden through the silk. ''Then tell him that it feels good. Only if it does, of course.''

''It does. Then what?''

''Use your imagination, woman. Talk him through the moves. Before you know it, he'll be eating out of your hand or eating out something else, I dare say.''

''Mac, you're terrible,'' she said with a smile.

Two hours later Mac had convinced Mrs. Roberts that she could turn every straight man in the Portola Heights golf club into a Valentino. He also managed to convince her that she might even get her husband to perform. As he zipped up his jeans, he said, ''Now, I'll expect a full report.''

''I'm not sure I'll want to tell my bedroom secrets to you anymore. After all, I'm going have my pick of lovers.'' She thought she was kidding, but Mac knew she was right.

One more charity case for San Francisco high society, thought Mac as he climbed into his pickup. He checked his watch. Perfect timing. At the bottom of the hill he turned left toward Whitman Junior High School.

He had just under two hours to collect his son from soccer practice, get him over to Martha's place, and then get back to his own place to shower before the evening lecture at BAU. As a part-time student at Golden Gate Technical College, Mac was entitled to take one course for credit at BAU. At the end of this quarter Mac would finally graduate with a B.S. in Biological Sciences. He had been working on the degree part-time for seven years, since Martha moved out.

Mac's interest in the biology of the immune system developed while he was in the army, but it took him eleven years after his return from Vietnam to do anything about it. The first two years were spent suffering through physical therapy to regain function of the lacerated leg that earned him his Purple Heart. Then Martha returned from her tour of duty and they tried to establish a civilian life together. They had met in Oakland Hospital in the military medical unit and were married just before their posting to the Far East.

The first years of married life were happy enough. Mac was busy setting up a San Francisco branch of his father's South Bay nursery business, one that specialized in "personalized garden design and implementation." The contacts with the San Francisco elite had come naturally, following several jobs for military brass obtained through the veterans' network. Martha seemed content to take up her former nursing duties at Oakland Hospital. It wasn't until a year after Mac, Jr., was born that the irresistible Julia Clayton was transferred to Oakland and Martha began to realize she was denying her true nature. In Vietnam, Martha and Julia had been inseparable, first as a nursing team, then as companions, and finally as lovers. When Mac, Jr., was five years old, his parents finally admitted their unsuitability, and Mac, Sr., began his services to the matrons of San Francisco. The same year Mac's head nurseryman died of AIDS. It was time then, Mac thought, to do something about immunology, and he enrolled in the part-time bachelor's degree program at Golden Gate Tech.

The breakup of the marriage had no obvious adverse effects on Mac, Jr. Though he occasionally felt persecuted by having two mothers and a father, he realized that many of his friends had as many as four parents, so he was marginally better off. This afternoon he was waiting in gym shorts and a sweatshirt on the palatial main steps of the junior high school. The fog had now reached that part of the city and swirled around the group of similarly dressed boys clustered on the steps. Their bare legs made them look vulnerable, not like the swift and powerful soccer players they imagined themselves to be. Mac, Jr., and his friends were on the cusp of adolescence, the age just before little boys become nasty. They were still proud of their parents and embraced life with enthusiasm. Mac, Jr., was particularly proud of his dad's vintage pickup truck and his military record.

On the opposite side of the school steps was a group of slightly older students, dressed in black. The girls were wearing purple lipstick and the boys were impaled with earrings in various orifices. The hair of both sexes was shaved off the sides of their heads. All of them were smoking cigarettes. They looked up furtively as Mac's truck pulled in and then returned to their business. He didn't look like anyone who would be so uncool as to report them. Mac wondered if his son would be among that group in a couple of years. He himself had participated in the equivalent rebellion, growing his hair down below his shoulders and wearing bell-bottomed jeans.

Mac, Jr., and a companion detached themselves from the rest of the team and came down the steps gingerly. Each had a backpack slung over one shoulder and was holding a specimen jar that sloshed with liquid.

"Hi, guys," said Mac as he leaned over from the driver's seat to open the passenger door. "What've you got there?"

"I've got the axolotl," said Mac, Jr., and with increased reverence, "Eric's got the fetal deer. We're supposed to compare and contrast their physiog-nomy. Can Eric come to Martha's with me?''

''Sure,'' said Mac, Sr., ''but it's phys-ion-omy. The *g* is silent.''

''Not the way Miss Fitch says it.''

''Well, you look it up in the dictionary at Martha's.''

After a lot of fussing and juggling of specimen jars, Mac, Jr., and Eric finally settled down on the front seat of the pickup. Mac, Jr., immediately turned on the radio full blast, drowning out further conversation with rap music until they reached Martha and Julia's house on Russian Hill.

Martha had just finished baking a batch of oatmeal raisin cookies, and the house smelled wonderful. The boys unloaded their treasures from the truck and then systematically raided the kitchen. Their flurry of activity finally swept up the stairs to Mac, Jr.'s, bedroom, leaving a peaceful vacuum behind them. Once Mac and Martha heard the bedroom door shut, they looked at each other with raised eyebrows.

''This PSE program is really good for the city schools,'' said Mac.

''The what?''

''Partnership in Science Education. Some of the grad students from BAU volunteer to organize science projects for the kids in the public schools.''

''Mmm,'' said Martha. She seemed distracted.

''Got any hints on the new orders?'' Mac asked her.

''No. That's what's bothering me. You must have read my mind. These top-secret projects are a pain in the butt. We've no hint of when we have to go or for how long they'll need us, if we do have to go. I simply don't like the idea of having to pick up and move to Texas at the drop of a hat.''

"Well," said Mac, "that's military life."

"Yeah, I s'pose it is," Martha said with a sigh. "The scuttlebutt is that the project could be a vaccination trial at the LBJ hospital. Julia overheard the sergeant talking on the phone a couple of days ago. That might involve a pretty serious time commitment. I'll let you know the second I get a glimmer of real information. You know that."

This last remark was said with an intimacy that belied the fact they hadn't been living together for seven years. They were still closer than many conventionally married couples.

"Well, I've gotta get over to the U," said Mac. "Don't forget Mac, Jr.'s, allergy shots are on Saturday. I can take him if you like. I need to use the library near the clinic this weekend."

"Great. If you can take him on Saturday, I'll ask Julia to pick him up from soccer practice tomorrow, before the night shift."

"Deal," said Mac. "Look, don't worry too much about moving. It'll be settled soon enough."

"I know. But I feel bad that you won't commit yourself to a graduate program until you know where I'm gonna be."

"Look, we decided already that we wouldn't separate completely until Mac, Jr., graduates from high school. As far as Ph.D. programs go, there's probably not that much difference between here and Texas. Both have enough immunology and virology that I can get the training I want to work on AIDS vaccines. And both programs offer financial support. It really doesn't matter to me."

"Must you be so understanding, Mac?" asked Martha with a teasing smile, but evidently relieved.

"That's what they all say." He pecked her lightly on the cheek as he left.

In the pickup Mac tuned the radio back to the classical music station. He started to think about his upcoming class. Having taken all the microbiology and immunology courses offered at Tech, he had qualified for Microbiology 214, the advanced virology course at BAU. Apparently there was a guest lecturer standing in for Dr. Braun tonight. Well, it would be kind of a relief from the pressure of continually trying to make a good impression. Dr. Braun had been far from receptive when he asked whether he could register for the course. She had become slightly less frosty when Mac told her about his 4.0 average at Tech and that he had been admitted to the BAU Ph.D. program for the fall, but he still felt he had to prove himself. The challenge was heightened by the fact that he found Dr. Braun attractive in an academic sort of way. But she was far too valuable to him as a potential referee for a recommendation to a good laboratory. So he stifled his more basic urges and studied hard to achieve a more intellectual goal.

THREE

Consultant's Contract

Celeste gave up trying to sleep. She looked at the digital clock next to the bed. It was twenty past six in the morning. More than an hour better than yesterday, when she was wide awake at five. At least yesterday's jet lag had worked to Celeste's advantage. She'd finally been awake at a convenient time to phone Jane and find out how she was doing.

Celeste was touched by Jane's evident relief in hearing from her, but it was a depressing conversation. Jane sounded tired and discouraged. She confided that she was seriously considering the early retirement option that Harvard had recently offered their senior faculty. Celeste, who had assumed that Jane's laboratory would exist as long as Jane did, urged her not to make a rash decision. What would she do if she gave up science? Surely this CSI business would be straightened out and blow over. But Jane had not been so sure. Celeste was distressed thinking about it.

She got out of bed and opened the curtains. It was a beautifully clear day. In the distance, beyond the high-rise buildings of Sapporo, Celeste could see the bare blue peak of the winter Olympics ski run, festooned with ski lifts. Fifteen floors below the window where Celeste stood lay a European-style city park, Nakajima Koen. Formal rose gardens flanked a man-made lake surrounded by willow trees. A number of empty, gaily colored rowboats were moored at the edge of the lake. The park was crisscrossed by paved paths that looked ideal for jogging. Not a soul was visible down below, so Celeste decided it was a perfect time to exercise in anonymity. A run would help her clear her head and, at least temporarily, ease some of her worry about Jane. She quickly donned shorts, her jogging bra, and T-shirt and headed downstairs, through the deserted hotel lobby and out into the fresh May morning air.

At the edge of the park, Celeste did a few stretches, releasing the tension in her shoulders and enjoying the feel of the sun on her bare arms and legs. Then the drumbeats started. A slow, steady rhythm came wafting across the park to where Celeste stood. She felt drawn to investigate, jogging loosely toward the source of the sounds.

Her search for the drummer led her through a clump of trees into a clearing. At the far edge was a large white, wooden building with elaborate Victorian-style gables, trimmed in light blue. The drummer was seated on the front steps of this structure, and the clearing was filled with elderly men and women dressed in soft trousers and sweatshirts in varied pastel colors. They were moving their arms and legs slowly, in time with the drummer, apparently doing their morning exercise. Celeste didn't want to invade the ceremonial atmosphere by lingering there, so she headed away from the clearing toward the far side of the park. But as the jogging path peaked over a small rise she once again found herself to be an intruder, looking down on two enormous sumo wrestlers swaddled in white loincloths. They looked equally startled by Celeste's appearance, though she was far more covered than they. Evidently the momentum of their moves was already under way and one of the wrestlers charged the other, landing them both on their backsides with a mutual grunt. Like two huge beetles that had been flipped over, they were unable to engage their limbs with the ground. Celeste did not wait to see how they managed to right themselves.

She followed the path back to the side of the park where the hotel tower stood, feeling a little sheepish, like an inadvertent voyeur. As she jogged through the formal rose garden where the low rosebushes were beginning to release their fragrance in the sun, Celeste felt uncomfortably exposed to the hotel windows. Then she noticed a wooden gate painted with white Japanese characters. Passing through the gate, on a narrow path lined with stone lanterns, Celeste found herself in a secret garden. It was as though the skyscrapers surrounding the park had disappeared. On previous trips to Japan Celeste had been struck by the contrast between its unrelated worlds of cheap ultramodernism and simple, old-fashioned tradition. But this was the first time she had truly entered the ancient world. In front of her lay a small pond with flowering lily pads. The water was perfectly still. A tiny island of rocks served as a landing place for a kingfisher with a turquoise stripe down its back. Celeste stood for a time, watching the bright bird and savoring the magic tranquillity of the moment, feeling that she had finally found her place in the park.

Back at the hotel, Celeste showered and put on her pinstripe suit. When she bought the suit in London a few years

earlier, she couldn't imagine that she would ever wear it.
Her mother had talked her into it. Now it seemed just the
thing for her lecture that afternoon. She inspected herself
in the mirror. Her dark hair was swept into a French twist,
and she was wearing the white pearl earrings she had pur-
chased at the end of her first trip to Japan with her speaker's
honorarium. She looked positively corporate.

Yesterday the real business of her trip was conducted in
a fairly informal atmosphere at the Biotechnology Division
of Fukuda in Sapporo. Today she was meeting Toshimi and
flying with him back to Fukuda headquarters in Osaka,
where she would lecture to the larger, more product-
oriented research department down there. Since Toshimi
had been appointed vice president, his former job as head
of the Biotechnology Division had been taken over by his
protégé Minoru Yamaguchi. Akira Hagai, who was Minoru's protégé, had just been made head of the new virology subdivision. All three had been at the meeting
yesterday, where Celeste reviewed the presentations by the
scientific staff of the new subdivision. The review had gone
well. Celeste easily found issues for discussion and advice.
Based on this "test consultancy" visit, it seemed the Fukuda management was unanimously in favor of formalizing
Celeste's advisory role. They also agreed, at Celeste's request, that in lieu of a consultant's salary they would make
a substantial donation to the postdoctoral research fellowship fund that the virology program at BAU was establishing.

Celeste was pleased to see the "Fukuda triumvirate"
again. The easy interaction among the three generations of
scientists always impressed her. Somehow they managed to
transcend the hierarchical behavior expected of them. Toshimi freely joked around with Minoru and often drew Ak-

ira into it. Their humor was self-effacing, almost British. Frequently, after a disparaging joke, Toshimi would say "sixty percent," and they would all giggle. Minoru finally explained there was a Japanese saying that all jokes contained 60 percent truth.

Packing her bags, Celeste anticipated an enjoyable trip to Osaka with Toshimi. Part of his freedom from traditional formality was due to his exalted position in the corporate ladder at Fukuda. Toshimi's staff treated him like royalty, and by association, Celeste was treated as visiting royalty. Though, largely because of their reaction to her gender, it was like being visiting royalty from Mars. That was actually the one disturbing element of Celeste's Japanese experience. She had yet to encounter a woman with any kind of position of authority in the Japanese scientific or business worlds. Recently she had thought of a plan for dealing with this problem and was anxious to get Toshimi alone to discuss it with him.

Later that afternoon, the Fukuda corporate lecture hall in Osaka was packed. Celeste concluded the scientific portion of her talk and pressed the slide advance button. The slide listing the members of her laboratory and collaborators flashed onto the screen. For a second, Celeste was taken aback. Then she remembered that she had removed the penultimate slide. It was a "joke" slide of her technician collecting samples at the slaughterhouse. She had recently learned that, in Japan, such references were politically incorrect, since people who worked in slaughterhouses and with leather tanning were traditionally a target for social discrimination. She quickly recovered from her lapse and went through the list of acknowledgments.

After the auditorium lights went back up, Celeste had a

chance to check out the audience while they applauded her. The crowd was predominantly male. Toshimi thanked her formally and then opened the floor to discussion. Celeste was impressed by the number and the depth of the questions. They had clearly been prepared and rehearsed, and though Celeste was able to handle them, she certainly felt challenged. By the end of the question period the room had heated up considerably, and Celeste could feel trickles of sweat running down the inside of her blouse and soaking into the waistband of her skirt. At last the audience was satisfied and dismissed her from the podium with a final round of applause.

She must have looked hot because when she finished removing her slides from the carousel, the gallant Toshimi handed her a fan decorated with three exquisitely drawn characters.

"Very well deserved," he said, obviously pleased with her presentation and its reception. "Calligraphy on this fan say 'In exhaust able.' One word each character. Like you."

"Thank you, Dr. Matsumoto. Just what I needed," said Celeste. She was quite sure she shouldn't call him Toshimi in this public domain. "Tell me, do all your speakers get a crowd that's so interested in the topic?"

"Oh, no," said Toshimi. "You have special audience because I tell everyone a beautiful woman is giving the lecture."

That explained why Toshimi insisted the consulting contract needed to be dealt with at the Osaka office. Celeste suspected his real motive had been to show her off. If Toshimi were not "honorably married" and had been a few years younger, the attraction between them might have manifested itself somewhat differently. Still, as it was, they both derived considerable pleasure from harmless flirtation, which enhanced their mutual professional respect.

Celeste had only partly guessed Toshimi's intent. Unknown to Celeste, there was another, more important reason that Toshimi felt some urgency to engage her services as a consultant. Profits from Protex were being threatened. And it wasn't just the political nonsense directed at Jane that Celeste had told Toshimi about. That was a ridiculous misunderstanding, which Toshimi hoped fervently he would be able to help set straight. No, this threat was technical, and they had no way of knowing, at the moment, whether it was valid.

Two weeks earlier, Toshimi had received a letter from the lawyers of Virotox, a small biotechnology company in the Bay Area. Apparently their CEO, Dr. Simon Phillipson, claimed to have a Protex replacement that he wanted Fukuda to evaluate as a potential product. While Toshimi had scientific confidence in his virology group in Sapporo, he was well aware of their shortcomings in molecular biology. He felt they needed someone with Celeste's additional expertise to advise them. Celeste's enthusiastic reception at the Osaka headquarters would make it that much easier for Toshimi to appoint her as a top security consultant, which would be necessary in this case. He was tremendously relieved, though not surprised, that she had made such a good impression. He was now sure he would be able to expedite her appointment in time to deal with the Virotox proposal. As it was, he was unable to discuss the matter with her until she had been given the top security clearance. Phillipson himself was due to visit Fukuda later in the week, and Toshimi felt that the situation was about to escalate.

That evening at dinner, Celeste at last had the opportunity to discuss with Toshimi her plan for a one-woman assault on Japanese sexism. She had to wait for the other members of the Fukuda staff to leave, including the one female scientist, Yukiko Tekiyama, who had obviously been invited as the inevitable female chaperone required for Celeste. Yukiko was extremely shy and childishly impressed with the restaurant, which had a three-star Michelin rating and was the best in Osaka. Celeste was touched by her delight in eating the very fine gold leaf that was served as decoration for the fois gras. It was clear that Yukiko was not accustomed to hobnobbing with men who were several ranks higher, and this made Celeste's case even stronger.

"Now that we're alone," Celeste said to Toshimi, "I'd like to ask you a favor."

"Ah, Celeste, you know I do anything for you."

"Well, maybe you'd better wait to see what it is."

"*Hai,* okay." Toshimi looked attentive.

"You know that Dr. Rosenthal, our chairman, plans to retire at the end of next year."

"*Hai,* I know Dr. Rosenthal very well."

"Well, he's decreasing the size of his laboratory and will be giving me another two benches in his lab, which is next door to mine. I already have a graduate student who needs one of the benches but I'd like to make a proposal regarding the other one."

"Now I read your mind. You are ready for visiting scientist from Fukuda, like we ask two years ago when you have no space."

"Yes, Toshimi, you have read my mind. But there's one condition I would like to make for this visitor."

"*Hai?*"

"I would like the visitor to be a woman scientist from your staff. I think this training would be a good way for her to gain respect from her colleagues and move up in the company when she returns."

"Ah," said Toshimi. "Interesting negotiation." He thought for a minute. "I believe this would be possible, but I must find good candidate. I will let you know."

This was clearly the end of the discussion for the moment. They finished the bottle of Château Margaux and talked of other things until Toshimi ushered Celeste into a taxi with his usual promise, "Next time we take bath together."

The following afternoon, when Celeste was airborne and facing the desiccated lump of meat touted as Club Class Filet Mignon, her thoughts returned to the three-star meal and Toshimi's reaction to her proposal. She was pleased by how receptive he had been. Possibly she had his good experience with Jane to thank for that. On her previous return flights from Japan, Celeste eagerly devoured the Western-style airline food, after several days of banqueting on Japanese seafood delicacies. Today, however, Celeste had no appetite, undoubtedly a credit to last night's Paris-trained Japanese chef who had produced a transcendental cross-cultural eating experience. With her meal half finished, she accepted a glass of port from the disapproving stewardess and pulled out her notes for the lecture that evening.

These return flights from Japan were always disconcerting. Celeste would arrive in San Francisco several hours before her scheduled takeoff from Osaka after spending eleven hours airborne. At least the timing meant she could stick to her lecture schedule. The plan was to revise her notes, drink enough after the meal to have a nap, and perhaps do some reading between waking up and landing at SFO. She would be back at her apartment in San Francisco sufficiently early to get a few hours of sound sleep before delivering the lecture at 6:00 P.M.

More or less on schedule, Celeste rapidly cleared customs at San Francisco and headed upstairs to United's "Premier" frequent flier booking desk. While it was on her mind, she decided to book her return trip to Sapporo next month for the follow-up meeting. Toshimi had been pretty insistent on an early return visit.

An elegant man stood in front of her, completing his transaction with the United Airlines agent. He was impeccable in beige corduroy trousers, a pale yellow cashmere sweater, pearl gray cotton turtleneck, and tweed jacket. While he spoke he pushed back his longish hair, prematurely approaching the color of his turtleneck.

"Right, then," he said with a British clip to the young woman behind the counter. "All set with a first-class return ticket to Osaka. Now, my dear, it's off to the Red Carpet Club. Ought to get some work done there before takeoff. Better than popping back to the office for only an hour, what?"

Phillipson turned away from the counter, and looking down, opened his jacket to put his ticket and boarding pass in the inside pocket. This gesture prevented him from seeing Celeste's carry-on, which she had set down on the floor behind him. He walked right into it and would have completely lost his balance if Celeste hadn't shot out her arm for him to catch hold of.

"Oh, madam! Terribly sorry. How clumsy of me," he exclaimed. Phillipson continued to hang on to Celeste's forearm, which he had grabbed reflexively, and looked her up and down quite boldly. In a solicitous tone that made it clear he liked what he saw, he said with concern, "I do hope I didn't hurt you."

"No, no, I'm fine," said Celeste, coloring, although he was the one who should have been embarrassed. She was as much startled by the man's overt assessment of her face and body as she was by the sudden physical contact. The appreciative once-over from a handsome stranger made the grunge of the eleven-hour flight evaporate instantly. But was he in fact a stranger? During the few seconds that they stared at each other, Celeste felt there was something familiar about this man. Don't be silly, she told herself. Just wishful thinking brought on by jet lag.

"Do forgive me," said Phillipson, recovering his composure. "I'd best be on my way through security." For a moment there, he was tempted to leave his card. But if he pursued every good-looking woman he came across, he'd never get any business done.

"This'll sound like I'm trying to follow him to Osaka," Celeste said jokingly to the agent at the counter, "but I actually do need to book a flight back to Japan next month."

"Well, I'd sure fly with him anytime!" said the agent, raising her eyebrows.

Several hours later, Celeste was flagging at the end of her lecture. She took a deep breath and started on the homestretch. The blackboard was covered with a diagram of the Eke virus life cycle after it infects a cell.

"Okay, so we've been discussing how a virus gets put together after it multiplies inside the cell it infects. Basically a virus is formed from DNA, surrounded by a coat. The coat is assembled from small building blocks of protein. These building blocks are first made in one large piece called a proprotein, which needs to be cleaved into smaller units. An enzyme called a pro-tee-ase, spelled protease, is responsible for cleaving the proprotein. This type of construction can make a virus vulnerable to two kinds of drugs. One type could block the protease and stop the cleavage process." Celeste then drew an "X" on the blackboard next to the step that could be blocked.

"The drug Protex, from Fukuda Pharmaceuticals, is the prototype for the first therapeutic approach. It was developed by Matsumoto and Stanley in the early sixties and blocks Eke virus protease activity. Coincidentally, earlier today I returned from a consultancy visit to Fukuda, where we discussed the potential for development of this therapeutic strategy for other known viruses.''

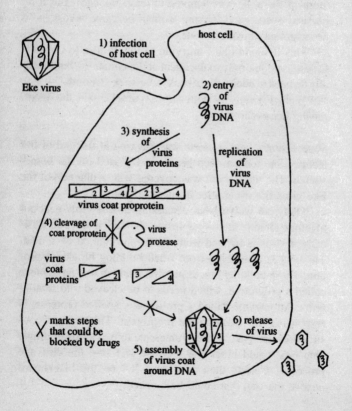

No wonder she looks so tired, thought Mac. This was definitely not one of her better lectures.

"A second type of drug could interfere with the so-called assembly of the coat, once the protein building blocks have already been produced," said Celeste. She added another X to the diagram on the blackboard. "This would require somewhat higher concentrations of the blocking compound because it would have to intercept each building block forming the virus coat."

Mac could not resist an interjection here. "Excuse me, Dr. Braun, but on the reading list there's a manuscript from Stanley's lab that explains why the approach you just described won't work. Apparently, assembly of the virus coat is too similar to the assembly process of some human proteins, so an assembly inhibitor will be toxic to human cells."

Damn this guy, thought Celeste. He was always trying to prove himself, though, she had to admit, his comments were at least substantiated in the scientific literature. It didn't help that he had one of those thin Clark Gable mustaches, which she found particularly unappealing.

To the class she said, "Yes, Mr. Macmillan, you have a point there. However, the studies that led to that manuscript were done exclusively on Eke virus. There have recently been a couple of instances of viruses from the pox family where this alternative approach looks more promising. These studies were reported at a recent conference and are not yet published, so I was unable to include them on your reading list." She knew she wasn't being fair, putting him in his place with unpublished information, but sometimes his interruptions bordered on the disruptive. Tonight she had little patience for losing the thread of her lecture.

The next day, reconsidering the incident, it occurred to

Celeste that this Tech exchange student was probably the
only student in the class who was actually reading the background material and thinking about it. The regular BAU
graduate students, used to being spoon-fed, were annoy-
ingly passive. She ought to be more appreciative of Mr.
Macmillan's interruptions, and she made a private resolution to try to be more tolerant and encouraging.

FOUR

Drug Deal

S imon Phillipson emerged from the automatic doors coated with reflective paint into the waiting throng at Osaka International Airport. Standing head and shoulders above most of the crowd, he easily spotted his name on a placard held by a young Japanese man in a dark suit. As he approached the placard a gray-haired, shorter man, also in a dark suit, rushed forward.

"Dr. Phillipson? Dr. Phillipson? I am Toshimi Matsumoto. Very pleased to meet you. Welcome to Osaka." He gave several sharp, shallow bows.

"Ah, Dr. Matsumoto. Likewise, pleased to meet you." Phillipson extended his hand. For such a powerful individual, Matsumoto had a rather weak handshake. But then, he was more accustomed to bowing, generally less deeply than the bow offered, as a sign of his higher rank.

"Dr. Phillipson . . ." Toshimi was clearly struggling with the double *l*, but remained dignified.

"Simon, please."

"*Hai*! Simon, we must hurry! Plane for Sapporo board in fifteen minutes from domestic terminal. We talk in flight."

Toshimi ushered Phillipson out of the international terminal and into the waiting Fukuda limousine. His gentle authority reminded Phillipson of a junior-school master. In the limousine, Toshimi and his aide sorted out the tickets and spoke quietly to each other in Japanese. Phillipson's sensation of being on a school trip, with grown-ups making the arrangements, was heightened. He sat passively in the back of the limousine, impressed by the aggressive progress the driver made through the congested airport traffic. At the domestic terminal they disembarked quickly and rushed to the departure gate. Hurrying down the jetway, Phillipson heard the connecting door to the airport shut behind them.

By the time they had settled into their seats in the stuffy first-class cabin of the commuter plane, Phillipson felt an unaccustomed nervous sweat prickling under his arms. Maybe it was the flashback to school that made him uncomfortable.

Catching his breath, Toshimi turned toward Phillipson. "Dr. Phillipson, Simon, your proposal has great interest for us. We look forward to discuss in Sapporo," he said with an ingratiating smile. "I suspect you tired after your trip."

"Oh, no. Quite comfortable. Thank you," lied Phillipson. Toshimi's remark was clearly a command that no business would be discussed until they were behind closed doors. Phillipson knew the rules from his previous encounters with the Japanese when he was scouting for venture capital.

"This week we enjoy a visit from Dr. Celeste Braun, at Fukuda, Osaka," said Toshimi. "Fantastic lecture! You also part of Stanley lab family. You know Celeste?"

"No, actually," said Phillipson, gritting his teeth. It challenged him to have to pretend the reference to his time with Stanley didn't bother him. "It's surprising I never met Dr. Braun. She joined the lab the year I left. I've heard of her success, of course. I gather she's well established at BAU. Quite a coup for them to get her over Harvard."

"*Hai, hai!* Wonderful woman. Like Jane Stanley, when I first met. I was Jane's first fellow, you know," Toshimi declared, with the same pride that Watson might announce his association with Holmes.

"Yes. Protex was a marvelous discovery. It must have been a very exciting time."

"*Hai,*" said Toshimi quietly. "Very exciting. Sometimes I think best time in life."

"Oh, no. You can't possibly believe that. You've helped establish Fukuda as the number one pharmaceutical company in Japan. Surely that's been as exciting," said Phillipson, hearing himself sound insincere.

They occupied themselves with further polite small talk for the rest of the flight to Sapporo. Phillipson would be relieved when they could actually get down to business in the boardroom. He had tried to befriend the Japanese but was continually frustrated by his inability to communicate. He found very little common ground for interaction, in spite of the fact that their excessive decorum and ironic sense of humor were often likened to British behavior.

"Well, gentlemen, I come before you to reveal the existence of a novel compound with potent antiviral effects."

They were in the inner sanctum of Minoru's office. Seated around the conference table were Toshimi, Minoru, and Akira. Phillipson noted that their heights were inversely proportional to their status, a useful mnemonic.

Phillipson stood in front of them to explain the data projected onto the screen. He had given them all copies of the same data, printed on paper with the Virotox, Inc., logo. Lurking in the back was the ever-present "office lady," ready to make cups of tea and fetch files as needed. This one had a Ph.D. in biochemistry and usually worked in the lab. But, as Akira's wife, she was called on to be office lady in cases of high confidentiality.

Phillipson pointed the red dot of his pocket laser pointer at a line on the graph projected in front of him. "Here we have a growth curve of Eke virus in the presence of increasing doses of Protex. Or rather, a death curve. You can see that the virus is rapidly killed after exposure to the drug. In the next slide, you see the effect of the same dosage of Protex on human cells in culture. As expected, there is no toxic effect on human cells.

"Now, here is the growth curve of Eke virus in the presence of Bazuran. Bazuran has the same effect as Protex." Phillipson flipped back two slides to make his point and then forward three.

"This is the effect of the same concentration of Bazuran on human cells. Again, like Protex, no toxicity." Phillipson paused to let his audience appreciate the data. "So you see, gentlemen, after all these years studying natural Amazonian toxins, I have finally found one that will inhibit Eke virus replication without harming human cells." Phillipson had decided that it was too complicated, at this stage of the negotiation, to explain that the Bazuran data were actually produced with a mutant strain of Eke virus. It was better strategy, he realized, to see if they managed to discover this for themselves. If they didn't discover he had been working with a mutant, then negotiations would remain simple. If they did, it could only help them appreciate the value of his offer.

"The final development regarding Bazuran that I would like to share with you is the unique formulation that my engineers have proposed for its use as a medication. Unlike Protex, Bazuran is stable in liquid form and easily vaporized, as are many of the plant toxins. Therefore, the drug can be delivered by nasal spray—you know, from an inhaler, like the ones used by asthmatics or allergy patients."

"*Hai,*" acknowledged Toshimi. "We have much allergy to ragweed here in Japan. Fukuda manufacturing very familiar with dispenser design for allergy products."

"Well, that's the end of my formal presentation, but I imagine there are at least two things you may be wondering at this point. The first is why Fukuda should be interested in exclusive rights to manufacture and distribute Bazuran. The second is how this compound could have been overlooked in the exhaustive studies done in Stanley's laboratory that apparently disproved this therapeutic approach.

"Well, to deal with the second issue first, those results were just plain wrong, as I have shown here. After I brought these compounds to the lab, Stanley distributed them among a number of the students and postdocs for testing. It would seem that the person testing this one was a particularly incompetent scientist. If I'm not mistaken, he eventually became a newspaper columnist. It's also possible that Stanley actually knew about these results but was hiding them from all of us, so as not to interfere with the Protex market. After all, the royalties on Protex did contribute significantly to her research funding. You may not yet have heard this over here, but she is currently being investigated by the U.S. Committee on Scientific Integrity for alleged misconduct with regard to her commercial interests.

"Now," continued Phillipson, "to address the first issue, of why Fukuda should be interested in a 'second Protex,' I think I should discuss this with Dr. Matsumoto in private."

Toshimi knew what Phillipson was about to propose, and his distaste for the man increased further at the reference to the CSI investigation. From Celeste's description it had seemed obvious that the CSI business was a clear-cut case of political overzealousness. In fact, it sounded to Toshimi more typical of the kinds of thing that occurred routinely in Japanese politics, which were so much more overtly connected to the business world. But if Phillipson intended to use Jane's discomfort to his advantage, Toshimi felt justified in taking extra precautions.

"Minoru and Akira hear anything confidential you will tell me," said Toshimi with a placating smile. "They are Matsumoto dynasty. She, the office lady," he continued, pointing at Mrs. Hagai, "does not understand English."

Mrs. Hagai, actually Dr. Kazuko Hagai, gave an appropriately vacant smile, in response to Toshimi's gesture. She would have to be on her guard not to respond to any commands or questions in English. In fact, her English was the best of the four Japanese in the room.

"Right. If you're comfortable with their presence, then so am I," said Phillipson tersely, if not totally truthfully. It would certainly be more awkward to put his proposition to three of them at once. He proceeded, "Roykan Limited was recently the number one pharmaceutical company in Japan until Fukuda, under the remarkable leadership of Dr. Matsumoto and his fellow officers, took over that desirable position. I am confident, gentlemen, that Roykan would like to be number one again. There is no question that they would be extremely interested in marketing a product to compete with Protex that would keep outbreaks of Eke virus under control. The rights to such a product would not be available to them, however, if Fukuda had the foresight to purchase exclusive rights to the manufacture and sale of such a product.

"The organic chemists at Virotox have recently completed the commercial protocol for extracting Bazuran from the original plant. We also have natives in Brazil who are 'farming' it in the rain forest. What we do not have is the facility for scale-up of production from the crude plant material, nor the quality control procedures for trials and manufacturing. I, personally, hold the patent rights to use of Bazuran, and a number of other natural toxins for pharmaceutical purposes."

Phillipson paused for a fraction of a second and looked at his audience for a possible reaction. Fortunately, there was none. Apparently they weren't sufficiently informed at this stage to question him on the consequences of the "Biodiversity Treaty" currently under debate in the U.S. Congress, and its potential threat to patents on rain forest products. He could have dealt with this pretty easily, but there was no reason to mention it if they weren't going to bring it up. After all, he was confident that by the time their lawyers got around to checking his patent, the treaty would have been voted down.

"I am sure you can see where this is leading, gentlemen. I am offering you the opportunity to purchase the production and distribution rights for Bazuran. My terms have to take into account that you will probably never actually manufacture Bazuran, since its production is somewhat more expensive than the production of Protex, at least as published in your stockholder reports. Roykan would of course be manufacturing, as they have no alternative and would probably garner a market share, of which I would retain eighty percent of the royalties to compensate for the extensive R&D that have gone into the product. I have therefore calculated the loss that we would suffer by selling out to you, based on the current world market for Protex, projected over the next seventeen years. I have accounted for that loss in the price of my offer, which now stands at twenty million dollars plus retention of eighty percent royalties should you ever decide to manufacture.

"You may wonder why I make you this offer without running to Roykan first. Well, although it may be poor business practice, I have loyalty to our joint heritage in the Stanley laboratory and want to do you a good turn."

Toshimi was disgusted, equally by the proposal and by Phillipson's hypocrisy. How could he insult Jane so disloyally one moment and then invoke laboratory solidarity the next? Toshimi's internal reaction was interrupted by a rapid-fire interjection from Akira in Japanese, which he considered for a moment, then nodded.

"Dr. Hagai suggest we test Bazuran here at Fukuda before we negotiate further. We are pleased if you agree and not contact Roykan before," said Toshimi.

"Certainly, gentlemen. I'll do better than that," Phillipson replied. He had come fully prepared for this eventuality. It would be a piece of cake to give them the Bazuran-sensitive virus mutant, along with a sample of the drug. Then it would be amusing to see whether they were smart enough to figure out it was a mutant. "I've brought with me a sample of Bazuran, as well as a new indicator strain of Eke virus that we recently engineered to make your test easier. We took the wild-type virus and engineered into it the gene for luciferase, the protein that makes fireflies light up. When the virus begins to replicate, the firefly protein is made, so any cell infected with the virus becomes luminescent. Thus, with this indicator strain, the test for virus growth is more sensitive and can be read within hours instead of waiting overnight.''

''Indicator strain is then wilder-type virus,'' said Minoru and all the Japanese present, except the office lady, giggled. The giggling was largely to relieve the overwhelming tension that had built up in the conference room, but Minoru felt obliged to explain. ''We always think 'wild-type' is funny way to describe normal.''

''Well, normal is called 'wild-type' because that's how it's found in the wild,'' said Phillipson stuffily. The Japanese tendency to giggle at moments of stress got on his nerves.

''*Hai*,'' said Toshimi conclusively, and barked some instructions to the office lady over his shoulder. ''She call Unami to take you to hotel now. We meet for dinner later. Limousine pick you up at seven and maybe you sleep off jet lag. Good sake tonight help, too!'' More giggling.

Phillipson nodded and, with a perfunctory smile, rose from the table, gathering up his papers into his briefcase. He hated sake. It tasted like lighter fluid smelled. But that was a small price to pay.

Following a discreet knock on the conference room door, the office lady returned with Unami in tow.

''You follow,'' said Unami with a quick bow and turned, leading Phillipson out of the room.

A short period of silence ensued, while the three Japanese men looked at each other.

"There is a word for this in English," said Minoru, "but it escapes me."

"Blackmail," said Kazuko Hagai from the back of the room. Her *l*'s were pronounced impeccably.

FIVE

Allergy Shots

C eleste was only thirty-five, but there was a large cultural generation gap between her and the postdoctoral fellows in her lab, who were in their late twenties. This was mainly because Celeste rarely watched television. But, once in a while, like Friday night after her return from Japan, Celeste needed to "switch on and switch off." Having never bothered to buy a VCR or connect to cable, she was stuck with the network offerings. So Celeste felt blessed with a rerun of the 1934 Frank Capra film *It Happened One Night*.

With a generous tumbler of red wine and a steaming plate of spaghetti with sausage smothered in Parmesan cheese, she settled down to combat jet lag with Claudette Colbert and Clark Gable. These combined treats had the desired effect. Two hours later, Celeste was sleeping soundly, dreaming of Clark Gable taking his shirt off as a prelude to demonstrating his uncontrollable desire for her. Under the circumstances, his mustache didn't put her off.

Celeste relished doing Saturday morning errands because it allowed her to escape the elitist academic world and blend in with the lives of ordinary people. Before going out, she carefully applied her lipstick. She had found that this simple adornment not only gave her authority in the classroom and at the conference table, where it often served as warpaint, but it also seemed to encourage nonacademic men to act more friendly toward her. After spending the night with Clark Gable, she could use a little male friendliness.

Celeste lived on the top floor of a three-story "painted lady" that, in the late seventies, had been split into two condominium units. In the shared garage underneath, Celeste lowered the roof of her MGB and turned the key in the ignition. The engine spluttered several times before catching. The car had never recovered from installation of the state-mandated smog protection device, though Celeste had finally convinced her mechanic to remove it. The mechanic loved the car almost as much as Celeste did. They called it the "wombat," in deference to its first owner, an Australian who had bought it in 1978, shortly before British Leyland stopped manufacturing MGBs.

Celeste pulled out of the sheltered side streets of the Castro, crossed Market, and drove up the side spur over the roller coaster of Seventeenth Street to the BAU campus. It was just before nine, and the streets were still empty. The little pastel houses, stacked precariously on the side of the hill, sparkled. Passing Mars and Uranus streets on her left, Celeste considered the suitability of these names. Sometimes it did seem that San Francisco constituted a separate planet.

She turned into the ramp leading to the parking garage across from the BAU hospital complex and opened the gate with a magnetic key card. On Saturdays the faculty could park in the public garage, which was a bit closer to the clinics, where Celeste was headed. Her first errand was to get her monthly allergy shots over with.

The waiting room at the BAU outpatient allergy clinic was already crowded. Allergies were rampant in northern California, where, during the height of spring, pollen was so thick that it formed a visible yellowish dust on anything left outdoors for more than a couple of hours. It was not unusual for migrants to the Bay Area to develop allergies to the fertile California plants within a few years of moving there, as had happened to Celeste. The BAU allergy clinic was one of the few clinics in the city that was open on Saturdays, so it was especially popular with young professionals. Celeste rarely went to get her allergy shots without running into someone she recognized.

To avoid being waylaid, Celeste didn't look around and walked purposefully through the maze of occupied arm-chairs and coffee tables strewn with dog-eared, out-of-date magazines. When she reached the nurses' station, Celeste added her name to the list on a clipboard hanging on the wall next to it. Five names were ahead of hers, so she had a good half-hour wait even before the injections, then at least twenty minutes after to make sure she didn't go into anaphylactic shock.

As the rest of the waiting area looked pretty full, Celeste plunked down in the row of chairs facing the entrance to the nurses' station to wait her turn. In anticipation of the need to kill time, Celeste had brought the mail that accumulated at home since her return from Japan, as well as the current detective novel she was devouring.

She opened a thick letter that looked like a wedding invitation. Celeste wondered which of her remaining single friends was about to abandon her. "The presence of your company is requested at a research symposium and testimonial dinner for Jane Stanley, M.D., on the occasion of her retirement from the Department of Microbiology." The symposium was scheduled for the last Saturday in May, exactly four weeks away. It would take place on the Harvard University undergraduate campus in Cambridge, Massachusetts and cocktails and dinner would follow at the Harvard Faculty Club.

Celeste was completely taken aback. She certainly hadn't expected things to move so fast. Jane must have already made up her mind, when Celeste had spoken to her from Japan on Monday. Celeste had evidently misunderstood and been under the impression that Jane was still debating the retirement decision. In fact, she had planned to give Jane a call on Sunday morning for a leisurely chat about it. Celeste knew these "golden handshake" deals had strict deadlines. Maybe Jane had been forced into a precipitous decision. At least the department was giving her the respect she was due, and Celeste hoped that the event might help raise Jane's spirits. Folded inside the invitation was a handwritten note. Celeste recognized the handwriting. It was from Evie Pritsker, the longtime administrator of the department.

Dear Celeste,

When you get this invitation, I'm sure you'll be as surprised as I was that Jane decided to take the early retirement option, and so suddenly! I guess the CSI business (which has been privately brewing up for months), on top of losing Roger, was just too much for her. She says she's planning to write a virology textbook, but I can't imagine Jane in the contemplative life. I really hope you can make it to the dinner because the chair (!) wants *you* (''Jane's star pupil'') to give the after-dinner speech. We're inviting everyone who ever worked with Jane, but I'm worried about a good turnout with such short notice. Please let me know ASAP if you can come.

All the best,
Evie.

Celeste was extremely flattered to be asked to be keynote speaker, but also somewhat apprehensive about it. She started thinking about what tone she should take and what she might say, and as wool-gathering goes, what she might wear. Her thoughts were interrupted by a conversation that started up behind her between a boy whom she had judged to be about twelve years old and a girl about half his age. Celeste didn't know it but the youth was her Tech graduate student's son, Mac, Jr.

''Are you here by yourself?'' asked the little girl with awe.

''Naw,'' said Mac, Jr. ''My dad's gone to get a cup of coffee.''

''Did you get shots?''

''' 'Course I got shots. What else would I be here for?''

''I'm here 'cause my mother is getting shots,'' said the girl.

''Goody for you,'' said Mac, Jr., without interest. He picked up the sports section of the newspaper lying in front of him on the coffee table, but he couldn't resist the temptation to show off his superior knowledge. ''Did you know that if you don't wait twenty minutes after getting allergy shots you could asphyxiate and,'' he said darkly, ''if that happens, you die?''

''What does that mean?'' she asked, worriedly looking

over at her mother being injected by a nurse. "You don't die from shots. They keep you well."

"Never mind," said Mac, Jr. "I shouldn't have wasted my time."

Suddenly there was a commotion at the nurses' station. The little girl's mother started to cough and wheeze.

"Quick, pass me that inhaler," said the nurse who had administered the injection. The assistant standing on the other side of the station pushed an inhaler across the table between them.

"I want two cc's of epinephrine," ordered the nurse as she held the inhaler to the woman's mouth, with her other hand at the woman's back. "Close your mouth over the opening and breathe deeply," she commanded. She spritzed the inhaler as the woman obliged. "Breathe again." After delivering a second spritz to the woman's respiratory passages, the nurse reached out to take the syringe of epinephrine from the assistant. She swabbed her patient's arm quickly with alcohol and injected the full dose. The little girl's mother looked shell-shocked by this whirlwind of treatment.

"You'd probably have recovered on your own, in about half an hour," said the nurse to her patient, "but we have to be extra cautious. We'll keep you under surveillance for another fifteen minutes to make sure the epinephrine has taken effect. Then you'll just be a little jittery until it wears off. Come back here with me, where you can sit quietly in one of the examination rooms."

"Mommy!" the little girl shrieked and jumped up to follow her mother and the nurse.

"What was that all about?" Celeste heard a familiar voice ask behind her back. Oh, dear, thought Celeste. It was that student from Tech, the one in her Micro 214 class. What was his name? Macmillan? Yeah, John Mac-millan.

She really wasn't in the mood to have a polite conversation with this guy, and especially wasn't in the mood to be introduced to his kid. Celeste figured if she just sat there with her back to them, she could pretend not to see them. She lay low, unwillingly continuing her eavesdropping.

"Oh, Dad!" said Mac, Jr., excitedly. "You missed an anaphylactic reaction. But she didn't choke to death, 'cause they injected her in time." He sounded disappointed. "What is it they inject with again? I heard her say it but I forgot already."

"Adrenaline," said Mac, Sr. "Only they probably called it epinephrine."

"Yeah, that's it," said Mac Jr. "Uh, Dad, can you explain again about the shots? I mean, how dangerous it is? I mean, how come reactions aren't supposed to happen?" He needed some parental reassurance.

Oh, boy, thought Celeste. Now we get to hear Dad explain why the sky is blue. That should be right up his alley, since he's such a know-it-all in class.

But in spite of herself, Celeste was just a little bit interested to hear how her student would instruct his son. She wondered if he'd get it right.

"Sure, kid," he said. "Lemme have a sip of coffee first. Here's your hot chocolate." Celeste could hear a paper bag being opened and cups being removed. The combined scent of fresh coffee and chocolate wafting over the back of the couch indicated the lids were off, confirmed by sounds of slurping.

"Okay. Let's get a piece of paper." After some more rustling, Mac, Sr., began his explanation. "First of all, you gotta remember that this is all about the immune response, right? It's like the body organizes a military attack on bad things like viruses or bacteria or parasites that make you sick. We'll just call 'em bugs for short. Now, these bugs all have proteins called antigens that are stuck on them. First the immune system does a little reconnaissance and it detects the antigens, so it knows there's a bug around that needs to be blown away. The first defense action is to make some other proteins, called antibodies, which bind onto the antigen." Celeste could hear the pencil scratching.

"Sure, sure, I'm way past that, Dad."

"I know you are, Mac, but it helps to start at the beginning to explain the tricky part. Now, the antibodies aren't really weapons. They're sorta like flags that signal which weapons the immune system should use. Remember, they have a Y shape, and the arms of the Y stick to the antigen and the tail or stem part sticks up and acts like the flag, signaling to the hit squads. The immune system has several hit squads, and depending on what kind of flag the antibody has, it tells the hit squads what kind of weapon to use."

"Are you sure this is gonna explain allergies? It sounds like a video game."

"Well, it is a kind of game, the way the immune system figures out what strategy to use to wipe something out. It doesn't always get it right, though. When it screws up, that's when we get allergies. Now just lemme get through this part about the hit squads."

"Okay, okay."

Celeste marveled at the patience of the parent but then thought smugly that he might be getting a little of his own medicine.

"So here we are on the battlefield with the bacteria wearing its antigen armor. Now, the most common kind of antibody or signal flag is called 'G.' Naming a Y-shaped thing 'G' sounds stupid, I know, but that's the way it is. Okay, so the 'G' antibodies can signal one type of hit squad to poke holes in the bugs. They can also mobilize these really greedy, Pacman-like white blood cells called macrophages to gobble up the bugs. Their name even means big eater. I call 'em the Fang Gang." Celeste heard the pencil scratching away, and Mac, Jr., snickered as his father added a ferocious-looking macrophage to his drawing. Celeste was getting curious to see this diagram.

"The 'G' antibody works great for wiping out bacteria and some viruses, but there's a special kind of antibody needed to wipe out parasites, called 'E.' Yup, you guessed it, another Y-shaped protein. What's special about 'E' is that it recruits a different hit squad. You thought the Fang Gang was bad, but these guys that 'E' recruits are even worse. They're called mast cells, and they spray the whole place with this chemical called histamine. What histamine does is basically cause a local flood, allowing a whole lot of white blood cells to sail in and fight the parasite. It's sorta like the army calling in the navy. For the parasite, it's a major flood and bad news. For us, it feels like swelling and itching. This 'E' antibody goes into action, for example, when you get bitten by a mosquito."

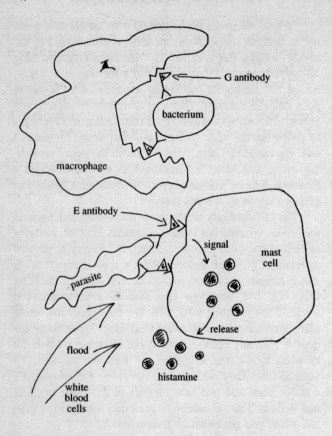

"Da-ad. This still doesn't have anything do with allergy shots," complained Mac, Jr.

"Just wait a sec, okay? In people who have allergies, the immune system gets mixed up. It produces 'E' antibodies that bind to harmless proteins in house dust or cat dandruff or grass pollen. The system somehow mistakes these for parasite antigens. When these harmless proteins are inhaled, the 'E' antibody binds in the lungs or the nose and does its stuff, causing the mast cells to spit out histamine all over the place. Then what do you think happens?''

"Flood time,'' said Mac, Jr. "In comes the navy.''

"You got it,'' said Mac. "If it's a major flood in the lungs, then you can't breathe. That's called anaphylaxis. If it's just a mild flood, then you got a runny nose.''

"So how come an allergy shot can fix it?''

"The idea with allergy shots is the patient gets injected with the harmless protein like house dust or grass pollen to try to fool the immune system into making the 'G' antibody instead of the 'E' antibody.''

"But you said that they're already making 'E,' so if you're injecting allergic people with the antigen, how come they don't choke and die?''

"Well, it all depends on how the antigen is delivered. If you breathe it in, it's all over. Same if you get it straight into the bloodstream. But if the antigen is injected into the muscle tissue, like for allergy shots, it leaks in real slowly, and the body can take it that way. When it leaks in slowly like that, the antibody lineup gets changed and no more calling in the navy. But you gotta be careful with the shots, see. 'Cause if the antigen gets directly in the blood, then—''

"Anaphylaxis!'' said Mac, Jr., with enthusiasm.

"Right on,'' said his father. "At least you'd know real soon if the shots got screwed up. An anaphylactic reaction happens almost immediately when the 'E' antibody in the blood zaps an antigen. They make you wait twenty minutes—here in the clinic, though—just to be extra sure everything is okay.''

"So is that what happened to that lady?'' asked Mac, Jr.

"Well, maybe," said Mac, Sr., not wanting to alarm his son by implying that the nurse was incompetent. "It's pretty unusual for that to happen. These nurses know what they're doing. They've got a lotta practice steering clear of blood vessels. Luckily, there's a natural substance called 'epinephrine.' The old-fashioned name is 'adrenaline.' This stuff has properties that reverse the effects of histamine. So immediate injection of epinephrine can prevent anaphylaxis."

"Phew," said Mac, Jr., massaging his arms. "I'm staying near the supply of epinephrine."

Celeste was impressed, very impressed. Mac had managed to get this kid to understand an incredibly complex process. At this point she just couldn't resist looking around. "Uh. Excuse me. I couldn't help overhearing. That was really an excellent explanation. So good, I almost understood it myself," she said with a smile.

Mac, Sr., went bright red under his workingman's tan. Celeste had never seen a man blush quite so profoundly. Then as she looked at him, she had an uncanny flashback to her dream about Clark Gable. Her stomach dropped uncontrollably to her pelvic region. Why was she having this "morning after" sensation, as though she had just spent a night of passion with the guy? It must be the damned mustache.

"Dr. Braun! 'Scuse me! I didn't see you there," said Mac, Sr., awkwardly. "Uh, this is my boy, Mac, Junior."

"Hello," said Celeste, extending her hand to Mac, Jr. It was touchingly tacky that his son was nicknamed after him.

"Celeste Braun!" bellowed the nurse from her station.

"I guess they've got my antigens ready," said Celeste. "See you shortly." She got up hastily, leaving her papers and book on the chair behind her.

When she returned, Celeste was disappointed to find no sign of the Macmillan family. They had evidently passed the critical period for anaphylaxis. She picked up her crime novel.

Celeste read a few paragraphs describing the sage detective Mulheisen ruminating over the embezzlement case in *Hit on the House*. It often struck her that putting together the evidence to solve a crime was not unlike drawing conclusions from experimental laboratory data. She particularly enjoyed following Mulheisen's shrewd insight during this process. Even so, she realized her thoughts were elsewhere as she read another paragraph without registering the content.

Well, I'll be, she thought. Her mind was preoccupied with next Tuesday night's lecture, when she would see Mac again. It's amazing how a dream can change your view of someone.

SIX

Control Experiment

Akira and Kazuko Hagai had lived in Sapporo all their lives. They met as doctoral students at Hokkaido University. At Fukuda Biotechnology Division, they shared the virology laboratory, of which Akira was nominally the head. Their parents believed it was a great tragedy that Akira and Kazuko were unable to have children. In fact, this gave Kazuko freedom for professional development that she wouldn't have had otherwise. Within the division it was generally acknowledged that Kazuko was one of the most insightful members of the scientific staff. Therefore it was not just because she was his wife that Akira sought her advice.

They were seated back to back on high stools, between the two benches in their small laboratory, each concentrating intensely on the experiments assembled in front of them. The laboratory was completely quiet, except for the hum of an incubator, cycling to keep the enclosed cultures at body temperature. Akira had about twenty petri dishes laid out in front of him. The bottom half of each dish was covered with a cloudy layer of cells cultured from human epithelial tissue, the kind of cells that coat the lung and nasal passages infected by Eke virus. Within these cells, Eke virus was replicating. When it reached sufficient numbers, the virus colony would produce a little clear patch, called a "plaque," as it burst the host cells. Viruses are the ultimately exploitive guests, growing inside the host before killing them and being liberated to infect the host next door.

Akira picked up each petri dish in turn and held it inside the opening created by a cardboard box standing on its side. Once in the shadow of the box, small spots decorating the layer of cells on the bottom of the dish glowed brightly, revealing the location of viral plaques. Akira was looking at the indicator strain of Eke virus that Phillipson had sent, and counting the number of plaques. As advertised by Phillipson, the replicating virus made firefly luciferase protein, which caused the virus plaques to glow in the dark.

"Kazuko, have a look at this!"

Kazuko swiveled around to face Akira's bench and slid off her stool. She picked up one of the petri dishes, placing it inside the shadow of the box to see the plaques glow.

"*Hai,*" she said. "Quite impressive. You can barely see some of these plaques with the naked eye, but in the dark they stand out clearly."

"That's what puzzles me," said Akira. "This strain from Phillipson seems to be very sensitive to killing by Bazuran. Yet I can't detect any response at all to the standard dose of Protex in my control experiment. First I thought I made a mistake, but then I tried several manufacturing lots of Protex, and none of them will kill this indicator strain."

Kazuko leaned over his shoulder, pulling his laboratory notebook toward her. She studied it intently for a few minutes. "I see no error in protocol," she said. "This is exactly how I would have done it."

"Well, I guess I should call Phillipson and check that he brought the right virus with him. As far as I know, there are no strains of Eke virus that are resistant to Protex."

"Perhaps the engineering of the indicator strain made it less sensitive to Protex, for some reason," suggested Kazuko. "You should test it with a tenfold higher amount of Protex."

"*Hai.* Good point," said Akira. "I'd also feel better if I could try Bazuran on the conventional strain of Eke virus. But Phillipson gave us only enough to test on the indicator strain. I'll have to request some more."

"I would check with Minoru before you contact Phillipson. I haven't heard anything about where the negotiations stand."

"Me either," said Akira. "I just wish I'd kept aside some Bazuran for even a limited test on our usual strain. I thought about it right after I put everything into the petri dishes." He began to replace the cultures in the incubator.

"Maybe you could reuse the Bazuran you already added to the indicator strain. I know it won't be exactly like testing it fresh, but as long as you retest it on the indicator strain, too, and show it still works, you can compare its effects on the two strains."

"Well, that might work, but it's Phillipson's responsibility to give us enough material so that we can perform tests to our satisfaction," Akira replied a little defensively as he finished tidying his bench.

"I'm not sure that responsibility is one of Phillipson's personal attributes," said Kazuko.

Downstairs, in the director's office, Minoru was glad to see Akira. Minoru had just completed a conference call with Toshimi and the Fukuda lawyers in Osaka, discussing the "Phillipson proposition." The whole business was distressing.

"How is number one son today?" asked Minoru, jokingly using the Chinese expression.

"I'd be better if I could understand these results with the virus from Phillipson," said Akira.

"Aha! This Bazuran compound doesn't really work, does it," Minoru gloated.

"On the contrary. It's Protex that I can't get to work. Something's wrong with the indicator strain. It was killed really efficiently by Bazuran, but none of the batches of Protex that I tried have any effect on its growth. Kazuko thinks that something in the engineering process might have caused the Eke virus to be less sensitive to Protex, so I'm planning to try higher doses of Protex. Still, I'd like to give Phillipson a call to ask if he can send me another batch of indicator strain, in case he made a mistake. I'll also need more Bazuran to repeat the test."

"Well, I ought to check with Toshimi to find out if it's okay for you to speak with Phillipson directly, given the legal situation. But darn it, Toshimi just left for New York, so I can't reach him until he lands. By then it will be the weekend and you won't be able to call Phillipson until Monday." Minoru continued to think aloud. "I really can't think of any legal reason why it wouldn't be okay for you to talk directly to Phillipson, especially considering that Toshimi wants us to get these results as soon as possible. You're just asking Phillipson for more sample to repeat the test, after all. I think you should go ahead and call. Maybe it will make him a little uncomfortable to know that things aren't going well with the testing. That would give me some satisfaction. He's such a condescending SOB."

Akira was surprised at Minoru's evident dislike. He was normally very mild-mannered, almost infuriatingly timid at times. "Glad to provide you with some satisfaction," said Akira with a smile. "I'll phone from upstairs, where my lab notes are."

As Akira turned to leave, Minoru was struck by a realization. "You know, if there was no mix-up of strains, then your results show that Eke virus could potentially mutate to be resistant to Protex. Then maybe we actually do need to buy the rights to this Bazuran. It would be like insurance, in case this mutation ever occurred in the wild."

"Well, it's completely improbable that a firefly luciferase gene could naturally insert into the wild-type virus and cause such a mutation," countered Akira. "But I suppose something similar could happen as a result of a more routine genetic process, though it's never been observed before. Let me at least confirm that we received the correct strain from Phillipson, before we alert Toshimi."

"*Hai,*" said Minoru. "That seems the best way to proceed."

Akira returned to his office cubbyhole at the back of the laboratory to place the call, shortly before 10:00 A.M.

It was shortly before 5:00 P.M. the previous day when the phone rang on Phillipson's secretary's desk in California.

"Hello. Virotox, Incorporated, here. This is Madeline Trotter speaking, secretary to Dr. Phillipson," said a pleasant voice with a British accent. Phillipson found that the best secretarial help came from the mother country.

"*Hai.* Dr. Hagai from Fukuda. Would like to speak to Dr. Phillipson, please."

"Just a moment," said Madeline. She put the phone on hold and pressed the intercom button for Phillipson's office.

"Someone from Fukuda, on the line for you, Dr. Phillipson," she said into the intercom. "A Doctor Hagai."

Hmph, thought Phillipson. One of the underlings. I wonder what he wants.

"Put him through," he said to Madeline.

The phone clicked, and he said, "Phillipson, here."

"Dr. Phillipson, I am Akira Hagai. I test Bazuran on indicator strain. I do control with Protex. It not kill indicator strain. I suspect some problem with indicator strain."

That was efficient of them, thought Phillipson. He needed to assess how much Akira had figured out and with whom he had shared his results. Phillipson knew he was treading a fine line between giving them enough information to sign the contract and too much information that might make them suspect his plans.

"That is odd," lied Phillipson. "Did you discuss your protocol with someone?" He used the same tone of voice he used when speaking to his lab assistant.

"*Hai*. Minoru say I should call. We suspect mutation in indicator strain, caused by insertion of firefly luciferase gene."

Perfect, thought Phillipson. They had come up with the wrong explanation for the right result. If they thought that Eke virus had the potential to become resistant to Protex, the contract for Bazuran was as good as signed. Now he just had to make sure that they didn't do any tests of Bazuran on wild-type virus until the signing actually took place. He had purposely provided only enough sample to test on the indicator strain. As long as they had run out of Bazuran and he was controlling the supply route, Phillipson had the matter well in hand.

To Akira he said, "Well, I suppose gene insertion could possibly cause Protex resistance, if regulation of protease levels is inherently unstable. Tell Minoru I suggest you repeat the experiment, with another batch of indicator strain. Unfortunately, the sample has to be hand-delivered, since Eke virus doesn't survive postal cargo flights. Let me see . . . I expect to see Toshimi at the Stanley symposium in Boston at the end of this month. I can give a new virus culture to Toshimi and he can carry it back to Osaka. Then you can fly down to pick it up.''

"Also, we need more Bazuran," said Akira. "I use everything you left behind to test indicator strain."

Excellent, thought Phillipson. He was now sure he had the situation under control. This confirmed that they hadn't tested Bazuran on the normal virus strain. And he was confident he could keep them from doing it by careful orchestration of the next set of experiments. Of course, the timing for delivery of the samples would be critical. He would give the indicator strain to Toshimi at the symposium. They would go ahead and confirm it was resistant to Protex, making Bazuran more desirable. He could easily stall on the second lot of Bazuran until he talked further to Toshimi to establish what they planned to do with it. If it sounded like this chap Akira planned to test the normal strain, there was one clear course of action Phillipson could take to inhibit progress on that front.

"Certainly," said Phillipson smoothly. "We have a new batch of Bazuran in production right now. I'm pretty sure it will be finished and quality-control tested by the week of the symposium. It shouldn't be a problem to bring it with me along with the virus."

"Thank you, Dr. Phillipson," said Akira. "I will tell Dr. Matsumoto to collect samples at Stanley symposium. Goodbye." After he hung up the receiver, Akira thought some more about his peculiar results with the indicator strain of

Eke virus. He should have asked Phillipson to send a double sample of Bazuran so he could test it on a conventional laboratory strain of Eke virus. When Toshimi went to the symposium, Akira would send with him a second request to Phillipson for more Bazuran, with a more thorough explanation of his experimental plans.

Good-bye to you, too, thought Phillipson and hung up. So far, so good. The Japanese had discovered the fallibility of Protex and would be prepared to sign the contract for Bazuran. As long as they didn't find out that Bazuran wouldn't work against wild-type Eke virus, there was no chance they would suspect his scheme. Even if they did the test, it was pretty improbable they would figure out his ultimate plans, but the bargaining clout of his threat to sell out to Roykan would be considerably reduced. Fortunately, in the locked cabinet of his private laboratory, he had everything at his disposal that was required for dealing with the situation. If he started tonight, he calculated, he would have just enough time before the Stanley symposium to prepare the sample he would bring with him.

Phillipson was anxious to begin his work as soon as possible, but he had to be sure of no interruptions when handling the toxins. He couldn't risk the possibility Madeline would still be putting calls through or that some ambitious technician would be working late and disturb him. To kill time, and to think out his strategy more clearly, he decided to go for a jog and then drive into San Mateo for a bite to eat. By the time he returned, the place would be empty.

Virotox, Inc., occupied one of a clone of buildings constructed to house high-technology companies. The surrounding Baylands Park was recently completed as part of the amenities for these tenants and included a jogging path that skirted a small artificial lake, bordering on a golf course. The landfill on which the park had been built still had a faint odor of fetid garbage, especially when it had baked in the sun all day.

As Phillipson pounded the path, he considered his options. He had known all along that implementation of his scheme might require eliminating some meddling individuals. Admittedly, he was pleased to be able to use his extensive knowledge of toxins and their actions. Now it was just a matter of deciding which one was appropriate, given the situation. It was pretty clear when and how he could administer it. But it wasn't totally clear if this extreme measure would be called for. And, of course, it would be a waste of a strategic tool if elimination turned out to be unnecessary. He needed a method that would give him the option of making a last-minute decision.

An hour later, Phillipson dined alone at La Grenouille, a popular and expensive haunt of the local business clientele. While dissecting the delicate layer of crust surrounding a coulibiac of salmon, he thought of the perfect solution. He recalled one of his shaman gurus telling him about Gouata toxin for sending gifts to your enemies. The toxin was inert in the dark, when wrapped in a package. As soon as it was exposed to light it vaporized instantly, and was absorbed by the skin and the respiratory system of the person opening the package. It rapidly dispersed into the air so that even bystanders were not affected by it. The best part was the symptoms. Once absorbed into the blood, the toxin accumulated in the liver, producing an effect like hepatitis, but a hepatitis from which the victim never recovered. The course of the poisoning would be no different from the course of the illness except the outcome.

SEVEN

Family Reunion

The last few weeks of spring quarter usually reached a peak of frustration for Celeste. She still had several more lectures to give and final exams to write and grade. By this time Celeste was itching to do some benchwork, if only to deal with some of the technical problems that her students and fellows had raised when she was otherwise occupied. At least her irregular forays into the lab kept her in touch with the reality of experimental work, a connection that many of her senior colleagues, dabbling in biotechnology ventures, had lost.

At the end of spring quarter this year, things didn't seem as bad as usual to Celeste. She traced her better mood to the encounter with Mac in the allergy clinic. She admitted she was acting adolescent, but having a slight crush on her disruptive student in Micro 214 certainly made teaching more tolerable. On several occasions the two of them got into an intense discussion about the design or interpretation of an experiment. Her didactic arguments were sharpened by the undertone of sexual tension she felt. It was good for the graduate students to hear scientific issues challenged, but Celeste flushed when she thought of how surprised they would be if they knew the source of her inspiration. Well, it was all harmless fantasy anyway. Celeste was glad to have the excuse of the Stanley symposium to get away for the weekend and put things in perspective.

Evie Pritsker's administrative efforts had been successful and she was pleased with the turnout for the symposium. Jane Stanley was deeply touched. The schedule featured talks by the most accomplished graduates of the Stanley laboratory, many of whom were now professors or high-level executives in drug companies. The venue was the Science Center on the Harvard undergraduate campus, where both Jane and Celeste had occasionally given lectures, although Jane's laboratory was across the river at the medical school. The site had been chosen for its proximity to the traditional Harvard faculty club, where the testimonial dinner would be held. The bright seventies upholstery in the Science Center lecture halls now looked dated to Celeste. Nonetheless, as she walked into the building she was hit by a flood of sensations, recalling the anxieties of her graduate student days. These were perhaps heightened by the nervousness she felt in anticipation of her speech at dinner.

Celeste had relatively little apprehension about her research talk during the symposium itself. She delivered a condensed version of her usual research seminar, and she enjoyed the opportunity to speak to an audience who didn't question the details of the experiments but were interested in the big picture. Celeste often acquired good ideas at such symposia, both from discussion after her own talk and from thinking about "big picture" presentations by other investigators.

At the morning coffee break after Celeste's talk, there were at least a hundred people milling about the lobby of the Science Center. Celeste picked up a Styrofoam cup of coffee from a table outside the lecture hall and scanned the crowd. Over by the wall she spotted Toshimi, speaking intently to a gray-haired man in a corduroy jacket, whose back was facing her. Celeste crossed the lobby toward them and watched Toshimi's companion push back his hair, with a fashion-model gesture, which gave Celeste a sense of déjà vu. As she approached, Celeste overheard him speaking to Toshimi. She immediately recognized the upper-class British accent of the mystery man who had tripped over her bag at the airport. Though she couldn't see his face, she needed no further confirmation of his identity, and her heart rate accelerated with enthusiasm. "I've got the sample for Hagai in the minibar fridge in my hotel room," the mystery man said to Toshimi. "I thought I would give it to you at the last possible moment, to maintain preservation. Now, perhaps we could review the data from Hagai's test experiments."

"*Hai, hai.*" Toshimi nodded and squatted to unlock his metal briefcase. He removed two sealed documents and set them on the floor beside the briefcase, then locked the briefcase. Still squatting, he handed the packets up to Phillipson. "This one is data you know about. This one is letter from Akira Hagai, he ask me to deliver. I suspect it propose new experiment." Then he caught sight of Celeste coming up behind Phillipson and jumped spryly to his feet.

Grinning widely, he extended his hand in exaggerated American style, barely bowing. "Aah, Dr. Braun. We must not meet like this."

"Toshimi," said Celeste, "so good to see you again, so soon." She took his hand and leaned over to kiss his cheek, something she would never have done in Japan. "An American custom," she explained to the beaming man.

"Please to meet Dr. Simon Phillipson," said Toshimi, snapping back into Japanese formality.

"Delighted to see you again, my dear," said Phillipson. He held out his right hand, and when she took it, he cupped her responding hand with his left, and his eyes sought hers. "If only I'd known that the good-looking woman who saved me from falling on my face at the airport was the famous Celeste Braun, I most certainly would have given in to my instinct to introduce myself. I find it difficult to forget a beautiful face."

Celeste was flustered and undeniably flattered by the intimate double-handed greeting and evident come-on. So there *was* an explanation for why this man had looked familiar when she encountered him at the airport. If he had been in the Stanley lab within a few years of her, she would surely have seen a picture of him, or maybe even been introduced to him if he had been back to visit. She should certainly have remembered meeting him, though, and suddenly it dawned on her: Wasn't he the guy whom Jane had thrown out? Then he certainly wouldn't have visited. But if he was, what was he doing here? Celeste hoped fervently she was wrong, but her intuition mocked her. Of all the people she could be attracted to, she had to pick this one. She needed to see Harry Freeman. He would be able to tell her if Phillipson was indeed the notorious fraud. Where was Harry, anyway? She hadn't seen him before her talk, and hoped he hadn't missed it.

Confused, Celeste withdrew her hand from Phillipson's.

She turned to Toshimi. "Toshimi, I wanted to ask you about—"

"*Hai,*" he cut her off. "Please. Excuse me, Celeste. I talk with Dr. Phillipson now." He bowed her away. "We talk later. Maybe take bath together." He giggled uneasily. In spite of the in-joke, Celeste definitely felt dismissed. Something was bothering Toshimi. It couldn't just be that he missed his usual trappings of power.

"I'll look forward to sitting with you at dinner," she said to Toshimi. She nodded to Phillipson. "Nice to have found out who you were, uh, are," she said awkwardly, and turned back to the crowded lobby quickly, to avoid a farewell handshake. What a bummer! Reappearance of a romantic encounter, only to discover he's a fraud. A damned attractive fraud, though.

Across the throng, Celeste caught sight of a burly man with a reddish beard. Harry was standing in the courtyard, just outside the glass doors leading into the lobby. His arm was around Jane Stanley's shoulders and they were talking with a young man in a jacket and tie who fiddled uncomfortably with his collar. Celeste hurriedly joined them.

"Celeste, dear. You must remember Harry Freeman," said Jane superfluously as Celeste and Harry greeted each other in an enthusiastic embrace.

"Jane," Celeste jokingly admonished her. "You know Harry was my heartthrob in the lab."

"Celeste, I'd like you to meet Bill Harrison, my last graduate student," said Jane, gesturing toward the young man in a tie. It sounded like Bill was the last of the Mohicans. "Bill is deciding what to do once he gets his degree, and our expert here is handing out free advice."

"Celeste Braun," said Celeste, extending her hand to

Bill. "Well, Harry *is* an authority on imaginative scientific careers."

"And an authority on being a graduate student, having spent twice as long as most students in Jane's lab," added Harry.

"That's no idle boast," Celeste said to Bill. "I'll bet it was at least ten years."

"Well, let's see," mused Harry. He counted off on his fingers. "One year of courses, one year of being a teaching fellow, two years on the toxin project after Phillipson arrived, two years trying to repeat my one promising result, one year setting up hybridoma technology, and two years to get out my first and only paper. Then six months to write a history of negative results for my thesis. So I guess it was nine years and six months altogether before retirement."

"You know, Harry," said Jane. "After all these years, I've never understood your elusive result with that toxin of Phillipson's. It's funny. I can still picture the original killing data and then those interminable experiments showing only slowed growth. Though I can't remember which toxin it was."

"I still use it as a curse," said Harry. Pointing his finger at Bill, as though he were holding him at gunpoint, he bellowed, "Bazuran!"

"That means your academic career will end and you will become a newspaper reporter," interpreted Celeste.

"Well, I doubt Bill is in danger of ending his academic career with a *Cell* and *Nature* paper already on his c.v.," said Jane defensively.

"Anyway, I'm not sure it's a curse to be science editor for the *New York Times*," said Bill politely.

"Well, let me reassure you on that score," countered

Harry. "My only moments of pleasure are when I get to see old lab friends passing through New York." He placed his large arm around Celeste's shoulders and gave her a squeeze.

Celeste felt herself blush, she hoped not too obviously. They had never been in love, but their physical relationship had started in the lab, when Harry's friendship helped Celeste recover from a particularly trying affair. It was a comfortable flirtation, and she and Harry had remained the best of friends, even after getting involved with other people. Whenever they met for dinner in New York and they were both single, their reminiscences usually didn't finish with dessert. His huge physical presence now stirred Celeste, and she wondered if she'd packed her diaphragm.

Further conversation was conveniently interrupted by Evie, who came by clapping her hands to usher the nattering scientists back into the lecture hall for the next session.

In the early days of her faculty appointment, Celeste adhered to a strict, self-imposed "lady scientist" dress code, afraid that otherwise she might not be taken seriously by her predominantly male colleagues. As her professional career developed, she became more relaxed about her appearance and enjoyed the few occasions for which she could dress to kill. Now she was feeling slick and sophisticated in a backless dark blue silk dress. One compensation for being small-breasted was that she could wear such dresses without a bra. And being braless made her feel bold.

As Celeste continued her speech, she knew she was on a roll. This was the first time she'd made an after-dinner speech, and it was clearly being well received. Undoubtedly the enthusiasm had something to do with the generous pouring of wine at dinner, but Celeste had also gauged the

mood just right and warmed to her audience. She surprised
herself with her own spontaneity and even made a few un-
planned jokes. So far, Celeste had managed to give an an-
ecdotal account of Jane's career with amusing slides of
many of the people in the room, without belittling the significance of Jane's scientific contributions. To wind up,
though, the occasion called for some more serious remarks.

"To finish, and allow you to proceed into the more alcoholic phase of this testimonial celebration, I would like
to share one of my personal legacies from Jane Stanley.
Before I took my oral examination in the second year of
graduate school, Jane insisted that I read the entire eleven
novels of C. P. Snow's *Strangers and Brothers*. Being a
diligent graduate student, I naturally resented the distraction
from reviewing mathematical equations for ultracentrifu-
gation." The audience laughed. "But, of course, the Snow
novels are now the only thing of value that I remember
from my pre-orals cramming." A reduced number of
laughs followed, responding to Celeste's change in tone.

Celeste continued, "As many of you probably know,
Snow trained as a scientist and worked for the British government during the Second World War. Afterward he remained a civil servant, interfacing between academic
science and society, in various capacities. In *Strangers and
Brothers* Snow deals with issues from his work, describing
academic life, the development of nuclear weapons, and
their subsequent regulation. He offers no magical solution
to the problem of scientists' responsibility for how their
discoveries are applied. But he does portray the scientific
community in a humane, positive light that is now in danger
of being completely extinguished.

"Reading C. P. Snow's *The Affair,* which is the eighth
novel in the series, reveals a sad contrast with the contem-

porary attitude toward fraud in science. In this novel, an academic physicist is accused of fraud. His case is dealt with by a tribunal of academic colleagues, entirely behind the closed doors of the Cambridge college of which he is a faculty member. The scientists themselves are the most anxious to establish the truth about the case. The college is anxious to avoid bad publicity for their academic enterprise. If we examine today's public sensationalism regarding cases of so-called scientific fraud, we are horrified by the suspicion that it has stirred up against the scientific enterprise in general. Evidently the Cambridge college's concerns, as portrayed by Snow, were justified.

"For example, the federal government's Committee on Scientific Integrity has had a seriously negative effect on both the execution and perception of science in our country. First of all, the mere establishment of a government committee to dig up cases of fraud obscures the fact that the scientific enterprise has built-in mechanisms for self-policing. Fraudulent work never stands the test of reproducibility and is rapidly discovered and weeded out. Second, the publicity generated by the CSI just by making accusations, whether they are right or wrong, is highly antiscience. These accusations reinforce the idea of the corrupt or *mad* scientist, which translates to the general public that science as a whole is evil. Witness the popularity of the film *Jurassic Park*. Interestingly, the major crime in *Jurassic Park*, besides the greed of the park developers, was that the premise of the park was based on bad science. According to the script, the scientists in the film made an error in their choice of 'filler DNA.' This sort of error would never happen in real-life science because there are too many checks and balances built into the way science is done. Within our community we know that those who are perceived as *mad* scientists are really just *bad* scientists, and their activities are soon limited by their lack of credibility.

"The retirement of Jane Stanley comes at a time when the value and integrity of our enterprise are being questioned. It is only to be hoped her retirement does not foreshadow retirement of our own role in society. The only way to reverse this trend is to follow in Jane Stanley's exemplary footsteps. Be honest, do good science, and educate."

The assembled guests had become quiet during Celeste's last remarks, and when she finished, the silence remained for a few seconds before enthusiastic applause broke out. Applause continued steadily as Celeste walked over to Jane, who stood up from her seat at the head table and hugged her. Both women were teary-eyed and had a lump in their throats. Several men surreptitiously removed handkerchiefs and blew their noses.

In the publike bar downstairs at the faculty club, the celebration continued. Celeste was showered with congratulations on her speech. Harry was encouraged to report it in the press, in view of the pending CSI investigation. Harry suggested that Celeste accompany him back to the hotel to give him a copy of her notes. Exhausted from her two public presentations that day, Celeste readily agreed. The party was apparently breaking up anyway.

Making her way out of the bar, Celeste arranged to meet Jane for brunch the following day. Then she sought out Toshimi to finalize their plans for her next trip. Simon Phillipson hadn't let him alone all evening, but fortunately she saw Phillipson head off to the men's room and was able to catch Toshimi's eye. Toshimi came over to her quickly.

"Celeste, we need you return sooner to Fukuda. Can you come next week?"

She shook her head. "Next week's impossible. Classes don't end till the following week. But I could try to change the reservation for just after that. I think, anyway. I'll have to check my schedule and call you. What's going on?"

"Can't talk now," said Toshimi, nodding at Phillipson emerging from the men's room. "But you must fly to Sapporo." The idea of a repeat encounter with Phillipson made Celeste uncomfortable, so she gave Toshimi another peck on the cheek and said, "I'll call you Sunday evening when I get back, Monday afternoon, your time." Toshimi didn't even have a chance to promise to bathe with her before she went off in search of Harry.

In the men's room, Phillipson had reread the letter from Akira Hagai. His comprehension of its contents would have dire consequences, so he wanted to be sure he understood it correctly. Phillipson had prepared two alternative packages to give to Toshimi for delivery to Hagai, and rereading the letter confirmed which one he should dispatch. Both packages contained a new sample of the Eke virus indicator strain. The only difference between the two samples was in the packaging material. One was more carefully sealed off to be sure it did not leak any contents before being opened by Hagai. Neither package contained any more Bazuran, which, as Phillipson explained to Toshimi, was slightly delayed in production and he would be sure to bring on his next visit. Phillipson also asked Toshimi to apologize to Hagai for the delay, especially considering the new experiment Hagai had proposed in his letter. Privately, Phillipson knew that Hagai would never have the opportunity to do that experiment.

By the time Celeste and Harry made it out the door of the faculty club, they were walking about half a block behind Toshimi and Phillipson. Still deep in conversation, those two were clearly headed to the same hotel at the corner of Quincy Street and Massachusetts Avenue.

"He's got balls showing up at this symposium," Harry muttered under his breath.

"Tell me about him," prompted Celeste. All day she had been secretly hoping that maybe the incident he was involved in had been some kind of misunderstanding. "I never knew what he did to cause Jane to kick him out."

"Well, first, he completely disrupted Jane's lab when he showed up with his precious toxins. For a couple of years, she had every new graduate student in the lab testing those damn compounds for antiviral activity. How he conned her into having *us* do it, I'll never know. I suppose I'm bitter because I was the main casualty. For some reason, I started off with a promising result and then could never repeat it. It's almost like the compound changed properties overnight.

"Then," continued Harry, "when Jane was finally convinced the toxin project was a bust, she insisted Phillipson work on something different. He was pretty pissed off, but agreed to help out with Tompkins' project and soon started taking credit for experiments that Tompkins had done. Finally Tompkins accused him of stealing from his notebook, and actually trapped Phillipson into doing a meaningless experiment to prove it. Jane, of course, backed Tompkins completely and asked Phillipson to leave. Naturally he denied any misdemeanor and insisted that he had just been checking Tompkins' notebook to be reminded of a protocol. The whole incident was pretty ugly, but I'm sure Jane was right to act as she did."

"I'm surprised Evie invited Phillipson to the symposium."

"He wasn't on the original invitation list but apparently

he contacted Evie and offered to pay for the wine. He said it was to make amends, but it did buy him space for the logo of his new company, Virotox, at the bottom of the menu.''

Celeste pulled the folded menu from her evening bag and checked it out. ''Hmph. I didn't notice that before.'' So the guy was a complete sleaze. Just her luck.

Celeste and Harry got out of the elevator on the fifth floor of the hotel. They were just in time to see Phillipson and Toshimi at the far end of the corridor disappear into what appeared to be Phillipson's room. But Celeste wasn't thinking about Phillipson anymore. In the elevator, Harry had stood behind her and, kissing the back of her neck, insinuated both hands under her wrap and through the sides of her backless dress to caress her bare breasts. She was ready to reciprocate.

EIGHT

Noodle Protocol

Exactly two weeks after the Stanley symposium, Celeste was airborne once again. Over Hawaii she got up to stretch. Standing in the aisle, Celeste raised both arms above her head and pressed against the luggage compartments on either side with the palms of her hands, disengaging her spine from a cramped curve. Thinking of her yoga teacher, she tried to press her tailbone toward the floor of the plane, drop her shoulders, and reach for the sky. What would this position be called? she wondered. The garment bag?

Celeste wandered down the aisle and between the curtains to see if the magazine rack in economy class contained something more interesting than two copies of *Business World*. Her search was rewarded with a well-thumbed copy of last month's issue of *Femina*. She'd been curious to look at this recently publicized fashion magazine for young professionals. Magazine in hand, Celeste headed back to club class by walking to the back of the plane and up the aisle on the other side. On the way she peered into the galley, where the stewardesses were picking at their meals. Celeste wondered whether their food was any more palatable than the passengers' or whether the job was selected by women who could live on cardboard.

"And then, after the Grand Hotel in Taipei, I didn't hear from him for months," one of the stewardesses complained to her colleague.

"Well, what did you expect, honey?" said a voice that Celeste found familiar.

"Debbie Kane!" Celeste exclaimed. "I didn't recognize you in uniform."

"Don't worry about it. We all look the same, hon," bantered Debbie automatically. Then she broke into a genuine smile as she recognized her visitor. "*You're* looking great, Celeste. Being a nerd must agree with you. Hey, I'm on break after I do the midmovie Cokes. Where's your seat?"

"Club class five C," said Celeste. "I'd enjoy some company." Almost a year earlier Celeste and Debbie had been in the same yoga class at the BAU gym. Debbie was intermittently living with a physician for the BAU outpatient clinics who had picked her up on a flight to London. Apparently the relationship had soured and Debbie had disappeared from the class. Celeste's acquaintance with Debbie was a classic locker room friendship. They were drawn together by the experience of sharing a particularly inspiring yoga teacher, but otherwise had little in common.

Celeste returned to 5C and opened *Femina*. She started to flip through the glossy fashion photographs and missed the table of contents. So far, the minimal text-to-advertisement ratio was typical of these sorts of magazines. Suddenly, staring up at Celeste was a full-page photographic portrait of the beautiful Senator Teresita Jiminez.

Apparently she was last month's *Femina* woman of the month. A complete account of her rise to political stardom, her wardrobe, and her doings in Congress was provided in that order, on the page opposite her exquisitely made-up face.

"Senator Jiminez is well known on Capitol Hill for her no-nonsense attitude," read Celeste. "She has made the scientific community pull up its socks in more than one arena. As chair of the Committee on Scientific Integrity, she is heading an investigation of misappropriation of biotechnology funds in academic laboratories. She has also shown no mercy for self-serving environmentalists by her strong opposition to congressional approval of the Biodiversity Treaty. The treaty, a Democratic initiative, proposes an international ban on patents for rain-forest products, on the premise that economic development will threaten biodiversity. Ms. Jiminez argues that the environmentalists' campaign to preserve their research domain is standing in the way of great medical advances in the form of new drugs that the rain forest has to offer. If these substances are not patented, they could fall into the wrong hands, and in this era of emerging diseases we could, as Jiminez points out, be at the mercy of some foreign drug company selling a life-saving therapeutic."

Appalled, Celeste read further. "While many men quake when Jiminez opens her mouth to speak from the Senate floor, she clearly has ardent admirers. At Washington parties, she is often escorted by General Ralph Johnson, M.D. Johnson is currently director of the Pentagon's biological warfare division and formerly acting chair of the Committee for Scientific Integrity, before its administration was taken over by Congress. It is rumored that Ms. Jiminez may be more than a political protégée to the recently widowed general.''

Before Celeste turned the page, Debbie perched herself on the arm of Celeste's seat.

''Now, there's a woman who's made something of her life,'' commented Debbie.

''I wouldn't admire *her*,'' said Celeste vehemently. ''She's positively insidious. Imagine, supporting exploitation of the rain forests in the name of medical progress. It looks like she's now set on destroying the natural world, as well as the reputations of those who study it.''

''Gosh, I wish I had some sense of purpose like you seem to. Or even like her, though I guess she's no good,'' said Debbie wistfully. ''The most I can do for the world is serve Cokes during turbulence. Lately I've been thinking about quitting and going back home, where I could help run the family farm in Montana. The second I graduated from high school, I traded on my good looks to get away from the hick life of the Bitterroot Valley. But all I dream about now is getting out of the 'Friendly Skies' and back to Big Sky. Ever since I broke up with Don, I've been so damn lonely. Life in the fast lane is not as glamorous as people think.''

Celeste sympathized, especially with this last remark. ''Look, you should come back to yoga class. Sheena and the gang would be really happy to see you.''

''I know,'' said Debbie. ''But every time I think about going, my flight schedule gets changed. Like next week they're switching me over to the SFO–London–Frankfurt route.''

''Well, why don't you give me a call when you know when you're in town. If you can't relax with yoga, you can at least relax with a beer.''

"I'd love to," said Debbie. As Celeste started fishing around in her purse for a card with her phone number, the stewardess call button rang twice in succession.

"Damn," said Debbie, "I said I'd take call, 'cause it's usually quiet during the movie. I better get going."

"Okay, but promise to give me a ring." They exchanged phone numbers, Debbie writing hers on the back of a frequent-flier program application, which Celeste tucked into her address book.

Celeste was met at the airport in Sapporo by Akira and Kazuko. Out of their white lab coats, they could have been any young Japanese couple, headed off for a weekend of taking pictures of each other.

"Toshimi-*san* wait for us in car," said Akira. "We drive to famous inn at Shikotsu-Toya National Park. Have conference there tomorrow. Today, get over jet lag."

They ushered Celeste into the backseat of a black sedan, where Toshimi was already sitting behind a white-gloved, uniformed driver. The seat backs were decorated with the lace doilies characteristic of Japanese taxicabs, and a box of Kleenex in a knitted cover rested on the immaculate back shelf. Celeste saw Akira get into the front seat of a tan car ahead of Toshimi's car, where Minoru was at the wheel. Kazuko got into the backseat of Minoru's car. Apparently they were driving to the inn in a convoy.

"It doesn't do a lot of good if my chaperone is in another car," said Celeste flirtatiously to Toshimi, referring to Kazuko.

"Chaperone just for appearance. Avoid international incident," replied Toshimi with a smile. "I hope Akira explain. No business today. Just lunch, then quiet drive to park. Tonight drink sake. Cure jet lag for clear head tomorrow.'' Sake certainly made it easier to sleep, but Celeste was skeptical about a clear head the following day.

Lunch was in a noodle restaurant in a rural town about fifty miles from the outskirts of Sapporo. The thin soba in salty brown broth tasted wonderful. It was a perfect antidote to the airline breakfast Celeste had consumed before changing planes at Osaka for Sapporo. Celeste felt comforted by the warm liquid filling her stomach. For a few minutes, noisy slurping replaced all conversation. Then Celeste realized that her companions had put down their chopsticks and were watching her eat, with concern on their faces.

"You not like soba?" asked Minoru.

"On the contrary. This is marvelous," said Celeste.

"You must make noise, then," said Minoru, seriously.

"Like this," said Akira and sucked in a mouthful of noodles with considerable gusto and sound effects.

"Oh, I see. I *am* sorry," said Celeste, and proceeded to suck up a few noodles, but not very loudly. "I guess it takes practice," she said, embarrassed. "You all know that I love Japanese food. Especially sushi," Celeste tried to reassure them to make up for her apparently bad manners.

Akira, realizing that they had made Celeste uncomfortable, attempted gallantly to change the subject. "Me, too," he said. "I did love sushi. Too much." He giggled.

"Yes," said Kazuko, giggling with her husband. "Three years ago Akira got hepatitis. He was greedy and ate bad sushi. He don't eat any more." Celeste was too tired to explain the immunology of hepatitis to these biochemists though she usually felt a responsibility to remind her more molecularly oriented colleagues about physiological issues. She also didn't want to increase their embarrassment. In fact, the strain of hepatitis carried in seafood can stimulate pretty good immunity, unlike the sexually transmitted strain, and Akira should now be able to eat even contaminated sushi with impunity.

The fatigue that was overwhelming Celeste in the noodle restaurant won out. Within five minutes of getting back into the car after lunch, she fell into a deep sleep, napping until the car stopped while the driver paid the guard at the entrance to the national park. She woke with a start, to see Toshimi smiling.

"Not to worry," he said. "I am very tired from Osaka. I sleep, too." He smiled more broadly. "Now we slept together," he said.

"But still no bath together," replied Celeste. She felt quite refreshed.

A heavy mist had set in, adding to the peacefulness of the national park. This was the first road that Celeste had been on in Japan that was not flanked by evidence of habitation or cultivation. They passed a metal roadside sign with a picture of a fox silhouette in white on a blue background. There were white Japanese characters underneath.

"What does that mean?" asked Celeste.

"Fox crossing," said Toshimi and giggled.

"I'm impressed," said Celeste. "Foxes are pretty rare in California."

The park road continued through an open forest of young birch trees, whose shiny white trunks contrasted with the low gray sky. Celeste and Toshimi rode in silence until they passed another sign displaying a picture of a deer.

"Deer crossing," said Toshimi quite solemnly, without breaking the spell surrounding them.

Shortly, the road became steeper and more winding and the birch forest was replaced by a denser wood of evergreen trees, a little too closely packed to have grown up naturally. But there were no obvious signs of human life until, coming around a bend, they confronted a large sign that said in English "Lake Toyako Inn," with the equivalent in Japanese characters underneath. The driver turned onto the side road leading up to the lake and the inn.

Then they passed another small blue-and-white sign displaying a picture of a fish.

"Trout crossing," said Toshimi, and giggled delightedly, at his own joke.

The inn, overlooking Lake Toyako, was built of red brick and glass. A well-manicured lawn spread below the inn and extended down to the water's edge, where there was a small wooden boat dock. Celeste left her bags in the lobby and wandered down to the shore. The scene before her had the stillness of a black-and-white photograph. The deep water of the lake reflected the black silhouettes of the mountains against the gray sky. A lone fisherman in a rowboat barely caused a ripple in the surface of the water. At that moment, Celeste was transported by the same aesthetic sense that had overtaken her in the Japanese garden in the park in Sapporo. She felt the beauty of nature's solitude represented in traditional Japanese art and, thinking of Debbie, understood her wish to escape the urban bustle and return to Montana.

The next morning Celeste was surprised by her alarm clock, a new experience in her four trips to Japan. Celeste remembered nothing about dinner the previous evening except that large quantities of sake were consumed. Perhaps Toshimi's theory about sake and jet lag was correct after all. She drew a deep hot bath and luxuriantly washed herself and her hair. She loved the way the Japanese soap and shampoo changed the way she smelled to herself. The scent was exotic and subtly erotic.

After a Western-style breakfast, the Fukuda meeting got

down to business. They convened in a small conference room overlooking the lawn and the lake. Although Kazuko was designated to take notes, there was no pretense that she was an office lady in this company.

"We must explain Phillipson proposal to Celeste," said Toshimi to his colleagues. Then to Celeste he said, "First I must repeat this is highly sensitive issue. Your presence here is secret and should remain so."

"Simon Phillipson?" asked Celeste, unsure if she had understood correctly, but remembering how inseparable he was from Toshimi at the Stanley symposium.

"Yes, Simon Phillipson. He offer to sell us rights to toxin that could replace Protex. If we don't buy, then he sell to Roykan, so they compete."

Having just heard Harry's account of Phillipson's spectacular failure to prove his toxins useful in Jane Stanley's lab, Celeste was puzzled. "He must have discovered a new toxin," she said. "What's the name of this one?"

"Bazuran," said Toshimi, Akira, and Minoru simultaneously.

"That's strange. It seems to me that's one they've already tested." Celeste's subconscious stimulated her to make a gun-pointing gesture with her finger and thumb, reiterating Harry's gesture at the recent symposium. "It sounds like the same toxin that Harry Freeman worked on," she said, "but I must not be remembering correctly. It simply couldn't be the same because Harry never got consistent results with his toxin, and believe me, he tried exhaustively." Nonetheless, she looked at her watch and did a quick calculation of the time in New York. "I could call him later to check. He'll be in the newsroom until at least lunchtime here."

"Well, Bazuran work well for us," said Akira. "And I

find evidence that Eke virus can show Protex resistance."

"So we think we must buy rights, as insurance policy," said Minoru.

"Hold on a minute, you're going too fast," said Celeste. "Let me look at your data."

"Honor to show you," said Akira, and he went over the data that he had already discussed with Kazuko and Minoru. "Phillipson give us indicator strain of Eke virus that make firefly luciferase when it multiply, so it glow in the dark. But indicator strain is not killed by Protex, even one hundred times normal dose. So then I think maybe he give us wrong virus indicator strain. So I ask him to send second sample of indicator strain and more Bazuran.

"While I wait, I try to reuse Bazuran on usual Eke virus test strain," continued Akira. "It still kill indicator strain at very low dose, not toxic to human cells. On usual Eke virus test strain same dose cause slow growth but not kill."

"Let me see if I'm understanding you correctly," said Celeste. "Phillipson gave you a special indicator strain. This strain is killed by Bazuran, but not at all sensitive to Protex. Then you reused Bazuran and it still kills the indicator strain but on the usual test strain of Eke virus, it only slows growth and doesn't kill it. Have you repeated these results with fresh Bazuran?"

"Not yet. Cannot repeat until Phillipson bring more. But I think results correct because new batch of indicator strain also killed by reused Bazuran, but also show no sensitivity to Protex like first batch."

Akira's confirmation of this last piece of data hung over the group, like a cloud of explosive gas. They sat in silence, as though recognizing its volatility would ignite it. Since Protex had been discovered, no resistant Eke virus mutants had ever been described. If such a mutant virus escaped the laboratory it would need to be dealt with efficiently and effectively or the world would be thrown back to the days before Protex, when threats of an Eke virus epidemic could be controlled only by complete annihilation of an infected community. Financial considerations aside, the potential global threat made it critical to develop an effective drug against such a mutant and thereby justified Fukuda's acquisition of Bazuran. In gaining the sole distribution rights for Protex years earlier, the management at Fukuda had essentially taken on responsibility for protecting the world from Eke virus.

But there was something else about Akira's data that worried Celeste, in addition to the obvious danger posed by a mutant Eke virus. She sensed there was something illegitimate and potentially threatening about Phillipson's dealings with Fukuda and was beginning to suspect that Phillipson might somehow be capitalizing on results that Harry had obtained earlier. The data from Akira sounded suspiciously like Harry's original data with whatever toxin he had been working with. She concentrated hard to remember the conversation between Jane and Harry at the Stanley symposium.

Celeste broke the silence and expressed her puzzlement out loud. "Maybe Bazuran *was* the toxin that Harry studied. I remember Jane mentioned something about slowing virus growth. But then again, they also mentioned that Harry's results were not reproducible." Celeste just couldn't be sure about her suspicions until she talked with Harry.

"Celeste, we have much confusion how to proceed," said Toshimi. "As businessmen, we cannot let Roykan have competitive product. As health care providers, we owe our patients that if Protex is not safe, we can provide alternative. Phillipson ask twenty million dollars for deal. This include patent rights to toxin and manufacture proto-col. They will supply plant from Amazon. This is a lot of money to risk for one product, even for us.''

"Well," said Celeste, drawing a breath. Here was clear further evidence of Phillipson's dishonesty. "Even if there is an Eke virus mutant and Phillipson's toxin can kill it, he can't offer you the toxin rights if the Biodiversity Treaty is passed. The treaty would effectively annul patents on any-thing produced in the rain forest. So you can at least hold off on that part of the agreement. On the other hand, what if it does turn out to be the same toxin Harry Freeman worked on? From the sound of Akira's data, Harry may have already observed the same effect with Bazuran, that it slowed the growth of the wild-type strain, suggesting it might have a greater effect on a mutant. So if the treaty fails and patents on rain-forest products are allowed, Harry would actually be the one with the rights to any patent using the toxin therapeutically. Have you told Phillipson yet about Akira's results with the conventional virus strain?"

"No, I reused original sample of Bazuran while I wait for new sample, so I don't tell him nothing yet," said Ak-ira.

Celeste's sense of betrayal by Phillipson was no longer mere personal regret. It had escalated into full-fledged dis-gust and the desire for revenge. She was formulating an experiment in the back of her mind that might help Fukuda counteract his threat. It involved a method of analysis that she had just recently developed in her own laboratory.

"Well, if you can stall another week, I can take the in-dicator strain back to my lab and do a different test my-self," suggested Celeste. As she proceeded to explain her theory, the Fukuda scientists looked increasingly shocked. "I think it's just possible that Phillipson may have cheated Harry out of his Ph.D. project. You see, Harry observed that one of Phillipson's toxins, possibly Bazuran, killed a particular Eke virus culture that he was working with. Then he was never able to repeat that result, but could only show that the toxin would slow the growth of Eke virus. Considering Akira's results, Harry's findings could be explained if he had discovered a mutant strain of Eke virus that was sensitive to Bazuran and Phillipson switched strains on him. Maybe the indicator strain Phillipson gave you is that same mutant strain of virus. The fact that it is insensitive to Protex certainly suggests it's a mutant."

"You mean," said Toshimi, his tone hardening, "he want us to pay so much money for Bazuran thinking that it kill wild-type strain, when it only kill a mutant laboratory strain? He think we are that stupid?" The barely controlled anger in his voice impressed Celeste. She knew there was a powerful side to Toshimi. This was the first time she had seen it for herself.

"Well, that's possible, but he must have known you would at least do the control with Protex on the indicator strain. Maybe he wanted you to figure out that Protex might not work on all strains and force you into buying Bazuran for 'insurance' purposes, as Minoru said earlier. Though I'm sure he didn't want you to realize that Harry may have actually discovered the properties of Bazuran before he did. And I doubt he wanted you to discover Bazuran doesn't kill the wild-type strain."

Toshimi had grown quite flushed and he almost spat out his response. "This Phillipson is not honorable. Even if we must have Bazuran, he cannot profit if it is not his to sell. We must know if this result is same as Harry found."

Celeste tried to sound calm and reassuring, though she agreed wholeheartedly with Toshimi's assessment of Phillipson. "I'll talk to Harry as soon he gets finished in the newsroom, which is usually about midnight New York time. But I'll still need to test the supposed mutant in my lab to be sure if it *is* a mutant. To explain Akira's data, its coat proteins should be a different size from the wild-type virus, and this is exactly what we've just set up to analyze."

"We stop by lab in Sapporo to send samples with you, when you return," said Toshimi. "Now we have lunch and wait for *New York Times* newsroom to close."

After lunch, Celeste made the two critical phone calls to the United States that were required to deal with Fukuda's problems. She hadn't spoken to Harry since they parted at the Stanley symposium, and he was pleased to hear from her.

"To answer your first question, Bazuran was definitely the name of the cursed compound. As for the second question, I threw out my old notebooks long ago. But there's a reasonable chance the original data is in my thesis, which is presumably gathering dust in some Harvard archive, as well as Jane's office and my mother's basement. Now, *you* answer *my* question," countered Harry. "When are you coming to New York? I miss your tits. Even if they *are* vestigial."

Celeste blushed in her hotel room. She enjoyed his down-to-earth attitude toward sex. "Talking dirty on international phone calls is probably a federal offense in this country," she said. "But you'll have to wait a while to do it in person. Unless you can meet me in D.C., when I go to review grant proposals for 'study section' in a couple of weeks. I can't remember exactly which nights I'll be there, but I could give you a call when I get back to San Francisco,'' she added hopefully.

''Mmmm. Sounds like a trip to the capital is definitely worth consideration. I look forward to hearing from you,'' said Harry.

The second phone call began considerably less successfully. Celeste needed someone from her lab to meet her at the airport the following evening, with a container of dry ice for transporting the virus. When no one picked up the receiver in the lab, she called her secretary's line.

''Oh,'' said Janice breezily, ''I guess I forgot to remind you, before you left. They've all gone to the department retreat at Asilomar and won't be back for two days.''

''Damn,'' said Celeste. She paused for a minute, thinking about what to do. This new secretary, Janice, irritated her. She was always defending the rest of the world against Celeste's demands rather than vice versa.

To fill the silence on the phone line, Janice said, ''Oh, by the way, Celeste, there's a man standing here in my office. He says he's a student at Tech and wants to know if you have any room in the lab for a summer student. I told him he'd have to wait until you get back.''

Mac! thought Celeste. This is too good to be true. ''Put him on the line, will you please, Janice.'' Celeste heard the receiver change hands.

''Hello, Mac?'' asked Celeste.

''Uh, yes, Dr. Braun. How'd you know it was me?''

''Just a lucky guess,'' said Celeste, smiling at the telephone. ''Look, Janice told me what you're interested in and—''

Mac interrupted her, ''It's not that I'm expecting you to pay me, Dr. Braun. I've made enough money this spring in my gardening business to take the summer off. I'd just like to get some bench experience before I start graduate school in the fall. I haven't had as much experience as most of the other students who will be starting at the same time.'' He spoke quickly and nervously.

Celeste was already a step ahead of him. ''Coincidentally, a short-term summer project has just come up that you might be able to help me with. We can discuss it when I get back. But meanwhile, I have a more immediate problem. I'm returning from Japan tomorrow evening and I'll be bringing a sample that has to be transferred immediately into dry ice. Apparently there's no one in my lab who will be around to meet me. Is there any chance you might be available?''

''I'd be glad to, Dr. Braun,'' said Mac. ''Let's see, I have to pick up Mac, Junior, at my ex-wife's place, before supper. But I could drop him at the movies while I go to the airport.''

Relieved, Celeste told Mac how to get the dry ice and instructed him where to meet her. When she hung up, she realized that she had acquired two new pieces of information. Mac was no longer attached to the mother of the child she had met in the allergy clinic. Also, he was a gardener. That explained a lot about his appearance, including the rough and grubby hands she had noticed.

The phone rang, bringing Celeste's thoughts back to the hotel room. It was Kazuko. Apparently Toshimi had decided they should drive back to Sapporo that afternoon to have time to prepare the sample properly before Celeste's flight the next day.

The return drive to Sapporo was less tedious than Celeste anticipated. About an hour south of the inn, the convoy turned off the main road.

''We make short visit to Showa Shinzan,'' explained Toshimi. "This mountain appear about sixty years ago from earthquake during Showa Emperor period. *Shin* mean 'recent.' *Zan* mean 'mountain.' "

Celeste was used to these little pilgrimages with her Japanese colleagues. Unspoiled natural sites were so rare in Japan that they had practically become shrines. Of course, this also meant they served as background for endless photographs of visiting tourists. Showa Shinzan was, however, in a league of its own. The energy with which the little bald mountain had pushed its way up out of the ground was very much in evidence. In the sultry overcast, the bare rock was brick red, contrasting with the green brush in the flat area around it. Vents and cracks in the rock spewed puffs of heavy white steam into the cool air. The mountain seemed alive. Celeste realized that Showa Shinzan and Toshimi were probably born in the same year.

NINE

Polyacrylamide Gel
Electrophoresis

M ac stood slightly apart from the crowd at the Customs exit. He was self-concious about his strange burden. Beneath the lid of the white Styrofoam box he held, wisps of cold steam were escaping from the dry ice inside. He watched as dazed passengers trickled out of the automatic doors leading from the Customs hall. Most were swallowed into family groups as soon as they emerged. The greetings were highly emotional, and Mac felt a lump forming in his throat. This is the stuff movies exploit, he thought, annoyed by his own sentimentality.

Captivated by the family reception of an ancient Japanese grandmother, or probably great-grandmother, Mac almost missed Celeste. He was suddenly aware that she was standing at the barrier in front of the Customs exit, scanning the crowd. He waved to catch her attention, and when she saw him, her face melted into a pleased smile, which he returned. Something undoubtedly passed between them. Another Hollywood cliché, thought Mac, dismissing the intensity of the look they had just exchanged.

Both Mac and Celeste were surprised and a little confused by being so glad to see each other. So it was just as well that the Styrofoam box prevented the intimate greeting the moment seemed to call for. Instead, Celeste touched Mac's arm gently and said, "Thanks a lot for coming. I hope it wasn't too inconvenient."

Mac felt a little awkward. "Oh, no, Dr. Braun. No trouble at all. Uh, should we do something about the sample?"

"Please, call me Celeste," she said, amused. "Actually, the sample is packed in my luggage, to avoid the silly rules about carrying dry ice. I think it would be better to unpack it at the car, though, not under the nose of Customs."

"Let me get this straight," said Mac, with an authoritative tone. "We're not doing anything illegal here, are we?"

Celeste blushed. Not realizing that he was teasing her, she hurriedly reassured him, "Oh, no, not really. Just bending the rules a little. You see, it's so tiresome explaining about biological samples and dealing with officials who don't realize that dry ice is nonexplosive, that I've got in the habit of avoiding the situation, so to speak. I guess it started when I was detained for several hours by a Customs official in Boston once. As soon as he saw my import letter from Harvard, he seized the opportunity to play a round of town-gown struggle."

Mac was surprised. He would have thought she was too straight for smuggling. This new angle added to the growing appeal of the woman. To Celeste he said, "My truck's up on level five. We'll have to go down one flight to get the elevator."

Level 5 was on the roof, and though the tailgate of the pickup was a perfect workbench, Mac and Celeste were buffeted by a fog-bearing wind while they transferred the samples from Celeste's luggage into fresh dry ice. Transfer completed, Mac held the passenger side door open for Celeste to climb in. She noticed the Macmillan's Nursery logo on the side.

When Mac joined her in the front seat, she said, "Tell me about your gardening business."

"Well, it's really my dad's business. I just run the San Francisco branch, which I'll soon turn over to my head nurseryman—uh woman—when I start grad school in the fall." Mac hesitated, debating whether to reveal his story. The story was highly effective for stimulating female sympathy, but for some reason Mac felt inhibited about employing his usual strategies with this woman. The inhibition passed, however. "My dad really helped me out when I came home wounded from Danang. I lost my best buddy and had to leave my wife behind. I was a mess. I think Dad training me to be a gardener was the best therapy I had."

Celeste sat pensively for a moment. "You know, for someone like me who's led such a prescribed life, these kinds of hardships are impossible to imagine," she said. "Still, you must enjoy the gardening, to have stayed with it so long."

"Yeah," said Mac, smiling to himself, "it has its compensations. But mostly I felt I was marking time until I registered for the B.S. degree. My education's really Jim's legacy—the guy who died in Danang."

"Tell me about him," encouraged Celeste.

"Jim—that is, Dr. James Weiner—ran the flu vaccine trials at Oakland Naval Hospital. I was a guinea pig when I first enlisted. Which I did 'cause I pulled a really low number in the draft lottery pick. I was against the war. The guinea pig stint was something I cooked up to keep out of combat. Didn't work though. We all got sent eventually—Jim, me, and my wife, Martha, who was a nurse in the unit. Anyway, Jim and I spent hours talking about vaccination, antibodies, and how the immune system works. Antibodies didn't do him any good in Danang, though. The medical corps got attacked by a sniper. I saw the guy next to him go down and tried to push Jim out of the line of fire. I was too late. Lucky for me the sniper took me for dead, too.''

"That sounds like a Purple Heart," remarked Celeste.

More of a broken heart, thought Mac. Then he said to Celeste, "Jim was a real inspiration to me. Whatever I manage to do in science will be thanks to him."

Not quite knowing what to say about Mac's heroism, Celeste returned to a more comfortable subject. "So I understand you're starting in our Ph.D. program in the fall."

"Well, I'm not exactly sure," said Mac. "My personal situation makes things pretty complicated. I'm choosing between two offers right now—one from your program and one from Dallas. Also, I'm on the waiting list for the military Ph.D. at the National Institutes of Health in D.C. But it's not really up to me. You see, we don't want to split up the family until Mac, Junior, finishes high school. I guess I should explain. Martha—that's my ex-wife—and her partner are both still in the military. They're waiting for orders for a new posting. Rumor says it's a hush-hush vaccination trial at the LBJ Hospital in Dallas. So far the brass have been so vague about the project that I can't tell if it's worth making a career decision for. Normally vaccine trials are a long-term commitment because the nurses are needed to draw blood for analysis after the immunizations. But this time there's been no indication that they'll be doing analysis. It all seems pretty weird to me. I mean, how can they have a decent trial if they don't do an analysis afterward? Anyway, we're trying to get more details so I can make my own commitments.''

''Well, your career decision was already made when you applied to grad school. I always tell students who are choosing between top programs that it doesn't really matter which one you attend. And from what I've seen of you in class, you can certainly make sure you get a good education. It must be frustrating, though, not even knowing which faculty you could potentially be working with.''

''It is, but, uh''—Mac became shy—''I was at least hoping I could work with you this summer. That would be good training for anywhere.''

Celeste was flattered. ''I think we can accommodate you,'' she said, smiling in the dark cab. ''While I was in Japan, I took on a new project. I think you can help me out with that. Have you ever run a gel before?''

''Uh, no. But I understand the principle,'' said Mac. ''It's basically putting an electric charge on a protein that's proportional to its size, isn't it? Then from the electrophoresis rate, its size can be established.''

''Exactly,'' said Celeste. ''For this particular project, the size of the protein we're going to look at could reveal a significant mutation in Eke virus. Mutation would explain some peculiar results observed by my colleagues at Fukuda. I've brought back the strain they've been working on to analyze here. Although they're competent with growth curves and genetics, they haven't got much experience with the techniques needed to analyze viral proteins. It's far more efficient for me to do it here, instead of sending them what they would need, and trying to explain how to set it up.''

''Uh, I'm not quite following, Dr. Braun, I mean Celeste,'' said Mac. ''You think the virus is making a protein of a different size?''

''Well, effectively yes, but it's more complicated than that. It's better explained with a diagram. Perhaps we could drop the sample off at the lab and go have a beer. I could draw it out for you,'' suggested Celeste.

''I'd love a beer,'' said Mac with a sigh, ''but I've got to pick up Mac, Junior, from the movies as soon as I drop you off. I'll look forward to a rain check, though.''

''Well, I can explain it just as well in the lab tomorrow morning,'' said Celeste, a little disappointed. ''You *can* start tomorrow, can't you? I need to get this project going as soon as possible.''

''Uh, sure,'' said Mac. He was a little taken aback at her sudden abruptness, as well as by her tacit assumption that he was joining her laboratory. Also, tomorrow *was* Saturday.

The rest of the trip to the laboratory was taken up with Celeste directing Mac through the streets of St. Francis Wood, up over the hill past Laguna Honda Hospital, and down into the Sunset District on Seventh Avenue.

When they pulled up to the front entrance of the BAU Medical Center, Celeste turned in the front seat to face Mac. Fatigue from the long flight over the Pacific washed over her, and she would have liked to collapse into an embrace. Instead she lightly touched his arm again and said, ''Thanks a lot for picking me up. I'm sorry if it meant losing an evening with your son, but it's all in a good cause. We'll start work tomorrow—say, about eleven? I've got a couple of things to take care of first thing in the morning.''

''Fine, I'll report for duty at eleven,'' said Mac. To himself he thought, Yes, certainly a good cause.

· · ·

In the midst of allergy season it seemed to Celeste that every time she turned around it was time to get another allergy shot. For some perverse reason known only to the mysteries of the immune system, more frequent exposure to pollen antigens through injections helps the body deal with more frequent exposure to pollen antigens in the atmosphere. At ten-thirty Saturday morning Celeste entered the BAU allergy clinic, her final errand before meeting Mac. She was running late and hoped that for once she didn't meet someone she knew. Thankfully there were only two names ahead of hers when she signed the injection waiting list. Relieved, Celeste turned around to take a seat, only to find herself face to face with Simon Phillipson. He was standing very close and she could smell his expensive aftershave cologne. The sharp woody scent pricked her nose while she adjusted to the shock of seeing him.

"Ah, Dr. Braun, we meet again," said Phillipson smoothly. "Terrible season for allergies, isn't it?" He must have been watching her sign in, and he planted himself in her path. Celeste took a defensive step back and bumped into the waist-high nurses' table, bruising her hip. How could she have been attracted to this guy? He was so obviously a manipulative creep. Not only was his handsomeness wasted on him, but also it was clearly a tool that he used to his advantage.

"I don't bite, you know," he said. "If you could please move aside, I'll sign myself in and then join you." Celeste sidestepped and with an exaggerated sweep of her hand, waved toward the list and said sarcastically, "Be my guest."

"Don't mind if I do," said Phillipson, signing his name with a flourish. Then he took Celeste by the arm and said, "Madam, come with me." He led her over to a vacant couch and directed her into the corner. He then sat down uncomfortably close, with his arm slung across the back of the couch, approaching Celeste's shoulder. "I'd heard a lot about your scientific reputation before I met you at the symposium, but never imagined you would be such a good-looking woman. How about having lunch when we're done here. I know a lovely British-style pub near Muir Woods. By the time we drive out there and take a walk on the beach—"

"I'm sorry," said Celeste quickly, "I've got to get to the lab. A new student's waiting for me to show him what to do." Even under the circumstances, it was difficult not to have one's head turned just a little bit. Academic women rarely received attention of this sort.

"Well, isn't he lucky," said Phillipson, almost leering. "Perhaps dinner, then."

"Celeste Braun," called the matronly head nurse.

"Excuse me," said Celeste, rising abruptly. She made her way hastily across the waiting room, only to hear the other nurse, a young cute one, call out "Simon Phillipson."

Phillipson and Celeste stood on opposite sides of the nurses' table. Both removed the sportsjackets they were wearing and rolled up their sleeves to receive injections. Phillipson was now definitely leering at Celeste, as though she had undressed more completely.

Celeste felt the cold swab of alcohol on her upper right arm, followed by a slight sting. Automatically, she turned to present her left arm for the second injection. As the nurse filled the second syringe, Celeste listened to the conversation across the table from her.

"Let me just double-check with you, Mr. Phillipson," said the pretty nurse brandishing her syringe. "I'm reducing the dosage of grass antigen because of your reaction last time, but I'm maintaining the other antigens at the same dose. You know, I'm surprised at your bad reaction. My other patients say the grass pollen count isn't too bad this year."

Phillipson settled his hornrimmed reading glasses on his nose and looked at his chart spread out on the table. He then turned to the nurse, bending closer than necessary to her prominent breasts to read her name badge. "Yes, that's right, uh, Kathy, my dear," he said. "Also, could you be a peach and check with the doc how long I can wait until the next injection? There's a good girl. I may need to be in Japan for a while, supervising a new project—that is if the Japanese can make it through their interminable formalities." Then to Celeste, across the table he said, "Don't you find the Japanese too tediously slow? They're driving me round the bend right now, holding up a project that's been ready to roll for months."

Phillipson's remark seemed to have been made innocently enough. But Celeste wondered if the sneaky bastard was probing to find out whether she was aware of his dealings with Fukuda. Obviously he was aware that she knew Toshimi, since Toshimi had introduced them at the Stanley symposium. But Toshimi had been very careful not to discuss her consultancy with Fukuda in Phillipson's presence and had been positively paranoid about confidentiality at their meeting two days previously. Circumspection appeared to be the appropriate course of action. "I wouldn't know," said Celeste. "I'm very fond of the Japanese as scientific colleagues and friends. I've only had limited business dealings with them, though."

That was easy, thought Celeste. It wasn't even a lie, really, since she had only just taken on the consultancy. It was interesting, she noted further, that Phillipson seemed anxious for Fukuda's timely cooperation. She wondered what the hurry was, or if he was just anxious to get the nastiness of blackmail over and done with.

A cold swab and sting in her left arm released Celeste from the captivity of Phillipson's attention. He was apparently trapped between injections until Kathy returned from consulting the "doc."

"Got to run to the lab now," Celeste said quickly to Phillipson. Anxious to avoid further invitations for intimate meals with him, she didn't even stop to put her jacket on. After all, her lab was close enough to the emergency room that if she had an anaphylactic reaction, she could probably make it to a source of epinephrine in time.

"These academic ladies are too neurotic for my taste," remarked Phillipson when Kathy returned. "What time do *you* get off for lunch?"

Mac was pacing up and down the corridor outside the locked door to Celeste's laboratory when she came hurrying around the corner. He reminded Celeste of a wolf she had seen at a place called Wolfhaven on the Washington–Oregon border, a sort of halfway house for wolves that people had tried to domesticate. For a second she thought, is this out of the frying pan into the fire? Then she realized she was being ridiculous. Mac's interest in her was purely for academic reasons, while Phillipson's had clearly been otherwise.

"Morning, Mac."

"Morning, Dr. Braun. Celeste."

"I guess no one's here yet." Celeste found the relaxed weekend schedule of her California students somewhat discouraging. On the East Coast, laboratory occupancy on evenings and weekends was indistinguishable from the rest of the week.

Celeste unlocked the laboratory and led Mac into her office at the back. "First I'll show you how to pour the gel. Then while it's polymerizing we can discuss the experimental plan." She hung her jacket on a peg on the office door. Her hair was tied back in a loose ponytail at the nape of her neck and a couple of strands had escaped, curling around her face. In her white shirt and jeans she looked very young and quite pretty, even vulnerable. Mac realized that he was probably slightly older than she. He had an irrational protective feeling toward this girlish-looking scientist.

As soon as Celeste opened her mouth, though, they seesawed back into teacher-student mode and she regained her authority over him. "The gel is a thin slab of material like Jell-O in a salt solution, through which an electrical current is conducted. We need to set up a mold between two glass plates separated on three sides with plastic strips, three quarters of a millimeter thick. The strips are sealed with melted agar so the mold doesn't leak. The gel material takes about thirty minutes to polymerize—that is, to solidify—after we make up the mixture. In its liquid form, acrylamide, it's a poisonous nerve toxin, but completely safe in the solid polyacrylamide form, so be careful when you're pouring it."

Celeste removed two pieces of glass from the dish rack next to the laboratory sink, scrubbed them first with Comet cleanser, then swabbed them with alcohol to dry them. Deftly she sandwiched three plastic strips between the plates, aligning the strips at the edges. Then she clipped the "sandwich" together with black binder clips, the kind used to clip heavy documents together. "Now you try it," Celeste said to Mac.

Mac copied her actions exactly with a second set of glass plates. He fumbled a little, but Celeste was impressed by the delicacy with which he moved his callused fingers.

Celeste then placed a small bottle in the microwave oven that was sitting on top of the refrigerator. "This is the agar for sealing the gel mold. It needs to be microwaved for two minutes to melt it." The door to the microwave had a hand-written sign on it reading "FOOD NOT." The refrigerator below had a bright yellow sticker on it with three purple triangles joined in the center, the international warning sign for radioactive material. It was also decorated with a deep orange sign with three overlapping circles, the international sign for biohazard material. With these ominous signs and the prospect of handling a nerve toxin, Mac wondered whether he should be uncomfortable. Celeste, however, seemed totally relaxed and was clearly enjoying handling the things in the lab.

They completed pouring the gel, with Celeste demonstrating and Mac imitating her actions. The last step was to add a layer of isobutanol, a kind of alcohol, over the top of the gel solution without mixing the two layers of liquid. The isobutanol had a heady, almost sweet smell that made Mac a little dizzy and a little high. This sensation, following his intense concentration on Celeste's physical movements, heightened his feeling of intimacy with her.

She smiled at him. "It's great to be working in the lab," she said. "I get horribly caught up in administration and supervision during the year. I always forget how satisfying it is to do things with my own hands." Celeste walked back into her office and returned wearing her jacket. "Let's get a bite to eat down in the cafeteria and I can explain what's going on here."

Over clam chowder left from Friday's menu, Celeste laid out Akira's results. "Here's the situation as I see it," she said. "There's a compound called Bazuran that slows the growth of wild-type Eke virus. Then there's a mutant strain of virus that is killed by Bazuran. This mutant has the additional property that it is no longer sensitive to the drug Protex. You remember Protex?"

"Uh, yeah," said Mac, hoping he was right. "Protex blocks the viral protease, which cuts up the proprotein into the building blocks needed for assembly of the virus coat."

"Perfect," said Celeste, smiling. "So if the virus is resistant to Protex, then what must have happened?"

"Its protease could have mutated?" suggested Mac.

"Right again. So if the protease mutates, what would change?"

"Well, it could cut differently, and the size of the coat protein building blocks would change. And that," said Mac, excited by getting the point of the experiment, "we could see on a gel." He paused. "But I still don't see how that explains a new sensitivity to Bazuran."

"Here, I'll draw it for you." Celeste pulled out a ball-point pen from her purse and started drawing on a napkin. "See, if the coat proteins are a different size, then they would have a different shape and they could bind to Bazuran better than wild-type coat proteins. And if something binds a coat protein, then what?"

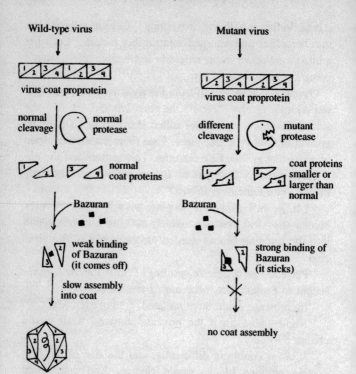

"Coat assembly would be blocked," said Mac with satisfaction. "But, if I recall correctly, coat assembly was a step that Stanley's work had ruled out as a possible target for drug prevention of Eke virus growth."

"Yes," said Celeste. She smiled, remembering how annoyed she'd been with Mac for bringing up that point in class. "What's even more ironic is that Harry Freeman, who developed that theory with Stanley, was probably the first person to observe the effect of Bazuran on Eke virus growth. In fact, I think he may have observed it killing the mutant strain, but the strain disappeared, so he couldn't confirm it.''

"What do you mean, 'disappeared'?" asked Mac.

"It's possible that someone may have switched the laboratory strains.''

"Well, if this mutant Eke virus ever got out of the lab, then anyone with commercial rights to Bazuran would clean up, since Protex would be useless," remarked Mac.

"Holy shit!" Celeste stared at the diagram on the napkin. The reality of the threat conveyed by the word "mutant" became all too clear. Carried away by the complex reasoning behind her hypothesis, Celeste had been talking about an Eke virus mutant like it was just another biological variant. But of course it wasn't. The unspoken dread that had arisen during the meeting at Fukuda returned in full force.

Celeste's expletive startled Mac, and he looked at her with concern. This was hardly an expression he expected from the highly professional Dr. Braun.

But she was completely oblivious to Mac's reaction. Her mind was now racing down the path of the worst possible scenario. What if Phillipson was in such a hurry to tie up the Fukuda deal because he planned to release the mutant virus to make money from Bazuran? Surely not. Phillipson as much as anyone should understand the consequences of risking an Eke virus epidemic. The only reason that Protex worked effectively to contain disease was that Eke virus outbreaks occurred in relatively isolated areas. Even releasing the wild-type virus, in spite of the known efficacy of Protex, would result in a far-reaching, potentially uncontrollable epidemic if it infiltrated into an urban area.

Celeste shook her head. It was inconceivable that Phillipson could even consider releasing the mutant virus.

"Nah, that would never happen," she said, trying to reassure herself. "First of all, Bazuran has probably never been tested on Eke virus infection in people. Second of all, it would be impossible to control the spread of a released virus to be sure that it could be contained by Bazuran. Third, people only do things like that in science fiction. Any real scientist would be wise to the fact that release of a mutant virus would be the equivalent of mass murder." Still, there was nothing about Phillipson that indicated he was wise. Devious and clever yes, but not necessarily wise. If this gel proved the existence of a mutant virus, Fukuda could be embroiled in a seriously dangerous situation. It was possibly no longer a question of patent rights but of world health. Celeste was gripped by the horrible realization that the results of the experiment she and Mac had just set up might have fatal implications.

"I'm not sure you're right about the fiction part," said Mac. "Having control of the only cure for a deadly virus is the pipe dream of every biological warfare strategist. I don't see why it wouldn't also be thought of as an industrial gold mine."

Celeste looked at Mac, simultaneously quizzical and fearful. He appeared to be reading her mind.

TEN

Hepatic Failure

The Fukuda Biotechnology Division in Sapporo was well protected from industrial spies by a high fence of electrified chicken wire. With all the fancy methods of surveillance that were now available, the chicken wire system was still the most effective deterrent. To Toshimi, the sight of this familiar barrier, delineating his empire, was reassuring. He recalled the days when he was recognized by the guard and simply waved through. But since his relocation to Osaka, corporate security measures had escalated dramatically. At the single entrance gate, Toshimi handed the guard his electronic pass key for scanning by the security computer. As soon as the guard read the videoscreen inside his sentry box, he made a respectful bow and indicated for Toshimi's taxi to proceed. At least respect was still forthcoming. Toshimi wondered if the computer specified how deep the bow should be.

The main entrance to the research laboratories was reached by a rabbit warren of alleys leading into the enclave from the main gate. Even if the taxi driver had been there before, he would be unlikely to remember his way without Toshimi's instructions. When the taxi pulled up in front of the glass doors to the laboratories, two men in white coats rushed out to escort Toshimi up the steps. In the lobby, a third man greeted him with a laboratory coat and white cloth slippers, for which Toshimi exchanged his suit jacket and shoes. Toshimi noted from the large digital clock in the lobby that it was a few minutes past ten.

Minoru hurried out of the doorway leading from the director's suite into the lobby just as Toshimi was buttoning up the lab coat. He bowed deeply. "Please excuse me for not being here to greet you in person," said Minoru breathlessly.

"Ah, number one son," said Toshimi teasingly. "You think I have already forgotten my way around?"

Minoru never felt at ease bantering in public. "I hope your trip was comfortable," he said for the benefit of the staff, who continued to surround them. Then he ushered Toshimi into the director's private office. Once they were alone, Minoru confessed, "I must get used to this, but I find their presence oppressive."

"*Hai, hai,*" said Toshimi dismissively. "I have always known you are too shy for this job. But too good a scientist for Fukuda not to have you. When Akira takes over from you, he will benefit from your wisdom and will not have a problem with shyness."

"*If* he takes over," said Minoru with concern. "This is why I was late greeting you. Kazuko informed me this morning that Akira is very ill. Apparently hepatitis again, and the liver tests show serious damage. He is now in the hospital detoxification unit. Kazuko is here to represent him at our meeting." Minoru opened the door on the opposite side of his office into the adjacent small conference room, where they had all met with Phillipson a few weeks earlier.

Kazuko was sitting at the conference table waiting for them. She rose, looking very pale and, Toshimi noted, very beautiful and dignified.

"I am so sorry to hear about Akira," said Toshimi.

"Thank you," said Kazuko, bowing. "I will tell him."

"Do they say how long he will have to stay in the detox unit?" asked Toshimi.

"Well, if it is like last time he had hepatitis, then he may be there about ten days. But this seems more acute than his last attack."

She was valiantly trying to hide it, but Kazuko's distress was evident. Toshimi's concern for Akira was accentuated by his perception of Kazuko's state of mind. He had an urge to reassure Kazuko with a hug, but it was simply not done.

Toshimi had spent enough time in the United States to observe the value of dispensing physical comfort, and not for the first time in his resumed Japanese life did he wish that Japanese customs were less formal.

Turning to Minoru, Kazuko said, "I must return soon to the hospital. May I present the opinion of Akira and myself?"

"Yes, please go ahead," said Minoru. "Phillipson will be here early this evening and before then we must decide how to proceed."

Kazuko briefly and professionally reviewed the evidence about Bazuran that Akira had collected. There was nothing substantially new since their meeting with Celeste the previous week. "Of course, we have not yet heard from Dr. Braun to confirm that there is a mutation in the virus. But it seems clearly suggested by the data that it is possible for

Eke virus to mutate and become resistant to Protex. It is also clear that Bazuran is effective, at least against the apparently mutant virus strain that we have received from Phillipson. We therefore recommend that Fukuda sign the contract with Phillipson.''

"Hai," agreed Toshimi. "Your arguments are good. It is our corporate honor to keep the Eke virus in check. We promised the WHO, in the hearings before Health, Inc., sold out, that we would not abandon our responsibility to world health, and that we would continue to make Protex as long as Eke virus persisted. If we discover resistance to Protex, I feel responsible to do something about it. It is not only our reputation but Japan's, whose honor we must uphold. For these reasons I understand why you do not see the need to wait for Dr. Braun's results. But perhaps we should telephone and hear if she knows anything further.''

"Of course," said Kazuko, rising from her seat and bowing again. "This will not change our opinion, so I request your permission to return to the hospital.''

Permission granted, Kazuko left the conference room with a final bow.

"If this were not Japan, she would be head of department," remarked Toshimi. "Akira is very good, but she is better.''

Minoru nodded in agreement. "Shall we telephone Dr. Braun?''

"Hai," said Toshimi. "We must listen to the opinion of the women.''

Half an hour later, Minoru's secretary informed them by intercom that Celeste was on the line. Minoru took the call on the speakerphone.

"Hello? Minoru? Toshimi? Your secretary tells me you're both there.''

"Hai!" said both men simultaneously.

After some internal debate, Celeste had decided not to burden them with her worst-case suspicions about Phillipson until she had the proof on a gel that a mutant virus really did exist. She was still unconvinced that anyone in his right mind would conceive of releasing a mutant virus, and her worries might seem alarmist and naive. Besides, there was nothing that could be done until they knew what they were dealing with, and Fukuda hadn't signed anything yet. Still, she was anxious to let them know that the analysis of the possible mutant was under way.

"I'm so glad you called," said Celeste's voice over the speakerphone. "I've been trying since eight A.M. your time to get through to Akira's office. I wanted to let him know that the gel is being exposed to film and we'll have the result at noon on Thursday."

"But that is almost two days from now. And Phillipson arrive at seven P.M. tonight," said Minoru. He paused to calculate. "About two A.M. your time. We must make decision before then. Are you sure gel need so much time to expose?"

"Well, I could develop it after half the calculated exposure time," said Celeste, thinking out loud. "I don't mind staying up past midnight to do it. It's just that I'm not sure the virus culture accumulated enough radioactivity to give a signal in half the time." She could hear the two men conferring in Japanese.

"We think you should develop at midnight," said Minoru. "If no signal, you reexpose to film. If signal, we make decision more easily. If you don't develop, then same as no signal. Nothing lost."

"Fine," said Celeste. "But I think you should ask Akira or Kazuko what they think."

"Akira very ill," said Toshimi. "In hospital with hepatitis. Bad liver. Kazuko stay with him."

"Oh, dear," said Celeste, worrying. "It must be pretty serious if he's hospitalized. I guess I'll just have to take the risk and develop the gel at midnight."

"Very good," said Toshimi. "Please call here as soon as you have result. Good-bye for now."

"'Bye," said Celeste, and hung up. She wished she could have talked to Akira, who was more familiar with the growth property of the virus sample. It would help her make a better guess about whether developing the film was worthwhile. But something else bothered her about the conversation, besides the obvious concern about Akira being hospitalized. She couldn't put her finger on it.

Celeste looked out of her office window. It was six P.M. and still light. Only three weeks from the summer solstice. So it would be safe in Golden Gate Park for another hour. Just enough time to go for a run before dinner to clear her brain for the long evening ahead.

Indeed, after fifteen minutes of breathing the park's eucalyptus-laden air, Celeste's mind began to solve problems on its own. By the time she jogged halfway around Stowe Lake, she suddenly realized what had bothered her during the conversation with Toshimi and Minoru. Abruptly, Celeste turned in her tracks and doubled back on the path she had just taken, dodging a surprised group of strolling Russian émigrés. She took the quickest route back to her office and sat there sweating, waiting for the phone connection to Fukuda.

"*Hai*, Toshimi Matsumoto speaking."

"Toshimi, this is Celeste. I'm calling back because I'm seriously worried about Akira. Did they say what kind of hepatitis he has?"

"Kazuko say they find antibodies to type A."

"And no antibodies to the other types?"

"No, I think not."

"Well, he can't have hepatitis A because he already had it and recovered. Remember he told us about the bad sushi he ate? He should be immune to any further infection by type A. The antibodies they detect are probably left from his earlier infection."

"What does this mean?" asked Toshimi. "What can be cause of his hepatitis?"

"Well, I don't know," replied Celeste. "But I suggest you get a more complete blood test. Check carefully for antibodies to types B and C. Also use HPLC analysis to check for the presence of toxic substances. Maybe he ate some toxic fugu. If he did, I think there's an antidote that should be administered as soon as possible." Celeste had always been suspicious of the Japanese delicacy called fugu, prepared from the poisonous pufferfish.

Toshimi understood the urgency. The antidote to fugu was sufficiently nasty itself that it couldn't be administered prophylactically. Unfortunately, it wasn't even guaranteed to be effective once symptoms developed. "We can do HPLC analysis here in drug metabolism lab. Minoru can take blood sample right away. He has medical qualification."

Celeste was concerned that the Fukuda drug metabolism lab might not recognize some of the more rare organic compounds they should look for. "If you fax me the HPLC data printout, I can have my colleague in the Drug Studies Unit have a look at it, too," she suggested.

"*Hai,* this is good idea," said Toshimi. "We leave right away for hospital. Must get back to prepare to meet with Phillipson."

"Good," said Celeste. "I'll call you later tonight, as soon as the film is developed." She hung up and noticed, with a start, that Mac had been standing in the doorway of her office, waiting for her to finish the conversation.

"Sorry to scare you," Mac apologized. "I was just on my way to use the library. So I thought I'd check in and find out what time you want to develop the gel on Thursday. But it sounds like you're gonna do it tonight. I thought it wasn't fully exposed yet. Did we make a mistake in our calculations?"

"No, but there's a parameter we didn't take into account. And since it turns out that Fukuda needs to know the result as soon as possible, it's probably worth taking the risk of developing the film early."

"What parameter?"

"We need to reconsider our assumptions. Let's start at the beginning." She took a deep breath. "We grew the virus in radioactive culture medium, so its proteins became radioactive and can be detected in the gel by exposing the gel to film. The radioactivity interacts with the film just like light, and makes a mark where it's exposed to the film."

"Yeah, I know that," said Mac.

His impatience reminded Celeste of his son's during his "lesson" at the allergy clinic. "Let me finish," she said. "The amount of time we have to wait to detect the proteins depends on how much radioactivity they accumulated during the culture period. Yesterday we calculated the time based on an average accumulation rate, but some proteins accumulate radioactivity faster than others. Unfortunately, I don't yet know the rate for the virus coat proteins, but it's a good bet they might be faster than the average."

"Yesterday we calculated it would be at least seventy-two hours to see a signal on the film," said Mac, feeling proprietary about his contribution to the experiment.

"Well, based on an average rate of accumulation, that's pretty accurate, but if the coat proteins accumulate twice as fast, then we'd have a chance of seeing something tonight by around midnight. Since the Japanese are so anxious to know the result, I think it's worth a try."

"Well, I'd really like to be there when you develop the film," said Mac. He didn't want to miss any part of his training. "I was planning to study in the library anyway. So I can come up to the lab when the library closes."

"Fine, I'll be working here all evening, until then." Celeste hesitated for a minute before she continued. "But first I was going to get a bite to eat. Would you like to join me?" The invitation sounded overly formal to her and made her self-conscious.

"Like that?" asked Mac. He was eyeing her bare legs appreciatively. He didn't seem to have been put off by the nature of the invitation.

Celeste blushed. She had completely forgotten she was still wearing her running gear. "No, I thought I would dress more casually," she said. "Look, I'll go shower in the gym and come by the library to pick you up. We can walk down to Ninth Avenue and decide which restaurant is the least crowded."

"Great," said Mac. "I'll be in the reading room near the Olympus Avenue entrance."

In the locker room, Celeste kicked off her running shoes and hastily stripped off her sweaty T-shirt and shorts. She stood in front of the full-length mirror near her locker completely naked, except for her socks. She inspected the legs that Mac had ogled. They were no longer the chunky appendages she had tried to hide by wearing floor-length "hippie" skirts in high school. Her latter-day running habits had slimmed them down, and above a pair of high heels they were quite passable. She was thankful, though, that high heels were not normal dress for academic women.

Celeste wondered if what Mac hadn't seen would also please him. At thirty-five, she at least finally understood that her body was beautiful, even if it wasn't the top-heavy shape that featured in popular male fantasies. She liked to think of herself as having the pear shape of women in Renaissance paintings. Above the waist, she still looked like a teenager, her conical, pink-tipped breasts sloping down from a flat breastbone. Her actual age was revealed by the womanly padding that had settled onto her belly and hips over the past few years. At first this change in shape had annoyed her, but now she considered it part of her sensuality. Harry seemed to like her body well enough, and she felt a quick pulse in her groin at the thought of his appreciation.

Glancing around at the other naked women in the locker room, Celeste was struck by the polymorphism of breast and body shape. Students with slim hips and pert breasts pranced around unselfconsciously. Older women shielded their bodies behind open locker doors as they dressed. A hugely pregnant woman carried her taut abdomen like a balloon that was about to pop, and two gay women, with rings through their nipples, were having an animated political discussion. They're all beautiful, she thought, as she went to the shower to prepare for her unexpected dinner date with Mac.

The date, however, turned out to be an unqualified disaster.

Once they were settled at a table for two in the neighborhood pizza parlor, Mac said, "I didn't mean to eavesdrop, but I was curious about something you said while you were on the phone, and wanted to know if it has anything to do with our experiment.''

''What's that?'' asked Celeste.

''HPLC,'' said Mac, a little embarrassed. ''It's probably something I should know about, but it doesn't ring a bell.''

''HPLC stands for high-pressure liquid chromatography,'' Celeste explained. ''It's a very sensitive way to analyze organic compounds such as natural poisons. Almost every molecule has characteristic properties when analyzed by HPLC, and identification of a toxin is practically unmistakable.'' Celeste went on to explain about Akira's supposed hepatitis and her suspicion that he may have eaten poisonous pufferfish.

Mac then started to quiz Celeste about the motivations of the Japanese in asking her to analyze the mutant virus. Could they be trusted with the knowledge that they had a mutant strain in their laboratory? He wanted to know how Celeste was sure of their integrity. After all, they were making money off of her advice.

Celeste figured that he must be reacting to the apparent interference of the Japanese with ''his'' experiment. But she was hypersensitive about the issue of Japanese integrity, and she couldn't control her irritation. She had defended the Japanese time and again in arguments with some of her more redneck colleagues, who displayed surprising xenophobia for supposedly intelligent people. Finding that Mac apparently had a similar attitude was an unexpected disappointment. Furthermore, under the circumstances, she felt as though Toshimi and his colleagues were being held hostage by Phillipson. She couldn't discuss the details with Mac, and her frustration about the situation made her even more wary of potential instances of Japanese-bashing. She lectured him about being open-minded toward other cultures.

Mac was shocked at the vehemence of her response. He thought he had asked a perfectly reasonable question, in view of their discussion the other day about taking advantage of exclusive drug rights. In spite of Celeste's skepticism, the situation wasn't necessarily science fiction. And it could be risky to tell a commercial enterprise about a potentially moneymaking mutant virus. Mac's concern was global and had nothing to do with the nationality of the company. He felt that Celeste had typecast him as an overly patriotic, bigoted Vietnam vet, and he told her so. More argumentative words were exchanged, and they finished their meal in silence. Mac refused to let Celeste pay for his share.

Leaving the restaurant, Celeste said, "I don't think I'll need your help in developing the gel tonight. Anyway, I'll probably have to reexpose it and develop it again in a couple of days. Come by the lab when you've cooled off and we can discuss what to do next."

Outside, it was a typical summer evening in the Sunset District. The fog had come in with a vengeance and the gusty, cold wind that accompanied it conveniently discouraged further communication. Celeste could barely hear what Mac said as he left her at the entrance to the library. He seemed to be apologizing, but it wasn't clear if he would show up again in the lab. At this point, Celeste was sufficiently irritated not to care.

At five minutes past midnight, Celeste had further cause to be irritated. She stood outside the darkroom by the slot where developed X-ray films dropped out of the automatic processing machine. The film she held up to the light was completely blank.

Damn it, she thought. Not even a whisper of a signal. In a hurry to set up a reexposure, Celeste slammed back into the dark room, through the tubular revolving door. But plunged into the dim red light, she was forced to catch her breath while her eyes adjusted, and the womb-like darkness had a soothing effect. By the time Celeste returned to her office to phone Japan, she had regained perspective.

"Well, Toshimi, we were too greedy. I won't be able to tell you anything further until the end of the week. I'm very sorry," she said.

"Do not worry," replied Toshimi. "We can figure out what to do about Phillipson contract."

"I'm still sorry that I couldn't clarify things for you," repeated Celeste with a sigh. Her frustration and anxiety were evident. "Don't forget to fax me the HPLC analysis and the antibody reports for Akira. At least maybe I can help there."

"You are tired," said Toshimi kindly. "Please go to sleep. HPLC report not ready until morning anyway. Even Japanese do not work all night."

ELEVEN

"Kampai!"

Two hours after Celeste reported her negative results to Toshimi, Phillipson's taxi wound its way through the Fukuda compound to the steps of the research building. He unfolded himself from the backseat and braced himself to meet the reception committee. He loathed giving up his shoes to the attendants and putting on those ridiculous slippers. At least he managed to keep his jacket this time. At his last visit the attendants had, with much giggling, discovered that all the lab coats available were too small for him. Thank God their courtesy extended to remembering this incident. The humiliation of undressing and dressing was not repeated.

Phillipson was ushered into the conference room next to the director's office. Minoru and Toshimi were waiting for him with official-looking documents laid out before them on the table. Phillipson was not surprised that Akira Hagai was absent. He thought there was a different office lady from the last meeting, but he wasn't sure.

"Good evening, Dr. Phillipson," said Toshimi. He stood up and inclined his head very slightly, in a gesture that couldn't really be called a bow but completely discouraged a handshake. "Fukuda prepared to do business."

"Excellent," said Phillipson, completely ignorant of the insulting greeting. "I see you have drawn up the papers."

"Yes, I think you find everything in order. Please take your time to read," said Toshimi. He motioned to the office lady and barked out a sentence in Japanese. She bolted from her hovering perch near the back of the room, picked up the pile of documents in front of Toshimi and Minoru, and brought them around the table, laying them out in front of Phillipson. She bowed and gestured for him to sit down.

"Sir, you like coffee?" she asked shyly.

"Why, yes, my dear, that would be lovely," said Phillipson, eyeing her. It must be a different office lady. He didn't remember such a smashing figure on the other one, and besides, she didn't speak English. He wondered how far the duties of office lady could be extended. He would ask Minoru later. Meanwhile, he needed to concentrate on the documents at hand.

While Phillipson looked over the documents, the three Japanese in the room sat unmoving and completely inexpressive. Phillipson broke the unnerving silence. "Here on page three, it refers to a subcontract about the production of Bazuran that is supposed to be detailed in another document, but I don't see that document here."

Minoru jumped up. "Oh, *hai, hai*. So sorry. That document checked by production manager this morning. I forgot to add to rest." Hastily he retrieved his briefcase from where it stood at the side of the room. He laid it on the table and fumbled with the combination lock. It popped open suddenly. In his confusion, Minoru had opened the briefcase upside down. A test tube of Akira's blood tumbled out onto the table and rolled down toward the end where Phillipson was sitting.

"What's this?" asked Phillipson. He picked up the tube as it came to rest in front of him and saw that it was a sample of blood. What the hell was Minoru doing with blood in his briefcase? "Is Fukuda getting into diagnostics?"

Phillipson's stomach tightened as another possibility occurred to him. He watched Minoru struggle for words. The others held their breath. Then, fulfilling his worst fears, Phillipson heard Minoru say, "That is Akira Hagai blood. He is very ill. Hospital say hepatitis but we think maybe he eat bad fugu. We test here."

Phillipson's mouth went dry. Presumably they would be doing an HPLC analysis, since that was about the only blood test a pharmaceutical company like Fukuda could do. There was absolutely no way he could allow that blood sample to reach the HPLC lab. It was too late to drop it on the floor without arousing suspicion. He had no choice except to hand the test tube back to Minoru, who accepted it with evident embarrassment and immediately restored it to his briefcase. Phillipson needed to keep an eye on that briefcase. He had to find a way to intercept the analysis.

After the blood incident, the tension in the small conference room increased by a significant order of magnitude.

Toshimi was considerably disturbed by Minoru's carelessness. Minoru just didn't have that corporate caution that was more instinctive to himself and to Akira. Somehow, it had skipped a generation. There was no obvious reason to hide their business from Phillipson, but it was never a good idea to reveal more than necessary about any internal affairs. Toshimi thought that the rogue test tube contained blood intended for an antibody test that was to be carried out by a contract lab. As far as Toshimi knew, Minoru should have already left the other blood sample in the drug metabolism lab for HPLC analysis, though his explanation made it seem otherwise. Toshimi certainly wasn't going to ask him now.

Minoru was upset with himself. He was annoyed at forgetting to add the last document to the contract. He was also frustrated by his relative inability to express himself in English.

Phillipson stared at the contract papers without reading a word. Mentally he reviewed his inventory of emergency measures. If they signed the contract tonight, there was sure to be an obligatory celebratory dinner. This would provide him with ample opportunity to use his bag of tricks. Given the late hour, he doubted that Minoru would deliver the blood sample before tomorrow morning. So Phillipson had the perfect remedy for the situation, as long as he could force the signing. And that's what he was there for anyway. It was too risky to the patent to let them try any more control experiments. He had managed to stall by saying that the new batch of Bazuran wasn't quite ready to bring over when he left for this trip. And now it was clear that Hagai was out of the picture and wouldn't be around to do the control experiment he proposed. But it was only a matter of time before someone else might try the same experiment, so the signing needed to be accelerated. Also, the sooner a deal was struck, the sooner he could get the rest of his scheme in gear. God knows that was turning into a bigger headache than he had bargained for, and delays would make it worse.

Phillipson already knew exactly what he had to do to get the contract signed. Recovering his composure, he turned his full attention back to the contract, to ensure that the deal he intended to force was going to meet his original demands. After another fifteen minutes of inspection, he was satisfied that he could proceed. Fukuda had accepted the $20 million purchase fee for exclusive rights to Bazuran but had reduced the royalty scheme from 80 to 75 percent. There was no point in quibbling about this 5 percent. Once his plan went into operation, even 10 percent of the royalties would be a fortune.

"Gentlemen," said Phillipson, "this all looks in order. I assume you're prepared to sign tonight."

In spite of the advice of his staff, Toshimi intended to hold out until he heard definitively from Celeste. If Phillipson did steal the original data from Stanley's laboratory, then he had no legal rights to Bazuran. Under those circumstances, there was no way Toshimi was going to pay this extortionist the enormous sum he was demanding. "We prefer to wait until tests complete. Must have new sample of Bazuran before final agreement," he said.

"That's a shame, gentlemen," replied Phillipson. "I have an appointment with the president of Roykan tomorrow morning. They're prepared to sign their contract and are just waiting for me to show up. I did promise you first option, however."

Toshimi mentally kicked himself. What a naive idiot, assuming he could catch Phillipson on the patent issue. He should have seen it coming. Kazuko saw it coming. Even at the beginning of their negotiations she had pegged Phillipson as a blackmailer. It was now evident that he was the most venomous kind—the sort who pretend to be aboveboard until they don't get cooperation. Toshimi was disgusted and felt contaminated from dealing with this swine. He promised himself revenge. But, for the present, they were backed into a corner. Fukuda had no choice. Toshimi, feeling sullied and resigned, took out his pen and signed the papers.

Later that evening, Toshimi left the celebratory dinner early. He wanted to check on Akira in the hospital and tell Kazuko that the contract with Phillipson had been signed. As he bowed out of the private dining room, he looked back in distaste at Phillipson, who was fondling the breast of the geisha girl kneeling next to him. Toshimi was glad Minoru had pretended not to understand when Phillipson asked him if the office lady could keep them company this evening. Western men had so little finesse in matters of sex.

As soon as Toshimi left, Phillipson said to Minoru, "I have a serious confession to make, now that Toshimi is gone. I have a much better solution to jet lag than drinking sake." The leer that had disgusted Celeste in the allergy clinic appeared on his face. He drew the geisha girl onto his lap, manipulating her with the hand that was still cupped around her breast. "Do you think you could arrange with the proprietor for her to, uh, help me with my jet lag, back at the hotel? Also, tell her to get me a large bottle of Sapporo beer. I absolutely detest sake." He released the woman, whose breast was hurting from the unaccustomed roughness, and squeezed her backside as she rose quickly.

Minoru said something to the woman in Japanese, presumably ordering the beer. She inclined her head obediently and responded in Japanese, using a pleasant, servile voice. She told Minoru, in no uncertain terms, that she wanted nothing to do with this Caucasian pig. Minoru waited until she passed through the curtain into the main part of the restaurant to fetch the beer.

"*Hai.* I go see what I can arrange for you," he said to Phillipson. He headed off to the men's room to wait for a spell before he returned to report an unsuccessful negotiation with the proprietor.

Alone in the private dining room, Phillipson made his own arrangements for a successful evening. After Minoru returned with his disappointing news, Phillipson shrugged and suggested they have another drink. As Japanese custom dictates, they poured out the drinks for each other. Phillipson poured for Minoru from the sake bottle they had shared all evening. Minoru poured for Phillipson from the newly arrived bottle of Sapporo beer. They toasted each other with the traditional *Kampai!*

Fifteen minutes later, Minoru started feeling a little dizzy and figured he'd reached his sake limit for the evening. He was finding it more and more difficult to think of civil English words for conversing with Phillipson. He looked quite unsteady by the time Phillipson saw him accept the ignition keys from the valet and get into his car with his briefcase. The valet had ushered many sozzled businessmen into their cars at this time of night and knew better than to challenge the judgment of a driver in that state. But Phillipson was confident that Minoru Yamaguchi and his briefcase would never make it home to the patiently waiting Mrs. Yamaguchi. Phillipson hailed a taxi to take him back to the hotel. He had completely forgotten about the missed opportunity with the geisha girl.

At 9:55 A.M. the following morning, the head technician in the drug metabolism laboratory at Fukuda finished the HPLC analysis of the blood sample that Dr. Yamaguchi had dropped off the previous afternoon. As instructed, she didn't wait to show the data to Yamaguchi but sent a copy immediately by fax to Dr. Braun, their consultant in the United States. Dr. Yamaguchi had given her two fax numbers but not clearly stated which one to use. His difficulty in issuing orders almost always led to confusion among the staff, who were used to more explicit directives. Anyway, it sort of seemed like he wanted her to use the first fax number, since he went out of his way to explain that she needed to call ahead to arrange for transmission. But the technician wasn't very confident of her English, so without strict instructions, she decided to use the other number, which went straight through.

Thus it was just after 5:00 P.M. on Wednesday when the fax was received by the machine in Celeste's department office, instead of by her Powerbook, which she would have had to connect to the phone line for reception in her own office. The secretaries had gone home for the day, so the fax lay in its tray all night while Celeste lay sleepless, worrying about whether there had been some problem in getting Akira's blood analyzed. It just hadn't occurred to her to check the office, since she was expecting a call to arrange for direct transmission to her computer. When Janice handed her the fax the following morning, Celeste experienced the first relief in tension she'd had since returning from Fukuda. But it was inevitably short-lived.

The squiggly lines of the HPLC data were completely incomprehensible to Celeste. Fax in hand, she ran down four flights of stairs to the drug studies unit on the eleventh floor to get an expert opinion. She had a special arrangement with Henry Wang, who ran the unit. On weekends he borrowed her tissue culture facility for propagating his prize-winning orchids. In exchange, he occasionally analyzed samples for her with his HPLC equipment.

Almost every surface in Wang's lab was occupied by a clicking, whirring HPLC machine and a partner computer terminal. Although Wang was the only human in the laboratory, the undertone of machine activity made it seem full of busy people. Wang spread the fax printout on a strip of lab bench in front of one of the machines. He was a stocky, jolly man, and his white lab coat barely closed across his belly. While he scrutinized the data, he made a soft, mechanical grunting noise, in tune with the humming machines around him. Celeste had heard him make the same noise while he was working with his orchids in her lab on the weekends.

"You say you think this might be fish toxin?" he asked skeptically. "There's no way this is fish toxin. This compound is clearly derived from plants. See this double peak here, followed by a sharp, single peak? That's typical of alkaloids, which only plants can synthesize."

"Do you think it could be a toxin or just some by-product of eating the usual Japanese vegetables?"

"I have no idea," said Wang, shaking his head. "There are so many weird compounds derived from plants. And so few have actually been analyzed. Most of the work has come from the botany labs at Oxford University, and most of that has never been published. Those guys are never in a hurry."

The botany laboratories at Oxford. Mentally, Celeste pictured the Victorian-style building that sat in the middle of the Parks Road science complex. She had walked by it almost every day during her first postdoctoral year, as a fellow at Oxford. She recalled the lab's chronically muddy garden, where the custodial staff had maintained a patch of Brussels sprouts among the more exotic specimens. She'd heard recently that it had been uprooted to make room for an industrially supported botanical institute.

It seemed to Celeste that this wasn't the first time she'd thought about the botany labs during the recent past, and she didn't have to probe her memory banks very deeply to find the connection. Phillipson and his work were haunting her. The uneasiness that accompanied her speculations about him these past few days overtook her once again. There was no escaping it. Phillipson had come from the botany laboratories. That was where he had first characterized the plant toxins he had brought to Jane's lab. And Bazuran, of course, had been among them. Maybe Akira had accidentally ingested some of what he was working with. If there were any Bazuran left, it would be easy to analyze by HPLC and compare to Akira's blood. But, Celeste recalled, Akira had mentioned during the last meeting at Fukuda that he had used up everything Phillipson had given him.

Suddenly Celeste had an inspiration. It was just possible that Jane Stanley would have among her records an HPLC analysis of the Phillipson toxins. Five minutes later, Celeste was back in her office, on the phone to Boston. As she was punching out Jane's number, it occurred to her that she could also ask Jane for a copy of the Bazuran data from Harry's thesis.

"Celeste," said Jane. "It's lovely to hear from you. How are you?"

"Fine, thanks," said Celeste, anxious to get to the issue at hand. "Awfully busy, actually. Since I saw you at the symposium, the quarter ended and I've been to Japan and back."

"That's my girl," said Jane with pride. Coming from her, the expression was far from demeaning. "Well, you've caught me in a hell of a mess—literally, that is. I've just finished packing up my office for cold storage, including all the old notebooks and files. It's taken me most of this month to sort through everything. You'd be amazed at some of the memorabilia I've unearthed and tossed out. It's been quite liberating. I've even taken care of all the 'pending' files on my desk for the first time in my entire career.'' Jane chuckled philosophically. ''I guess it's the last time, too.'' She paused, savoring the significance of this. ''But then, you didn't call to hear about my house cleaning therapy. What can I do for you?''

''It's quite a coincidence, but what I'm calling about sort of relates to that, in a way,'' said Celeste. ''I'm actually looking for two things. I was hoping you might have some old HPLC printouts of the Phillipson toxins. I've run across some data on a peculiar plant compound and was curious whether it might be in the same family. The other thing I'm looking for is a copy of Harry Freeman's thesis.''

''Wow, you're talking ancient history there. If you'd asked me six weeks ago, I would have rummaged around and perhaps been able to help you out. But today, I can say with the certainty of a newly purged soul that I'm afraid I'm totally useless to you. It's ironic that I'd hung on to printouts of those HPLC analyses of the Phillipson toxins for years, and only last week sent them to be incinerated along with a lot of other rubbish. I specifically remember adding the printouts to the pile. It was like finally erasing the last traces of the Phillipson incident from my life. I figured that anyone who wanted information on those useless toxins could always look up his thesis in the Bodleian Library. You know, once I asked him why they never bothered to publish all that work in a proper journal, and he said, in that snooty accent of his, 'a bound thesis in Oxford's Bodleian Library *is* a recognized publication.' '' Jane mimicked Phillipson's BBC tones rather well. ''He always insisted on referencing that damn thesis. Personally, I found it academically offensive, since it's not exactly a publication that's readily available to the community at large."

"So if I want to see the data, I've got to get access to his thesis in Oxford?"

"That's about it," confirmed Jane. "He, of course, took his copy away with him when he left the lab. And I must say I wasn't sorry to see the back of both of them."

"Do you happen to know if the Bodleian has any kind of reference service?"

"I'm sorry, dear. I really don't know. I always used to call Sir Andrew when I needed something from over there. He would get his lab assistant to look it up for me. But since his own lab shut down with his retirement, he's been spending all his time in the House of Lords."

Celeste could just imagine the reference service in Oxford, if one did exist. An ancient retainer in a blue smock might poke around for days in the dusty stacks and then grudgingly photocopy a page or two. She would have to figure out a more efficient way to get the information.

"Well, thanks for the lead. Maybe I'll just have to fly over myself for the weekend and look it up," joked Celeste.

"It's too bad you're on the other coast," said Jane, taking Celeste seriously. "You know, every so often, Roger and I would fly over from Boston for a weekend in London. It was a marvelous break from the routine—" Jane's reminiscences were cut short by the arrival of two men in physical plant uniforms. They were standing in the doorway of her office contemplating the huge pile of cardboard cartons, as though they had never seen such objects before. "Oh, dear, I've got to go. It looks like the movers are here."

"Quickly, just tell me if I'm out of luck with Harry's thesis as well."

"Sorry, I forgot you asked for that, too. Why, though, I can't imagine. But I guess you'll have to tell me another time. Anyway, you've been preempted again by my purge. Addison Library has been after me for more than a year to lend them my copies of the lab theses. Apparently a flood in their archives damaged the thesis collection, which they had just boxed for microfilming. Filling their request was one of my last desk-clearing acts. If it helps you at all, I should have the theses back in about four to five weeks, though. You know, I don't recall even coming across Harry's old notebooks. But, if I did, they would already be in storage with the first lot of boxes that were picked up last week. Your timing really couldn't have been worse. Anyway, the physical plant guys are here to cart away the rest."

"Not my day, I guess," said Celeste. "At least I know you'll eventually have Harry's thesis back, if I don't manage to see a copy any other way. I'd better let you go, but let's talk again soon."

"I'll look forward to it. And sorry I wasn't more helpful, dear," said Jane and hung up.

Celeste was just as glad that she didn't have to explain her unusual requests more fully to Jane at this point. But she made a note in her calendar to give Jane a call the following week. After all, packing up thirty years of lab records for cold storage must be like burying part of yourself. Jane had sounded remarkably cheerful, but it was highly likely that her mood might change when she realized how much the lack of familiar clutter symbolized her retirement.

Jane had at least pointed Celeste in the right direction to find the information she needed. And inspired by Jane's recollections about weekends abroad, Celeste decided to call United Airlines to see if she could use her frequent-flier miles to get a flight to London that evening. If she arrived early Friday morning in London, she could be at the Bodleian Library in Oxford by noon. After looking up Phillipson's thesis, she could spend Saturday in London and return Sunday. Certainly, if the youthful Jane and Roger could do it, so could Celeste. It was only double the flying time from Boston and three hours' extra jet lag.

But the woman at United just laughed at her. "Honey," she said, "the freebie seats have been booked since March. This is the height of the tourist season, you know. You couldn't even *pay* for a first-class seat at this short notice."

Well, Celeste thought, it was kind of unrealistic anyway. Now, do I still know anyone in Oxford who could get the information for me? The head of the genetics lab where she spent her fellowship year had since moved to a professorship in Australia, taking his group of collaborators with him and effectively cleaning out the department. Then she remembered Jennifer Dickens. Jenny was a Berkeley undergraduate who did a project in Celeste's lab during the summers of her sophomore and junior years. She had gone to Oxford on a Marshall Scholarship two years earlier. Celeste fished her address book out of her briefcase to see if she had a number for Jenny, and the piece of paper on which Debbie Kane, the flight attendant, had scribbled her number fell onto the desk. Maybe Debbie could help her out. Hadn't she said she was about to change to the London–Frankfurt route?

Luckily, Debbie was home, and even luckier, she was working the evening flight for London. She was delighted by the possibility of seeing London with a friend, and it didn't take her long to figure out how she could get Celeste a seat. "I've got a really cool idea," she said. "If you were a trainee, you'd be allowed to fly even without completing the safety course, so it wouldn't be illegal. And we're always short-staffed on the European flights during the summer, so the extra help would be welcome. Look, the head steward owes me one. I've subbed plenty when he's found a nice young man to spend the weekend with in San Francisco. I'll just tell him you're a friend thinking about applying to the flight attendant program. Are you up for it?''

Celeste didn't hesitate. ''I'll go home and get my passport,'' she said gratefully.

Celeste inspected herself in the mirror in the staff changing room at the airport. The only parts of the image she recognized were the black high-heeled pumps she had brought from home. She and Debbie had to raid the lockers of two different stewardesses to find a size 12 skirt that would accommodate Celeste's hips and a size 10 blouse that didn't balloon out below the bow tie. The stewardesses were incredibly friendly, and happy to help out the new ''recruit.'' One of them even insisted on doing Celeste's makeup. When Celeste smiled, she felt the unaccustomed tightness of foundation on her cheeks. Its masklike properties contributed to the sensation of being in disguise.

The flight went quite smoothly. Constantly having some little task to fulfill and the freedom to walk around the plane made the journey a lot more tolerable than it usually was, sitting in an assigned club class seat. In college, Celeste had waitressed at a seaside resort, and like riding a bicycle, the skills of waiting on people came back instinctively. It interested Celeste to see how people reacted to her, based on their expectations of someone in a flight attendant's uniform. Particularly amusing was the encounter with one of her colleagues from BAU.

Bryan Baird, M.D., was chief of psychiatry at the BAU hospital. Six months ago he married his fourth wife, a virologist at one of the Bay Area's biotechnology companies and a peripheral colleague of Celeste's. Celeste occasionally shared the elevator with Dr. Baird and had recently seen him at some of the molecular biology seminars. His research work, although medically based, apparently bordered on molecular neurobiology. Between wives three and four he had a flagrant affair with one of the neurobiology Ph.D. students, leaving the poor girl devastated when he chose a new companion from his own age group.

Celeste was working club class when she first encountered Dr. Baird. She hadn't looked carefully at the next row of passengers as she moved along collecting drink orders. Consulting the passenger seating list, so that she could say his name when she took the order, she realized she was in danger of being discovered. But Dr. Baird looked straight at her without a glimmer of recognition.

He's probably never noticed me at BAU, she thought. I'm certainly not his type. Both the new wife and the graduate student were petite but well-endowed women. Besides, the extra eye makeup and dark lipstick changed Celeste's appearance dramatically.

"I'll have a malt whiskey with ice, and a soda water with lime, my dear," said the chief of psychiatry, looking Celeste up and down appreciatively.

Later, Celeste was "tending bar" in the galley and Dr. Baird wandered by for a refill. He'd already had several whiskies by this time. His leathery California complexion glowed.

"I'll have some more of that Glenfiddich, if you're still pouring," he said. "Not so good for the figure, but great for a transatlantic nap." He was clearly vain about his physique. And justifiably so. Only the gray in his boyishly cut hair revealed his seniority.

Celeste overtly gave him the once-over, imitating his earlier inspection of her. She decided to have some fun with him.

"You look pretty good to me," she said. "Now, let's see. A distinguished-looking guy like you, flying club class . . . I'll bet you're some kind of executive, or no, maybe a doctor. Yeah, you have a doctoring kind of look that would give a patient confidence in you. You could be a gynecologist or a psychiatrist, or something."

"You must be psychic, young lady," said Dr. Baird. "Or have we met before? You do look familiar."

"I doubt it," said Celeste. "I just started flying out of San Francisco."

"Anyway, let me introduce myself. Bryan Baird, chief of psychiatry at Short Hospital, BAU." He executed the predictable double-handed clasp, meaningful look included. "And you are Francine?" he asked, bending close to read the name badge she had borrowed. "Ah, you smell nice, Francine."

"Regulation-issue *Deneuve*," said Celeste.

"As in Catherine Deneuve?" asked Baird, stepping even closer and inhaling again. "Yes, the scent is evocative, or should I say provocative?" He raised one eyebrow at his prey. "Deneuve, the actress, *is* one of my favorites. You're quite different, though. In fact, I hope you don't mind my saying so, but you're unusual-looking for a stewardess. You're like a woman in a Klimt painting—*The Kiss,* for example."

"It must be the long nose," said Celeste, self-deprecatingly, but she was rather impressed by the intellectual nature of the come-on. She didn't have to wonder where it was leading.

"Look, Francine, are you stopping in London or carrying

on through to Frankfurt? 'Cause if you're going to be in London, I'm looking for someone to go to the theater with Saturday evening, and if you're available I'd love to get to know you better.''

Celeste couldn't resist the temptation, on behalf of his new wife. She wondered if she would be the first woman who ever stood him up. "That sounds wonderful, Dr. Baird. What are we going to see?''

"Don't know yet. I'll see what's on in the West End. Why don't you meet me at my hotel, The Dorchester, at, say, six o'clock? Then we can have a drink before curtain time.''

"Fine, that'll be perfect, since I'll be coming back to London on Saturday after visiting friends in Oxford.''

"Looking forward to it, Francine,'' said Baird. He was extremely close to her now, and evidently about to kiss her.

She was saved by the call button ringing insistently several times. She traced the signal to Debbie, sitting in the stewardess's enclosure, grinning.

"It's a little safety mechanism we have,'' she said. "We look out for each other. If a passenger gets obnoxious, this extra call button is quite handy.''

"Thanks, Deb,'' said Celeste. "I don't know how much longer I could have kept up that charade. I actually know the guy from work, but he didn't recognize me. It's lucky he's into research and doesn't practice psychiatry anymore. Otherwise BAU would be up to its ears in sexual harassment suits.''

Debbie and Celeste spent the next couple of hours chatting in the curtained-off area where the flight attendants rest. Debbie was obsessed with plans for returning to the Bitterroot Valley, and her conversation was like a travelogue for Montana. When she discovered that Celeste had never been there, Debbie made her promise to come with her on a visit to her parents' ranch sometime. Celeste was curious to see this fabulous Big Sky country.

The rest of the flight was uneventful. In deference to her request, Celeste was transferred to economy class for the duration. Flight attendants cleared Customs through a private gate, so that as long as Celeste serviced only the less privileged passengers, Dr. Baird could be avoided.

At Heathrow, Debbie remained in the transit lounge to continue on to Frankfurt and take the short leg back to London, where she would meet Celeste on Saturday afternoon. Celeste accompanied the few crew members disembarking in London down the yellow corridors of Heathrow and out into the cool, wet June morning. As she boarded the bus for Oxford, she felt she had come home. Her year there had been a formative one, a sort of "coming of age." It was her first experience of being a real person and no longer a student, and she felt Britain embodied her adult roots. These thoughts entered Celeste's mind only subconsciously. She was asleep long before the bus traversed the complex series of roundabouts through the suburbs of northwestern London and pulled onto the M40, heading for the City of Spires.

TWELVE

Poison Pen

By the time the bus arrived at the Gloucester Green depot, the early-morning fog had burned off, and it promised to be a gorgeous day. Such sunny June days in Oxford were characterized by strawberries and champagne on the college lawns and students dressed in black and white, taking their final exams. Unlike Cambridge, Oxford University maintained the requirement that students take their final exams wearing academic dress, known as sub-fusc. As Celeste made her way up George Street, she was passed by packs of students on bicycles with their academic gowns flapping, joking and shouting to each other to deny their pre-exam butterflies.

Celeste made a quick stop at the bank on the corner of George Street and Cornmarket, where she had kept an account since her fellowship days. Then she walked up the Broad toward the Bodleian Library. The emperors' heads surrounding the Sheldonian Theatre looked benign in the sunlight and greeted Celeste like old friends. The barmaid at the King's Arms pub was putting out a blackboard advertising morning coffee and pub lunches as Celeste turned left onto Parks Road. Promising herself a pint in the pub that evening, Celeste passed up the advertised temptations and turned right just beyond the pub into the familiar entryway of her college. There sat the same grouchy porter who had monitored the students' comings and goings when Celeste lived in Oxford. He rummaged around for the key to the college guest room. The sunshine melted even this old curmudgeon, who treated Celeste to a smile containing less than half a dozen teeth and the remark, "Good to see you again, luv." Celeste had often wondered whether the Oxford colleges went to Central Casting to hire their employees.

In the college guest room, with the surprise luxury of a private bathroom, Celeste quickly removed the flight attendant's uniform and drew on blue jeans, a long-sleeved T-shirt, and a bulky sweater. She wasn't sure how long she might be stuck in the Bodleian and recalled that the warmest setting on the Oxford library thermostats was "Icy Blast." From her passport wallet, she dug out a tattered light green "reader's ticket" from her fellowship days. On it was printed the oath that all users of the Bodleian Library had to swear before being admitted to the stacks. In addition to promising to obey the rules of the library, the reader specifically had to promise not to deface or remove any library property and "not to bring into the Library or kindle therein any fire or flame, and not to smoke in the Library." Celeste's signature of nine years earlier, below the oath, looked childish. It was practically a historical document. Celeste assumed that Oxford was one place where library privileges did not have to be renewed every year.

But she was wrong. The guard at the entrance to the main building proudly informed Celeste that she needed a new computerized card with a photograph and would have to report to the administration office. She followed his directions to a wooden door in the stone archway leading to the courtyard of the most ancient part of the library.

Acquiring the new card was surprisingly straightforward. Celeste had only to show her BAU faculty identification card to certify her academic intent. The office was equipped with a passport photo machine for instant production of cards. Everything about the procedure was thoroughly modern except the user fees. Celeste paid twelve pounds— fewer than twenty dollars—for five years of library privileges. Evidently the recent fundraising campaign for Oxford University hadn't yet figured out how to tap all their assets.

Celeste asked the registrar where she could find a catalog of dissertations and was directed farther into the old part of the library. The courtyard entrance was crowded with tourists waiting to see Duke Humfrey's library, where Celeste was headed. She bypassed the tour groups at the entrance by showing her newly issued "reader's ticket."

At the top of two flights of stone stairs, Celeste found the dissertation catalog in the Renaissance reading room, which ironically she had never visited during her fellowship year. The vaulted ceiling was supported by intricately carved wooden beams and divided into individual panels decorated with university shields. Light entered from a stained-glass window at the far end of the churchlike room. Celeste expected a Shakespearean character to emerge from the wooden stacks and offer assistance. But ultimately unassisted, she found the handwritten card listing Phillipson's thesis. She needed to return to the main library building, where she had begun her assault on the system.

Now the guard at the entrance was happy to direct Celeste to the D.Phil. thesis repository in the basement of the library. She was grateful for his prompt cooperation, since it was 12:30 P.M. by this time and she knew that all library services shut down religiously from 1:00 P.M. to 2:00 P.M. for lunch. Much to her annoyance, someone was ahead of her at the thesis repository, negotiating loudly with the inevitable grizzled guardian in a blue smock.

The negotiator was a sandy-haired young man wearing wire-rimmed National Health–style spectacles and a very tweedy jacket over a Shetland sweater and khaki trousers. If the excessive Englishness above the ankles didn't give him away, his white socks and Top-Sider moccasins confirmed his identity as a Rhodes Scholar. Celeste had encountered the species previously. She even dated a few before she realized that their culture was very different from the one she had come to England to experience. They tended to roam in packs, complain loudly, and never mix with the natives. This one was clearly reverting to type.

"I'm telling you, it's gotta be there. I was just looking at it last week. Are you all sure you got the author's name?"

"Grass, like you said, isn't it?"

"No, Gri-ce. G, R, I, C, E," the young man said with a thick Southern drawl.

"Oh, Grace, as in no saving," said the man in the blue smock.

"No, here, lemme write it," and the young man scratched aggressively with his pencil on a piece of scrap paper, which he pushed at the thesis custodian.

"Oh. Grice," said the custodian. "Well, perhaps we do have a Grice. I'll have a look after me lunch."

"Oh, for God's sake," said the young man, thoroughly exasperated.

While Celeste watched this interchange with some exasperation of her own, she looked around the reading room. It seemed to be almost exclusively populated by her compatriots, or barely differentiated Canadians, who were distinguishable only by the maple leaf flags sewn to their backpacks. Things hadn't changed much since her year in Oxford. The thesis custodian started to lower the metal grille, closing off the counter and thereby terminating his conversation with the young man in front of Celeste. Quickly, Celeste scribbled onto one of the request forms "Phillipson, Simon, 1977. 'Organic Chemistry of Amazonian Toxins,'" and shoved the form under the lowering grille into the man's cage.

"Excuse me, sir," she said as politely as possible, "I've just flown all the way from San Francisco today, to have a look at this thesis, and I only have this afternoon to read it. Would you mind looking this up as well?" Then she added, smiling sweetly, "After your lunch, of course."

Smiles had no effect on him. "Bloody Americans," he muttered. "Always in a hurry." Absolutely no one was going to stand between him and his cheese and pickle sandwich. But he did snatch up the paper that Celeste had pushed toward him.

As the custodian disappeared into the depths of the thesis room, the young man turned to Celeste and said, "Looks like we'll have to come back after lunch, ma'am. If you all are just visiting I can show you a nice place to eat that won't take forever for service."

"Why, thank you, that would be lovely," said Celeste. The stewardess rations had long been metabolized and by now she was quite hungry.

"Lemme introduce myself. Ralph O. Johnson the Fourth. My friends call me Ollie, on account of my dad is Ralph, too. 'Course, everyone calls him Buck, though. My middle name's Oliver. It's kinda cute, since my big sister is Kathleen and my little brother is Franklin. Dad calls us Kukla, Fran, and Ollie. You know, after those children's puppets on TV."

"Celeste Braun," said Celeste, extending her hand to meet his polite handshake. "Actually, I knew Oxford quite well when I was here as a visiting fellow. But I'm not sure I would know where to get a quick lunch these days."

Ollie led Celeste out of the library. They blinked in the June sunlight. It was ten degrees warmer outside than in the library. Tweed jacket and bulky sweater were immediately shed.

"I suppose you recall how unusual this sort of weather is," said Ollie. "I was gonna take you to a place above the covered market, but maybe we should go to a pub with tables outside."

"Oh, I thought you were going to take me to the private dining room at Rhodes House," teased Celeste.

"Why, how'd you know I'm a Rhodes Scholar?"

"Just a guess. Actually, I'd prefer to eat in the market, if you don't mind. I'm spoiled by good weather in San Francisco, and I'm anxious to get back promptly to have a look at that thesis. Our friendly guard may require more prodding after lunch."

"Oh, God," commiserated Ollie. "These guys just burn me up. They're so slow and bureaucratic. Say, Ms. Braun, whaddya do in 'Frisco?"

"I'm an assistant professor at Bay Area University. I teach and do medical research, mostly virology."

"Whoa! Heavy-duty. My dad knows about that stuff, but

not me. Unh-unh. Strictly classics for yours truly."

"Who's your father?" asked Celeste.

"Aw, he's not really a scientist. He's General Ralph Johnson, at the Pentagon. He got an M.D. years ago and now he thinks about germ warfare. Just lately he's obsessed with viruses in a big way. It's like a hobby. That's all he could talk about when I was home at Christmas. That, and his new gal, the senator from Massachusetts. I'd say she's got the Pentagon in her pocket, if she wanted it. It'll be tough on my dad if she don't."

From a surprising memory bank of trivia, Celeste dredged up a recollection of the *Femina* article about Teresita Jiminez and her involvement with some general at the Pentagon. Why was it she could remember gossip pertaining to two individuals she hoped never to meet, when she always had to look up the chemical structures of the less common amino acids? Celeste appreciated that she was hobnobbing with a son of the establishment, and found his candor refreshing, considering his pedigree. She warmed to him as his story unfolded. Ollie, it transpired, was fanatically devoted to reading classical Greek literature. Celeste was surprised that a modern youth would have even heard of Greek literature, much less be captivated by it. Ollie had developed his unusual interest while working as a security guard at nights, the summer after he finished boarding school. Apparently Papa Johnson believed in his offspring earning their own pocket money for college, even though he could have provided for them handsomely.

Ollie regarded his sojourn in Oxford as a last fling before having to face the reality of returning to business school, to learn how to manage the family estate. "I always wished I had an older brother, so I could be disinherited and study Greek," he told Celeste.

Celeste learned all of this as they lunched at Georgina's, a vegetarian café, above a flight of narrow stairs in the middle of the covered market. She found the restaurant exactly as it had been nine years earlier, including the smell of stale urine and garbage at the bottom of the stairs that made you hold your breath until reaching the food smells of the café at the top. The market, too, was unchanged. The aroma of roasted coffee mingled with the sharp smell of decaying meat and the heavy, sweet smell of hothouse flowers. The fruit and vegetable vendors still wore their fingerless, woolly gloves, as the temperature hovered around 50°F the entire year. Leaving the market after lunch, Celeste and Ollie were glad to be warmed up again by the renegade June sun. It seemed a shame to reenter the Bodleian, but they resolutely donned their warm clothing and went to do battle with the thesis custodian.

Celeste quickly forgot all about privileged youth and Greek classics as she pored over the HPLC diagrams in Phillipson's thesis. Wang's suspicion of a plant-derived compound in Akira's blood was correct. The HPLC analysis of Akira's blood was an almost exact match with the HPLC data on page 318 of Phillipson's thesis. But the data weren't from Bazuran, as Celeste had suspected. They were from a different toxin, called Mingou toxin, apparently one of a family of alkaloid toxins that included Perouata and Gouata toxin. Only a few minor peaks were different from the pattern of the Fukuda data. This indicated that the substance in Akira's blood was a toxin with a similar structure and slight chemical modification, perhaps Gouata or Perouata toxin.

With a growing sense of distress, Celeste rapidly flipped back through the thesis to see if she could find any information about symptoms of toxicity. Oddly, Phillipson had organized his description of the toxins by their effects and applications. Celeste would have expected a student of organic chemistry to organize the data according to chemical structure rather than anthropological hearsay. But the thesis appeared to be more of an analytical curiosity than a scholarly work. From a subjective point of view, it was practically a "how to" book for poisoning your enemies. The descriptions of symptoms were written with great relish.

"Gouata toxin results in an agonizing liver failure, which manifests initially as mild hepatitis," Celeste read. "Within a week the liver is reduced to pulp and the victim essentially dies of autotoxicity. Unable to clear the naturally toxic substances that are generated by the body, the victim first turns bright yellow and then dark green. The final color change is accompanied by severe itching of the entire body, before the then longed-for relief of death."

It was 3:00 P.M. by the time Celeste was convinced that Akira had been dosed with Gouata toxin. The ominous sign on the window to the thesis archives indicated that all theses had to be returned by 3:30 P.M. to allow for reshelving before the reading room closed for tea at four. There was not sufficient time to copy the entire 350-page volume, so Celeste had to be satisfied with making a copy of the 50-page appendix of HPLC printouts, illustrating examples of each family of toxins. She also copied the chapter describing toxins with hepatitislike effects. At 3:25 P.M., the blue-smocked custodian stood impatiently waiting at Celeste's elbow, as she completed the detailed paperwork required to get a photocopy of the rest of the thesis sent to her in San Francisco. Intuition told her that it might be useful to have descriptions of the biological effects of the other toxins as well. As long as the reproduction department didn't use sea mail by mistake, she might even receive the copy before

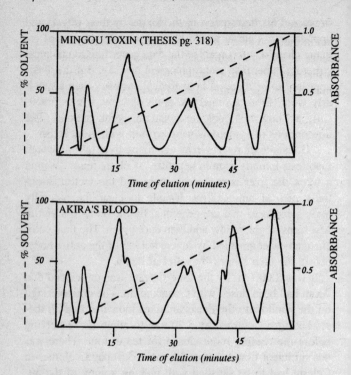

High-pressure liquid chromatography (HPLC) analyzes the properties of drugs, proteins, or toxins bound by a device, called a column, in the HPLC machine. The analysis determines how much solvent (over time) it takes to wash (elute) the bound substances from the column. Substances are detected by absorbance of light. The positions and shapes of the elution peaks are characteristic for each substance.

the end of the month. Looking at the custodian's retreating blue back, Celeste thought the slowest part of the transaction might be the intralibrary transport.

Celeste's perusal of the thesis had required such concentration that she didn't have a chance to register the significance of what she had found out. Now she sat at the table in the reading room, completely dazed, staring blankly in front of her. She should alert Minoru and Toshimi immediately, though it was undoubtedly too late to get a transfusion for Akira since, given his symptoms, the toxin must already have concentrated in his liver.

And what did this mean with respect to Phillipson? On the face of it, the evidence Celeste had found suggested murder. Poisoning by Bazuran might have been an accident. But a totally unrelated toxin had shown up in Akira's blood. Phillipson was the obvious person who could have had access to that toxin and come into contact with Akira. Celeste already knew the guy was a cheat and a charlatan. But a murderer? She couldn't take it in. She shivered as she thought of their several encounters over the past month.

What aspect of the Bazuran project could be so important that Phillipson felt he had to commit murder? Was there more to this project than her colleagues at Fukuda knew? Celeste wondered why Akira had been targeted. Had he come too close to the evidence that Phillipson stole the mutant from Harry? Hopefully, the answer was waiting on film back at her lab. If Phillipson had murdered Akira, then he had obviously crossed a barrier of human sensibility. And it was human sensibility that Celeste had assumed would prevent Phillipson from enacting Mac's suspicions. Still, release of a killer virus was murder on a different scale. After all, there was a good chance that such an act might even threaten the perpetrator. But were such things differentiated in the mind of a criminal? Celeste had no idea. She was an expert in virology, not criminal psychology. She felt completely and utterly out of her depth, and momentarily seized by panic.

Pulling herself together, Celeste's first instinct was to find a fax machine and send the data and a message to Fukuda. Then she thought it might be too risky sending this sensitive information by fax. It would be better to phone Toshimi and discuss it privately. But, damn it, it was already Saturday in Osaka. She'd have to call Janice to get Toshimi's home phone number off of her computer file. She checked her watch. It was 4:00 P.M., 8:00 A.M. in San Francisco. Only an hour until Janice would be at her desk.

"You all look like you've seen a ghost," said Ollie. He had been standing by her side for a good few minutes before she noticed him.

"Well, I have, in a way," said Celeste and thought, Akira's ghost.

"Come on, let's go have cream tea in Holywell Street."

"Thanks, but I'm saving myself for a pub supper of sausage, eggs, beans, and chips," said Celeste.

"You gotta be kidding." Ollie was incredulous. "You eat that stuff?"

"When in Rome," said Celeste. She suddenly felt dog tired.

The following day seemed endless to Celeste. She had returned to London on a morning train and spent the afternoon showing Debbie around the city. She couldn't discuss her discovery with Debbie, and it lurked in the back of her mind to torment her, whenever she had a moment to herself. A large part of the torment was that she was helpless to do anything about it until she could contact Toshimi. She'd successfully reached Janice yesterday afternoon, but there was no answer at Toshimi's home, which she had been calling every few hours since Janice gave her the number. Neither had she been able to get through to him at the office, which she tried in desperation, even though it was Sunday by then. Toshimi's apparent silence disturbed Celeste further.

Debbie, happily oblivious of Celeste's situation, was thrilled to get a table booked at Ronnie Scott's. In the course of their afternoon together Celeste and Debbie had discovered that they were both avid jazz fans, though neither could claim to be a connoisseur. Debbie had been introduced to jazz by her first noncowboy lover the year she left Montana. Celeste was a relatively new recruit, from listening to KJAZ since her move to San Francisco. She missed it tremendously after their frequency was outbid by talk radio, and she was surprised to discover that KJAZ had been the last commercial all-jazz radio station in the country.

As the two women hailed a taxi for their evening of wailing saxophone, Dr. Bryan Baird finally admitted defeat. He'd been waiting almost two hours for that stewardess to show up. With less than half an hour until curtain time, he figured he better head over to the theater. Maybe he could unload the extra ticket, if people were waiting for returns. It was a long time since he'd spent an evening alone without intending to do so.

By late Sunday afternoon, when the return flight from London arrived in San Francisco, the crew was slaphappy. The distraction of working the flight had helped Celeste shelve her worries about Phillipson and Fukuda, at least temporarily. She was caught up by the camaraderie of the exhausted crew, and the satisfaction of being part of a team brought back pleasant memories of rowing in college. As soon as she opened the door of her apartment, however, her sense of well-being evaporated. The red light on her answering machine blinked insistently, its demand for attention restoring the anxiety of the past couple of days. She punched the button with apprehension.

"Hi, Celeste. This is Janice," said the machine. "I thought you should know that Dr. Toshimi from Fukuda called on Friday morning, about two hours after you did, and left a different phone number than the one I gave you. He wants you to call him at that number this weekend. He sounded like it was pretty urgent. I didn't know how to get ahold of you, but I figured you'd at least call in to get your messages here." Janice's voice then recited and repeated the ten-digit phone number that Toshimi had given her, which Celeste copied onto the jacket of the phone book.

Celeste realized that Janice meant well, and that being unable to get ahold of her, it made sense to do what she did—that is, if Celeste used the phone like normal people. But Celeste was not in the habit of checking her messages while she was away. In fact, she didn't even know how to do it. The best part about going away was escaping the world of messages. But now Celeste reluctantly admitted her habits might have to change. She'd been inadvertently thrust into this situation, and she was going to have to take advantage of everything at her disposal to stay on top of it—even if it meant participating in the technological nightmare of the "information superhighway."

Celeste checked her watch. It was Monday afternoon in Japan. Toshimi would be back in the office by now, and probably extremely anxious that he hadn't heard from her. The phone still blinked, with further messages. They would have to wait. Celeste consulted her address book and dialed the number for Fukuda headquarters in Osaka. She put the receiver down and pushed the speaker phone button to listen for the connection. This freed her to retrieve the copy of the appendix to Phillipson's thesis from the depths of the overstuffed, regulation flight attendant's bag that had accompanied her to Oxford and back. The unfamiliar bag reminded her she was still in uniform and she kicked off her pumps, to the enormous relief of her stockinged toes, which spread out gratefully on the hardwood floor.

Toshimi's personal secretary, whose English was far better than his, told Celeste she had instructions to interrupt him in conference if Dr. Braun called. Within a minute, Toshimi was on the line. The strain in his voice was evident.

"Ah, Celeste," he said. "Finally I hear from you. I was hoping you call to the funeral this weekend. We are very busy here and very sad. My two 'sons' have joined the spirits. They are happy but we must bear the loss."

Two? Celeste wondered. "Toshimi, what's happened?" His spirituality was probably comforting but not very useful for conveying facts.

"Minoru in fatal car accident, Wednesday night. Then Akira pass away only few hours later, early Thursday morning."

Celeste was dumbstruck. Either it was a horrible coincidence or Phillipson was on the rampage. "Oh, Toshimi. I'm so sorry," was all Celeste could manage while she tried to collect her thoughts.

Then she told Toshimi about the toxin data in Phillipson's thesis. "I just can't bring myself to believe it, but it certainly looks like Phillipson poisoned Akira. Do you think he could have had anything to do with Minoru's accident?" Celeste felt herself babbling into the phone.

"Interesting question," said Toshimi thoughtfully. "You

suspect, maybe not coincidence?'' He told Celeste about the escaped sample of Akira's blood.

"Minoru's 'accident' could have been Phillipson's attempt to stop delivery of the blood sample for analysis,'' Celeste suggested. "Did Phillipson know that the HPLC analysis of Akira's blood had already been done?''

"I think not," said Toshimi.

"Is there any way you can get an HPLC analysis of Minoru's blood? I brought back photocopies of data for some of the toxins that Phillipson studied, and I ordered copies of the rest. We could see if any of these show up in Minoru's blood.''

"Police think Minoru drunk. Must have taken blood sample for alcohol test. I call inspector right away to see if we can do HPLC.''

"Ever since I saw the toxin data in the thesis, I've been trying to figure out why Phillipson would need to kill Akira. All I can think is that I must have been right about Phillipson stealing Harry's original findings. Maybe Akira suggested an experiment that would have revealed this. It would certainly put Phillipson's patent in jeopardy.''

"Now I recall letter Akira send to Phillipson at Stanley symposium,'' said Toshimi. "I think he ask for more Bazuran to test wild-type strain.''

"That's got to be it, then,'' said Celeste. "As soon as I saw that test on the wild-type strain, it made me think of Harry's earlier results. Phillipson doesn't know that Akira actually did that experiment, does he?''

"No, Akira not supposed to have done it. He reuse first sample of Bazuran because Phillipson did not send more.''

"I bet he planned for Akira to die before he got around to testing the wild-type strain. Did he bring more Bazuran with him?''

"No. He say it was still in production."

"Well, I think it's academic now, but at least the gel I have on film will prove we're dealing with a mutant strain. It would certainly be worth knowing if Phillipson really did switch strains on Harry." Celeste was still reluctant to confess her worst fears to Toshimi until she knew about the mutant for sure. But she was already thinking about how to broach the suggestion that Phillipson might be planning to release the virus to make money. She realized from Toshimi's next comment that he was likely to be skeptical.

"To suspect is to suspect," said Toshimi. "Data is data. Result from gel very important." He paused. But his own private suspicions confirmed his resolve. "Celeste, I must ask favor," he said. "I worry about Kazuko now. She is alone and also involved in Bazuran project. I think she is best away from Fukuda. Could she work in your lab for a while? We, of course, pay support."

"Oh, Toshimi," exclaimed Celeste. "This is exactly what I proposed to you last month. I only wish it had happened for different reasons."

"*Hai*," said Toshimi, "me also." A brief silence followed. "I send her to arrive Tuesday, evening flight, Japan Air Lines. If we can get it, she bring HPLC data of Minoru blood. I must call police right now."

"Fine," said Celeste. "I'll meet the flight. But if there's any change of plans, I'll be calling Monday—uh, tomorrow, anyway, since the film of the gel should be ready to develop."

"*Hai, hai.* Call at home, even if late. I want to know result."

THIRTEEN

Infection Connection

The hospital foyer was deserted when Celeste arrived at the medical center at 6:00 A.M. Monday morning. Returning from Europe was almost as bad as flying to Japan for her bodily clock. Though she would have to wait until noon to develop the gel film, she knew there was plenty of work to keep her occupied, lying in piles on her desk.

Crossing the lobby, Celeste walked past the serene portrait of the benefactress who had donated money to redecorate the surgery waiting area. The portrait didn't look as incongruous as usual, since the lounge was empty of anxious relatives that early in the morning. It was still a relief, though, to pass between the swinging doors into the research tower. Normally Celeste had time to peruse the notices of upcoming lectures and seminars while she waited for the elevator, but two cars were standing empty, ready for ascent. As the doors shut, the words ''Virotox, Inc.'' at the bottom of a neon pink notice flashed at her from among the colored flyers tacked to the bulletin board across the lobby.

As soon as she got to her office, Celeste hurriedly sorted through the pile of mail on her desk to find a copy of the provocative announcement. Sure enough, Virotox, Inc., was sponsoring a lecture at three o'clock that afternoon. The invited speaker was a well-known viral epidemiologist. He was one of the first to characterize patterns of virus spread between animals and humans. She would have to attend.

Celeste spent the next few hours at her computer, revising her graduate student's latest effort in writing his first scientific manuscript. She was so absorbed in the work that Mac had to clear his throat to get her to notice him in the doorway.

Celeste looked around. "Yes?" she said, sounding unintentionally frosty. She was embarrassed that she had let the argument get out of hand the other night.

"Uh, I hope you're still speaking to me," said Mac. He still hadn't been able to figure out what he had done to make her so angry with him.

She smiled. He was obviously equally chagrined. She teased him gently to ease the tension. "I wouldn't count on it," she said.

Mac smiled back, and their gazes locked for a few seconds, each trying to read the thoughts of the other person.

"But I don't have to speak to you to show you how to develop a gel film," said Celeste, "so let's do it."

She beckoned to Mac to follow her out of the office and led him through the maze of corridors crowded with humming equipment. Celeste removed the metal film cassette from the −70°C freezer where it had been stored, holding it by the corners to avoid being burned by the extreme cold.

"Even the asbestos fingers I've developed won't tolerate this," she said.

In the darkroom there was barely enough room for the two of them. Mac was so close that Celeste could feel the heat from his body and smell his scent, in spite of the strong odor of darkroom chemicals. He smelled fresh, a soapy smell from her childhood, not like most of the men she'd been with recently, whose aftershave often made her sneeze. Celeste removed the film from the cassette and fed it through the automatic developer. "We can't open the door until the buzzer goes off. Otherwise light leaks into the developing system."

"Okeydoke," said Mac. Celeste sensed him tensing up, being careful not to touch her. So much for my Clark Gable fantasies, she thought as they stood in awkward silence in the dark.

Released by the buzzer, they emerged self-consciously into the bright corridor. But all awkwardness was instantly forgotten as the film emerged from the slot in the wall of the darkroom. The patterns were clear, dark, and easily interpretable. The samples had been applied to the gel so that the wild-type virus coat proteins were always next to the equivalent proteins from the suspected mutant. Without even consulting the key as to which was which, it was obvious from the film that every pair of samples differed from each other, showing that the two virus strains had proteins of different sizes.

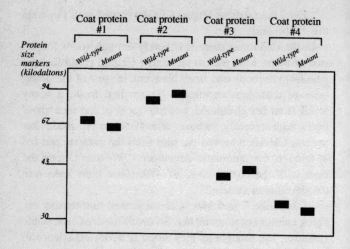

"Amazing," said Celeste. "Look at these paired lanes. Every coat protein is a different size between the wild-type and indicator strain! So the indicator strain must have a mutant protease. This would totally explain the change in sensitivity to the drugs. Assembly of the different coat proteins in the mutant must be more sensitive to Bazuran than assembly of coat proteins in the wild-type. And the mutated protease must no longer be sensitive to Protex."

"Whoa," said Mac, briefly laying a large hand on her shoulder, as though slowing her down. "Mercy on the ignorant. Please translate."

"Sorry. I'll try to explain it more clearly." The hand flustered her a little. "It's just that it's incredible that I was right about the kind of mutation that had changed the virus. No, wait a minute, maybe it's not incredible. Maybe I'd heard this idea before." She was overwhelmed by a sense of déjà vu.

"You know, this data looks kind of familiar," she said slowly, dredging her memory. "In fact, I'm almost positive Harry found something similar. I remember him trying to explain it to me. In one experiment he did, in the period when Bazuran was working, he saw that several Eke virus coat proteins had changed size and hypothesized that the protease might have mutated because that would affect several coat proteins at once. But when he went back to check protease activity, it seemed normal. Then he couldn't reproduce either the Bazuran sensitivity or the protein data. In the end he concluded he must have made some gross error or discovered a mutant strain that got overgrown by the wild-type strain and was lost. Here it is again, though. Phillipson claims to have discovered it, but it's not original."

"What's not original?" asked Mac. He felt a little uncomfortable standing in the middle of the main passageway through the laboratory while Celeste went through her elaborate recollections. But lab personnel were evidently used to discussions of data in the corridor. They paid no attention to Mac and Celeste and brushed past them, laden with racks of test tubes and buckets of ice, heading for the nearby row of centrifuges.

Celeste was still in a focused trance, thinking about the data. "Well, this guy Phillipson wants to convince Fukuda to buy the rights to Bazuran. He claims that Eke virus could mutate to become sensitive to Bazuran and insensitive to Protex. Here we have a clear demonstration that this is feasible. But this supposed new finding of Phillipson's may be a rediscovery of something already found by Harry Freeman when he was in Jane's lab. If the details of the mutation are exactly the same, then Phillipson's patent won't hold up. I've got to call Toshimi right away."

Mac was just about following this. "If you challenge a patent claim, you'll need evidence that the work was done before. I suppose it's all in Freeman's lab notebook."

"You're right, in principle. But Harry's work was done in the days before fraud mania. There was no legal obligation to keep your notebooks after you left a lab, just common sense. And Harry didn't have much common sense when it came to his career in Jane Stanley's lab. He told me last week that he had tossed out all his old notebooks. I'm sure it was a dramatic gesture on his part." Celeste paused. "But you know, I wasn't actually in Jane's lab when Harry did that work. He did it when Phillipson was still there. So I must have known about it from proofreading Harry's thesis, which he wrote later, while I was there. Now I've definitely got to see a copy of his thesis."

Celeste headed back to her office, calculating what time it was in New York, and where Harry might be. Mac followed her, feeling doglike. "Uh, Dr. Braun, I mean Celeste, now that we're done with this experiment, what will I do next?"

"Oh, yes," Celeste said distractedly. "We do have to make some plans for you. Remind me how long you'll be here."

Mac became a little annoyed. Here he was giving up a lucrative summer of gardening to work in the lab for this woman and she couldn't even bother to remember his situation. He replied as though speaking to a forgetful child. "Well, I'm not totally sure when I'll have to leave, or even where I'm going. I'm waiting to hear where my ex-wife will be posted before I decide on a graduate program. Then if it's Texas, I'll leave in mid-August. The other programs start in September, so I can stay till the end of August."

Mac's petulant tone made Celeste stop and turn around

to face him. She focused on him and smiled. "I'm sorry," she said. "I just got so caught up in thinking about this result. You see, it may have a lot of significance. More than I can discuss freely right now." She looked strained. "I remember now, your wife's involved in some top-secret government vaccine trial, and you're waiting for orders."

"My ex-wife," corrected Mac.

Celeste carried on, as though she hadn't heard. But she was puzzled by the mixed signals from this guy. "I need to give a little thought to the next step, and also figure out whether this is really the best project for you to be involved in, under the circumstances. Would you mind coming back tomorrow or Wednesday, so we can discuss it in more depth?"

"Okay, but if we're not going to do any more today, I'll probably head over to my last gardening job and do some tidying up. When you know when you wanna meet again, call me on my beeper." Mac handed Celeste a business card from his wallet. He didn't understand why, but he felt mildly frustrated from the encounter with Celeste this morning. Digging in Mrs. Roberts's garden might be just the antidote.

"Fine," said Celeste. "I'll give you a call." She laid Mac's card on top of a pile of papers on her desk and started to dial Harry's number at the *New York Times*.

"Darling," said Harry, when she had identified herself, "great to hear from you. To what do I owe this pleasure? Feeling horny?"

"Harry," Celeste admonished. Occasionally, but only occasionally, his preoccupation with sex irritated her. "Something's come up in the lab that I need to check out in your thesis. I found out from Jane that her copy is out being microfilmed. So I think your mother's copy is the only one available at the moment.''

''Well, that's a waste of microfilm,'' said Harry. ''I s'pose I could find the thesis at my mother's, but I'm not sure it's even on a shelf. There's a bunch of boxes in the basement from graduate school that I never unpacked.''

''Is there any way you could get it fairly soon?''

''If you make it worth my while, I might even go visit the mater this week. What's on offer?''

Celeste looked at her calendar. ''Next Sunday I'm flying out to D.C. for my study section meeting. How about bed and breakfast Tuesday night in Washington?''

''I'll take the bed. Skip the breakfast, I'm on a diet.''

''Maybe you could fax me the chapter on Bazuran when you get the thesis.''

''You *are* single-minded,'' said Harry. ''But not as single-minded as I am.''

''No, probably not,'' replied Celeste, feeling her underpants moisten in anticipation of a night with Harry. In the absence of romance, good sex and good friendship had a lot going for it. Besides, romance was full of strained silences and unrequited love. A good friendship made it easy to relax and enjoy sex.

Sex and romance were the farthest things from Celeste's mind, on her way to the lecture hall later that afternoon, for the virology seminar. Jet lag was taking its toll as she slipped into a seat near the back of the auditorium. Celeste hoped she would be able to stay awake for the duration of the talk. However, a glimpse of Bryan Baird and his wife chatting with the speaker in the front row got her adrenaline pumping. Celeste now recalled that Baird's wife had recently moved to Virotox. She must have been hosting the speaker's visit to the Bay Area.

Sure enough, Bryan Baird introduced the speaker. He thanked Virotox for their generosity in giving the speaker a break from his consulting duties and allowing him to contribute to the BAU seminar series. Baird was predictably unctuous, and Celeste's disgust for him increased.

The lecture room was packed. General interest in AIDS epidemiology was enormous. In addition to the usual graduate students, fellows, and basic science faculty, there was a huge contingent of clinical faculty. It was easy to assign the assembled crowd into these two groups. The scientists, young and old, male and female, were uniformly dressed in jeans. The clinical faculty wore white coats and power ties or the female equivalent. And in case their dress code was too subtle a status symbol, their beepers went off with some regularity.

The speaker talked about the frightening numbers of individuals afflicted with HIV in East Africa. He discussed the feasibility of the theory that the virus was originally a monkey virus that made its way into the human population through tribal practices of consuming monkey blood. His data were compelling and delivered in a dry, old-fashioned academic manner with none of the bells and whistles in the form of colored slides and cute jokes that characterized lectures from Celeste's generation of scientists. Normally Celeste would have appreciated this straightforward, thoughtful delivery, but today her mind wandered, giving way to the fatigue and stress of the past few days.

Celeste considered this man's long and distinguished career. He was an excellent scientist, but also a testimony to the fact that it helps to be in the right place at the right time. He had just joined the Centers for Disease Control and Prevention in Atlanta, when he had the opportunity to make his reputation. As Celeste heard it, he was single-handedly responsible for tracking down the cause of the famous *Haemophilus* epidemic in young children, which resulted from a batch of contaminated whooping cough vaccine. That epidemic was particularly insidious because of the widespread campaign to vaccinate against an equally insidious disease. It proved to be such an effective way to spread an infectious agent that the regulations for vaccine production were made highly stringent. Now it was mandatory that all vaccines to be used in children be tested on military volunteers.

The thought of military vaccination brought Celeste's wandering mind around to Mac, and their findings that morning. She would be able to call Toshimi as soon as the seminar let out. It would be about nine on Tuesday morning in Japan. She was now completely convinced that Phillipson had stolen Harry's experiment and that he believed Akira's work would result in discovery of the theft and threaten his patent. But concern about a patent seemed hardly a motive for murder, particularly if Bazuran was effective only against a mutant strain of virus generated in the laboratory. Bazuran wouldn't even be manufactured—unless, of course, it was needed in an emergency, such as escape of the mutant virus from the laboratory. Celeste had to face it: She could no longer dismiss Mac's idea as science fiction.

She made herself say the words in her head: Phillipson is a killer and a thief. Everything about him suggested he would be reckless enough to release a mutant virus to make money off the cure.

Sitting there in the lecture hall and surrounded by dozing colleagues, Celeste was gripped again by the sickening, panicky feeling she felt in the Bodleian Library when she looked at Phillipson's thesis. But her mind, ignoring her debilitating emotions, prodded her to pay attention to where she was and led her through a series of deductions.

She reminded herself that the speaker she was listening to was sponsored by Virotox. Evidently he was consulting for them. His area of expertise was predicting patterns of virus spread. He discovered the danger of accidental disease dissemination through vaccine administration. Could there be a connection between Virotox and vaccine production or testing? Would this be their strategy for releasing the mutant virus? Celeste was suddenly wide awake. She knew two ways she might find out.

A few minutes later the speaker finished his lecture and the surrounding audience applauded. A number of people got up to leave before the question period, and Celeste took advantage of the shifting crowd to move closer to where Baird and his wife were sitting. After about ten minutes of general questions from the audience, Baird thanked the speaker once again and dismissed the remaining crowd. A few persistent questioners then surrounded the speaker at the podium and a lively discussion continued, into which Baird's wife was drawn from her ringside seat. Celeste seized her opportunity and, coming down the side aisle, sat down next to Baird.

"Hi, Bryan," said Celeste. "Sorry I couldn't make it the other night."

Baird looked puzzled and then blushed. "I know you. You're Celeste Braun from Microbiology. But aren't you . . . ?" Celeste realized he couldn't even remember the name of the stewardess he had propositioned.

"Francine, that's right," said Celeste, smiling sweetly. "Just moonlighting." She didn't feel the need to explain herself further. Baird was the married one of the two of them. He should do the explaining.

Celeste continued. "I should congratulate your wife on her new job at Virotox. In fact, there's something I'd like to know about Virotox. But I see she's tied up at the moment. Perhaps if you could find out the information for me, then I wouldn't need to talk to her." Celeste gave Baird a calculated look.

He caught Celeste's drift immediately, and was relieved that there appeared to be a simple solution to prevent her from squawking to his wife. "Sure, uh, Celeste. Anything you'd like to know, assuming, of course, that you'll be discreet."

"I think that's a reasonable exchange," said Celeste. "I'm just curious about the composition of the Virotox board of directors and would be interested to see a list of investors putting up venture capital. I imagine that someone at your wife's level would have access to that information."

"I think I can get that for you. Just give me a few days and I'll drop it off with your secretary." Baird looked at her venomously. "Don't let me keep you any longer," he said with acidic sweetness.

"Nice to see you again, Bryan," said Celeste, flashing her stewardess smile.

Back in her office, Celeste had to force herself to call Toshimi. She was unbelievably tired and felt soiled from her attempt at blackmail. Baird might be a greaseball, but she had been playing on his court.

In spite of the fact that Celeste was finally able to report the results of her experiment, the conversation with Toshimi was far from satisfactory. If anything, it compounded Celeste's uneasiness. Now that she had proven there was a mutant, Toshimi seemed to think that the patent issue would be sufficient motive for murder. As she had feared, he wouldn't even entertain Celeste's suggestion that Phillipson planned to release the virus, dismissing it for lack of evidence and for the obvious, unthinkable danger of such an act. He urged Celeste to get the information from Harry's thesis. He also wanted to initiate Phillipson's prosecution as soon as the blood analysis from both Akira and Minoru could be correlated with the printouts from Phillipson's thesis. Toshimi confirmed that Kazuko would bring an HPLC analysis of Minoru's blood when she arrived in San Francisco the following day.

There was no question that Toshimi was right about the danger of releasing a mutant virus. Even if Bazuran was effective against the mutant, there was little chance it could control spread of the infection in an urban population. And a widespread epidemic of Eke virus would make the recent Ebola virus outbreaks seem like local incidents of food poisoning. But Celeste didn't think that Toshimi was right to assume Phillipson would not take the risk. Furthermore, if Phillipson intended to release the virus, he could blackmail Fukuda into doing whatever he wanted by threatening to implicate them. Bazuran would be needed to counteract the released virus, and it would be easy to pin the blame on the Japanese. By forcing Fukuda to sign the contract for Bazuran, Phillipson had effectively put himself in the position of being able to blackmail the entire Japanese government.

If Celeste was right about Phillipson's plan, she would need to prove it before Fukuda accused Phillipson of the poisonings. Otherwise he could retaliate, with a much larger bargaining chip. Ironically, there might be one time factor in her favor, giving her a few days to come up with further evidence of Phillipson's intentions. With any luck, they would have to wait for the rest of Phillipson's thesis data to arrive from the Bodleian to implicate him in Minoru's death. But there was no guarantee that she didn't already have the information they needed in the photocopies she made in Oxford. She wouldn't know where she stood until Kazuko arrived.

Exhausted but feeling a pressing urgency to pursue her second line of investigation into a possible military vaccine trial connection for Virotox, Celeste punched Mac's beeper number. As instructed, she entered her own number after the tone and pressed the "#" sign. Then she lay down on the couch in her office to wait for his call and promptly fell asleep.

Mac paused to breathe. He looked up at the soft belly above him and beyond that at the two flattened pancakes of breasts splayed over Mrs. Roberts's rib cage. Between them he could just make out her chin, arched toward the ceiling. He resumed his task. Suddenly her whole body shuddered. She grabbed his hair and pushed his head out of her groin. With a practiced move, he slid himself up onto her front, between her spread legs. As he entered her, his beeper emitted a shrill noise from the chair where he had thrown his clothes.

FOURTEEN

Hay Fever

The naked body stretched out beside Simon Phillipson had fewer creases at the edges than the one on which Mac had just collapsed. The skin's smooth surface moved gently with the shallow breathing of his companion, who had fallen asleep almost immediately after the climax of their furious coupling. Phillipson had become flaccid. But he lay taut and sleepless, listening to the street sounds of Georgetown at three o'clock in the morning. He probably shouldn't have come to Washington, but since his return from Japan he felt an urgency to move things along.

It didn't help that Teri Jiminez was irritated with him. Well, that wasn't entirely true. The conflict introduced an exciting undercurrent of violence in bed. But Teri had already planned to spend the weekend with him in San Francisco after her talk at the Congressional Women's Fundraiser, and was vexed by this disruption in her plans. Phillipson thought she was far too concerned about that stuffy old fart of a general whom she was leading on.

Pleading stomach flu, she managed to get out of her date last night, when Phillipson had shown up. But the general insisted she come by on her way to Dulles International Airport so he could say good-bye. It was quite possible that Phillipson and Teri would be at the general's house at the same time. Phillipson relished the potential charade of being formal to each other in the general's presence. Teri had made it clear that she did not.

Her political correctness exasperated Phillipson. If she weren't so useful, he'd have dumped her long ago. But actually, how useful was she now? The Biodiversity Treaty was well on its way to being rejected by the Senate, thanks to the legislation Teri had introduced. Discreditation of Stanley was also essentially completed, having been taken over by the media. Teri's timely appearance on *Spotlight on Health* had certainly moved that along, a clever move on his part to introduce her to DiMaggio. Still, there was no question Teri was a good lay. Under the circumstances, she was probably worth keeping around for further congressional favors. Also, the direct connection with the general might continue to prove useful.

The general was another matter. Phillipson found nothing redeeming about him and resented his dependence on the man for the ultimate success of his plan. The general was simply too egocentric to take orders. He would have to be prodded into appropriate action another way. Phillipson lay awake another hour, working out his strategy. At last, satisfied he had a solution, he fell into a fitful doze until Teri's automatic coffeemaker ground into action, inducing her to roll out of bed and shut herself in the bathroom.

The coffeemaker sat on a pristine kitchenette counter next to the microwave oven, the automatic pastamaker, and the automatic breadmaker. The white plastic finish on these appliances matched the white plastic electric toothbrush and hair dryer in the bathroom, and the white shag carpet that blanketed Teri's apartment. The blond wood dining set and the white leather couch did nothing to alleviate the air of hospital sterility. Nor did the muted pastel tones of the expensive but innocuous prints on the wall. Phillipson was convinced there was a clone of such apartments in the capital, all decorated by the same "PC" designers.

There were only two items in the whole place that revealed occupancy by a nonclonal human being. One was a dog-eared looseleaf notebook with a pink plastic cover that sat on the bottom shelf of the nightstand on Teri's side of the bed. Phillipson had been completely puzzled by this uncharacteristically shoddy object and privately inspected it on a previous visit while Teri was in the shower. It turned out to be a homemade scrapbook, hand-captioned in white ink on black paper, in unfamiliar handwriting. Phillipson guessed it was the work of Teri's mother, whose photograph appeared on the first page. She was standing in a barrio backyard, holding a baby in one arm and the hand of a young girl with the other. It was captioned "In the beginning."

The other discordant object in the apartment was the red telephone. It was Teri's one display of her local power. As did all red telephones in Washington, this one connected directly to a private line at the Pentagon. Phillipson fully intended to use this line, but it would be another hour before his prey could be reached by that means.

Phillipson heard Teri turn off her shower behind the closed door of the bathroom, and he became aroused at the thought of her stepping out, dripping wet. He would wait until she finished her toilette, though. With her hair freshly cemented into place with the latest "natural-looking" spray, she would insist on being entered from behind. It was less disruptive to her hairdo, and Phillipson vastly preferred it. Hammering away, facing a slim back, brought back provocative memories of his school days. He figured she found it a welcome change from the fumbling frontal assaults by the general.

Phillipson calculated correctly. His needs met—and co-operatively, too—he showered, dressed, and made his connection on the red telephone. The advantage of the direct line was that no secretary was aware of his call. Phillipson suspected, however, that this discretionary privilege did not bypass the CIA, so he identified himself with an agreed code name. The general's reaction to his call validated his suspicion. Phillipson could hear him take a deep breath before he responded. His voice was chillingly polite, as only a Southerner can be.

"Well, I didn't reckon on hearing from you so soon, uh, after your last defeat. You must be anxious to get back on that golf course."

Good cover, General, thought Phillipson. He hadn't expected any subtlety from the U.S. military brass. "I most certainly am," he said into the red receiver. "In fact, I'm leaving town tonight, and was hoping to get a game in this afternoon. I've been practicing my drives all weekend."

"Well, that suits me just fine," cooed the general in his thick southern drawl. "I was intending to be out at the house in Virginia this afternoon, anyway. When'd you like to tee off?"

"I'll be there at noon. If you'd like a spot of lunch, we could be at the tee by half past one," said Phillipson.

"All right," said the general with a sigh. "The earlier the better. I'm expecting another visitor later in the afternoon."

"Looking forward to it, Ralph," said Phillipson.

"See ya later," said the general. As he hung up he realized that Phillipson had phoned on a red line. Jeez, he'd have to keep a closer eye on that guy. He must have some other high-up connections. Lucky his automatic response to Phillipson's code name was the golf partner routine, so the CIA wouldn't be any the wiser. Damn the CIA, anyway. He would have liked to get them to trace the red-line call. But that would raise a flag. He'd have to wait to check his monthly incoming-call list. An unusual red-line number ought to stand out. He wrote down the date and time of the call: June 8, 9:15 A.M. Then he opened his desk drawer, pulled out a well-worn, leather-bound hip flask, and took his second hit of bourbon for the day.

"I wish you wouldn't use my private line to talk Biotech business with the general," complained Teri. "I know you think he's a gomer, but he could track the call. It's a risk to our power base."

"You mean you'd lose your political protector if he found out you're sharing your favors with someone else. I've got nothing to lose myself," said Phillipson. "Virotox already has his money and I have no doubt of his further cooperation."

This last remark sounded ominous. Teri knew Phillipson could be a ruthless bastard under his refined exterior. His disdain for the rest of the world reminded her of the barrio toughs to whom she deliberately lost her virginity when she was fourteen. She had adopted that disdain, as well as the toughness, and responded to the kindred spirit in Phillipson when he had propositioned her at the California fundraiser two years earlier. It puzzled her then, this protectiveness she felt toward the general. Although the affair with the general was completely calculated, she had become fond of him. The accumulated years of his bourbon habit meant his sexual advances rarely resulted in penetration. They were more like heavy petting sessions, and Teri found the physical attention a relaxing release. Emotionally, the general had become a substitute for her nonexistent father, and she would regret it if he were hurt unnecessarily.

"Be gentle with him, Simon," she said. "He's not a young man."

"That," said Phillipson, "is precisely the problem. He's a pompous old fool with a chip on his shoulder. He fancies himself a self-taught scientist, doing brilliant experiments for the Pentagon. Out of control, he could be dangerous. I note your concern, however. Rather touching, in fact. You're not going soft on me, are you?" He drew her roughly toward him.

Teri stiffened against his grasp. "Not when I'm dressed for work. There'll be plenty of time for that in California. Now let me go," she said with considerable authority.

"Yes, Madam Senator," said Phillipson. "See you at Ralphie's."

Teri shot him a furious look. "His nickname's Buck," she said and slammed out the door of her apartment. Phillipson watched her from the window. The driver of her car held the door, taking in the view of her long brown legs as she maneuvered her well-fitted business suit into the backseat.

Maybe she is dispensable after all, Phillipson thought. He turned away from the window and phoned for a taxi to take him to Virginia.

In preparation for the journey, Phillipson took another shower and put on his lightest cotton shirt and rolled up the sleeves. In spite of these precautions, he was soaked to the skin with sweat within five minutes of getting into the taxi. Thick, heavy air sat on the city, and the sun barely penetrated the breezeless, leafy canopy of the Friendship Heights neighborhood through which they drove. The houses, with their neat little ghost gardens, were shut tight against the sauna outside. The supercilious taxi driver made no excuses for the fact that the air-conditioning in the cab didn't work. The only defense against a complete sap of Phillipson's energy was to fall into an uneasy doze, until a warm breeze from the open windows of the taxi speeding along the Beltway toward Virginia woke him up.

The general did not look good. His nose was already glowing from a series of prelunch bourbons. He slapped Phillipson on the back too heartily, making his shirt stick to his back under the crumpled blue linen jacket he had donned before entering the club. There was only one other couple in the club restaurant, a pair of blue-haired matrons wearing matching pink golfing shirts, with the club logo over each left breast. They were so interested in the general's presence that Phillipson decided to save his discussion for the privacy of the golf course. He patiently consumed a tasteless seafood salad and sipped iced tea while the general polished off a small steak and baked potato, accompanied by another bourbon, and the usual southern-style courtesies that passed for conversation.

Finally, ensconced in the golf cart heading toward the second hole, the general lit up his cigar, and Phillipson got down to business.

"I gather your son's a Rhodes Scholar at Oxford."

"Why, yes, we're real proud of him," drawled the general. "Though I wish he was a little more inclined to the family business."

"I also gather that he has other inclinations," said Phillipson.

The general shot Phillipson a warning look. "Now, whaddya mean by that?" he demanded.

"Well, let's put it this way," said Phillipson. "I was an Oxford man myself and still have a lot of connections to the dons—that is, the faculty there. One in particular, Dr. Nicholas Hunt of Bailliol. Did your son ever mention him?"

"Not that I can recollect. The boy keeps his academic business to himself."

"Well, if I recall, Dr. Hunt can be quite seductive. The unfortunate part about his vice is that he also likes to take photographs."

The general turned purple. "What the fuck are you driving at, Phillipson? You better not be making improper suggestions about my boy, Ollie. I'd watch your ass if I were you."

"Photographs don't lie," said Phillipson coolly. "However, they can be destroyed. They can also be released to the tabloids. The headlines would be marvelous. 'Clinton's Heritage: Gay Times for the Modern Rhodes Scholar.' "

"I wouldn't do that if I was you, bud," threatened the general. He braked the golf cart abruptly and turned his heavy body to face Phillipson. Phillipson just sat there with a self-satisfied smirk. "Well, Jesus H. Christ. I guess you would." The general was livid, and Phillipson had him exactly where he wanted him. "All right," he growled. "What'll it take to call off your dogs?"

"Ah, General. I knew you would see my point of view. I've merely established an insurance policy that I will continue to have the full cooperation of the Pentagon. I'm anxious to get our little experiment under way as soon as possible. We can't afford any more of these delays for protocol. I want the order signed by the end of the week."

"I told you, it doesn't make sense if we haven't got the control population lined up."

"You bloody fool," said Phillipson quietly. "If you think the purpose of our plan is to give you the chance to do the perfect experiment in germ warfare, think again. I don't give a damn about your protocols, nor about your precious son. Hunt is prepared to send off the photos unless he hears otherwise. I've a good mind to let him go through with it."

The general was fuming. He was furious with himself for being at the mercy of this bullying foreigner, and he was furious with Ollie for his fucking free spirit. He should have kept that boy in military academy. He chewed ferociously on the end of his cigar, considering how to deal with Phillipson, then stomped on the accelerator, jerking the golf cart back into motion. They rode the rest of the way to the green in silence.

Phillipson's drive had landed just short of the green. It shouldn't have been difficult to get it within putting range. However, the general's drive had already landed on the green. This impressively good shot for someone so sozzled took Phillipson by surprise. It must have been the tension of the moment, since it was hardly his sense of fair play, that made Phillipson completely overshoot the green. He saw the ball roll into the rough on the other side and come to rest near a heap of grass clippings piled discreetly off to the side.

It was the general's turn to smirk, at least momentarily. They climbed back into the cart and the general drove, a bit too fast, over to where Phillipson's ball had landed. As he braked, the wheels of the cart caught the edge of the pile of grass clippings, stirring up a dusty green cloud.

Immediately Phillipson began to cough. He gasped for

breath, as though being strangled, then lapsed into heavy wheezing. "Quick. The clubhouse. Adrenaline," he whispered hoarsely. He was as purple as the general had been a few moments earlier.

The general didn't start up the cart immediately. He looked carefully at Phillipson. From the ancient history of his medical training he recognized the symptoms of an allergy-induced asthma attack. It looked like the kind of attack that could develop into anaphylaxis if Phillipson didn't get some help.

So the bastard has a chink in his armor, thought the general. The bourbon coursing through his veins urged him to let the fucker choke to death. Then he remembered the photographs. Hadn't Phillipson said they would be sent off *unless* he canceled the instructions? It was too big a risk. The general gunned the golf cart accelerator and hurried back to the clubhouse, taking the shortest route he could without driving on the green.

Later the same day, in San Francisco, Celeste was anticipating Kazuko's arrival from Japan. She phoned the airline to learn that Kazuko's flight would be on time, leaving a little more than an hour to get some work done before heading for the airport. Celeste reached under her desk and dragged out the huge cardboard box containing the eighty-two grant proposals that would be read and reviewed by her study section committee in Washington next week. The amount of paper that was flown back and forth across the country to make the peer review system work was phenomenal. This would be reduced only marginally once Celeste was hooked up to the Internet, because so much of the evaluation still depended on photographic data. Anyway, the Internet connection was waiting for the BAU electricians to complete the campus wiring job that had been in progress for the past eighteen months, and Celeste wasn't holding her breath. In fact, she wasn't really that anxious to be plugged in, fearful of the inevitable escalation of trivial correspondence.

Celeste was assigned as primary or secondary reviewer for seven of the grant proposals to be considered by the study section. This meant she had to produce a written report for each of these and ingest sufficient detail that she could advocate in their favor if they were good. Then there would be four more to read closely to be able to provide verbal commentary, as the third reviewer. But Celeste still had two reports to write before she could even start reading those. She had saved the two most difficult for last. These were competitive times, and one of these proposals was in for its fourth submission. Apparently the laboratory in question had all but shut down and the principal investigator was the only one left to do both the experimental work and write the grant proposals. The criminal part was that the work proposed was original and sound and there was no question it should be supported. It just didn't use the trendy genetic approaches that fascinated some of Celeste's colleagues on the review committee, so had been seen as dispensable in favor of the more flashy proposals. She would have to go out of her way to argue in favor of funding this time around or the work would be lost to the scientific community.

Celeste's contemplation of the injustice of the current funding situation was interrupted by the phone. Normally she would have left the call to answer later, but in response to the answering machine click she heard, "Bryan Baird, here. I have the information you requested. You can reach me at—"

"Hi, this is Celeste," she said, picking up the receiver. "I heard your voice on the answering machine."

"Yeah," said Baird flatly. "I have that information you wanted. How do you want to get it?"

"You can fax it to my Powerbook, at this same number, if you don't mind."

"Okay, I'll get my secretary to do it in a few minutes," said Baird grudgingly. "I hope that's all you'll be asking for."

"As far as I know," said Celeste. "And Bryan," she added sweetly, "I appreciate your cooperation."

Celeste hung up and plugged her Powerbook into the phone line to receive Baird's fax. As she waited for the transmission, Celeste's Luddite self grudgingly admitted that E-mail would have been quicker.

However, speed would only have made her disappointed sooner. After careful scrutiny, Celeste had to face the fact that there was nothing about the list of Virotox investors that brought her any closer to enlightenment regarding Phillipson's activities. The venture capital contributors were all firms with addresses back East, except for one based in Hong Kong. There were six altogether. The first three were apparently named after the conglomeration of wealthy people whose money they represented. These names meant nothing to Celeste. The names of the last three backers revealed that profits from a variety of enterprises were now diversified into Biotech. Virotox was evidently supported by soft-drink money from the Fountain Bottling Co., sportswear money courtesy of Aerobic Gear Ltd. from Hong Kong, and even an entertainment outfit called KFO Puppet Productions, Inc. As a whole, it was a completely unrevealing if gullible group. Celeste was crushed that her blackmail effort was so unproductive, but really, what had she expected? She had foolishly hoped that one of the major vaccine-producing companies might be on the list. But, considering it further, that would have been unlikely, since they usually produce and test their own vaccines. She supposed it had been worth a try, but now she had to rely on what she could find out from Mac about the military vaccine trials. When he had finally answered his page, he'd been rather aloof, and said he couldn't talk. She'd have to wait until tomorrow morning, when they had an appointment to discuss the next stage of his project.

Fewer than two hours later, at San Francisco International Airport, Teresita and Phillipson waited at the curbside for the limousine to pick them up. Teri was mulling over the events of the day. She had certainly not been prepared for the scene waiting for her at the general's home in Virginia. A very subdued, wan-looking Phillipson was sitting like an invalid, in a huge armchair in the general's living room. The general was playing the genial host.

"Teri, my dear. I'd like you to meet my business associate Simon Phillipson. Poor boy suffers from serious hay fever. He's been resting up from a bad attack. It'd be real nice if you could take him to the airport."

"Of course, I'd be happy to." Extending her hand for Phillipson to shake, she said, "Teresita Jiminez, pleased to meet you."

"Ah, Senator, the pleasure's all mine. I've heard so much about you." Phillipson's leer could simply have been read as appreciation for an attractive woman.

It had been easy from there on. Phillipson's delicate state made it possible to avoid any awkward moments with the general. It had provided them with a perfect excuse to go to the airport together.

Phillipson looked fine to her now. He had brightened up when they stepped out of the terminal and were greeted by the cool, sharp breeze signaling the start of a foggy evening. Teri supposed that Londoners always preferred to be in the fog. Usually she was very careful to avoid any physical contact with him in public. But no one expected her in San Francisco until tomorrow, so there were no press hanging around. She took his arm, in an uncharacteristic gesture of affection.

Two terminals away, Celeste stowed Kazuko's luggage in the trunk of Celeste's MGB. Kazuko was so enchanted by the old-fashioned sports car that Celeste took the roof down for her. Then she handed Kazuko one of the wool challis scarves she kept in the trunk for passengers and tied her own scarf around her neck.

Celeste nosed the "wombat" into the poky flow of traffic. It was a peak time for flight arrivals. The airport was the usual battleground between taxi drivers and overweight wives in leisurewear who were guarding family vans while their errant husbands awaited baggage. Dodging through this war zone usually made Celeste stew about the "hub" management of the airport. What was economically sound for the airlines inevitably created havoc for the passengers. But this evening Celeste was concentrating so hard on listening to what Kazuko was saying about the tragedies at Fukuda that she barely noticed the traffic. She missed the exit into the left lane of traffic leaving the airport.

Trapped in the next battlefield, in front of the American and United domestic arrival gates, the MGB inched along in the lane next to the terminals. From twenty-five yards, Celeste spotted him. That mane of gray hair was unmistakable. Her stomach tightened, as the face that had been haunting her thoughts came into focus. They were about to drive right past Phillipson, with Kazuko in full view, in the open car.

The chance that Phillipson would even see Kazuko, or recognize her if he did, was pretty slim. But Celeste remembered Toshimi's concern and knew she couldn't take any chances at all.

"Quick, Kazuko, duck."

Kazuko looked at Celeste blankly.

They had practically reached Phillipson. Celeste noticed he was standing next to a woman who held his arm possessively. She was wearing a shiny, black vinyl raincoat and had her back to the flow of traffic. A space was clearing in front of them into which Celeste was pushed by the surge of vehicles. She watched the woman in the raincoat lean intimately up against Phillipson and say something into his ear.

Celeste dawdled, checking her rearview mirror for an opportunity to move into the left lane. The taxi driver behind her started to honk. Suddenly a passsenger van came swooping in from the left and filled the spot in front of Phillipson and his companion. On the back of the van there were white letters that said "How's my driving? Dial 1-800-KURTESY."

Almost as bad as your spelling, thank God, thought Celeste. Sheltered by the blessedly rude van, she leaned over and in one gesture pulled the shawl over Kazuko's head and pushed her head down onto her knees, into airplane crash brace position.

"Stay down, it's Phillipson," said Celeste. Then she pulled out from behind the van with a squeal of tires.

After they passed the waiting couple, Celeste once again checked her rearview mirror, this time to see if her driving acrobatics had attracted their attention. But they were completely oblivious to the traffic. Phillipson had drawn the woman up against him into a kissing embrace. Celeste could imagine the plasticky feel of the vinyl raincoat against Phillipson's hand. It was an unusually brash-looking garment for the kind of woman Celeste imagined Phillipson might be comfortable being seen with. In spite of the fact that vinyl raincoats had recently been hailed as a fashionable return to sixties mod style, to Celeste the coat advertised a bimbo.

Finally, the MGB made it out to the freeway entrance ramp. Celeste touched Kazuko gently on the shoulder. "It's okay, you can sit up now," she said. Kazuko rose stiffly. She looked like a doll that had been shoved inappropriately into a toy car by a careless child playing with her. A few long black strands had escaped from her smooth hairdo and were whipped back by the breeze.

"I have been foolish," Kazuko said. "We must have the roof."

"No, no, it's not *your* fault! San Francisco is such a small town. I almost always run into someone I know at the airport. Besides, that guy seems to hang out here a lot," said Celeste, recalling her first encounter with him at the United desk a few weeks back. "But for that matter, so do I." She wondered how many times she and Phillipson had crossed paths before she had been introduced to him. The thought gave her a creepy sensation. Had they been destined to meet?

Feeling extremely vulnerable for a supposed protector, Celeste pulled off at the next exit and raised the roof, latching them into anonymity for the remainder of the drive into the city.

Back at Celeste's apartment, Kazuko refused to go to bed until she and Celeste went over the HPLC analysis of Minoru's blood. They sat at Celeste's dining table poring over the squiggly peaks and valleys of the HPLC printout. Kazuko's cup of steaming tea held down one side of the scroll, across which the data meandered. Celeste's bottle of beer held down the other side. The huge round, maple table was the center of Celeste's life in the apartment. Half of the dining table was piled with folders and copies of articles from scientific journals. The clear space in the middle of these mounds of paper was just large enough for Celeste's Powerbook, when it was in residence. In the center of the table stood a blue ceramic pitcher, serving as a vase for a fading bunch of red and pink dahlias. A few of their petals had dropped onto a pile of papers sitting next to the vase. The HPLC printout stretched across the half of the table that Celeste tried, with occasional success, to keep empty for dining.

Kazuko and Celeste divided up the data from Phillipson's thesis that Celeste had copied in Oxford. As though they were playing an elaborate parlor game, each leafed through a stack, looking for similarities with the printout on the table. Neither of them found anything close to a perfect match, but one in Kazuko's pile had some resemblance to the analysis in front of them.

"I agree with you that Minoru's blood tracing looks a little like this Dunga toxin. Except all the peaks are in a slightly different location, as though it has been consistently modified," said Celeste.

"Maybe it has modification from the solution in which it dissolve," suggested Kazuko.

"Yes, that's a possibility, it might have had a chemical reaction with something. The data is too similar for this not to be related to Dunga toxin. We'll have to wait for the rest of Phillipson's thesis to arrive from the Bodleian. The chapter on Dunga or related toxins might say if there's anything special about its activation or administration.''

''When do you expect rest of thesis?''

''They said it would take about ten days—three for the copying and a week for the mail. Though I'm not sure that accounts for the exponential effects of combining the Royal Mail with the U.S. Postal Service. It's only been forty-eight hours since I returned from London. Also, I placed the order Friday afternoon, so I'm sure the soonest they would have started processing it would have been Monday morning.''

''Toshimi need hard data for prosecution. We must wait.''

Privately, Celeste was relieved. It seemed to her that the evidence for Phillipson's involvement in the deaths of both Akira and Minoru was overwhelming. But this insistence on formalities gave her the brief reprieve she was hoping for to pursue her tenuous investigation of what Phillipson was up to. She was convinced that the situation was incredibly volatile, and if Phillipson felt threatened at this point, who knew what would happen? Celeste was agonizingly aware that because of Toshimi's perhaps justifiable skepticism, she bore the entire responsibility for finding evidence of what Phillipson might be planning. So far she had hit a wall.

''Still, we should probably start to prepare some kind of report,'' said Celeste to Kazuko. ''I'll write a summary of the data we have already that links the Fukuda deaths to Phillipson's toxins. Then when we get the rest of the thesis, we can finalize the report for delivery to Toshimi.''

''This is a good plan,'' said Kazuko.

''Now, while I write, you are going to sleep,'' insisted Celeste. She led Kazuko into her bedroom. ''You'll sleep here; I changed the sheets this morning. I'll sleep on the couch when I'm finished with the report."

"You are very kind," said Kazuko with a slight bow. She was too exhausted to protest.

The self-possession of this woman, who had just lost her husband and gone into exile in an unknown country, inspired Celeste. But when she finished the report at one in the morning, inspiration did not extend itself to the domestic activity of making up the sofa bed. Kazuko found her the next morning, sleeping fully dressed under a duvet, nestled into the cushions of the living-room couch.

FIFTEEN

Trial Run

Wednesday morning Mac shaved carefully. He skirted the edge of his mustache and thought about Elaine Roberts. Then he thought about Celeste Braun. He knew she was giving him a chance to start his new career. Yet, he had run from his feeling of inadequacy in the lab straight into Elaine's bed. Having sex with Elaine represented all that was easy for him. Too easy, in fact. In the early hours of Tuesday morning, he had finally convinced her to pursue the new attentions of her husband's golf partner. This one was difficult to release back into the stream.

"Come on, Mac, grow up," he said out loud to himself. Then he opened the medicine cabinet and took out the scissors for trimming his mustache. He clipped boldly across his upper lip, then pulled it down, clamping it taut with his front teeth, and finished the job with a razor. Might as well have a new face for a new career, he thought.

He made pancakes for Mac, Jr., who was so excited about his first day at the Academy of Sciences summer program that he ate three before he noticed the negative shadow on his father's upper lip. Mac dropped his son off in Golden Gate Park just before nine and parked the truck near the Academy of Sciences. Then he hiked up the hill to the Medical Center, surrounded by swirling fog.

Celeste's laboratory was dark, and the door to her office was shut. Without the bustling students and postdocs, the lab looked small. Each workstation was composed of a low desk next to the wall attached to a waist-high bench projecting out into the room. And each station reflected the character of the student or fellow who occupied it. Desks piled high with papers were coupled to benches covered with dirty glassware and equipment. Tidy desks were paired with benches covered with protective paper, with neatly labeled bottles of solutions placed carefully in a row. At some of the desks, corkboards displayed photographs of children or technical notes, but all of them displayed copies of cartoons, of goofy Gary Larson scientists in white coats, of Calvin and Hobbes, or of the occasional cartoon from *The New Yorker*. Mac amused himself making the rounds of the desks, reading these wry comments on the human condition.

"Need some light?" asked a perky female voice as the fluorescent room lights flickered on. It was Celeste's technician, Barbie.

"Thanks, Barbie," said Mac. "I'm just waiting for Dr. Braun." He felt a little silly, caught in the act of reading cartoons. Maybe he should have been reading a scientific journal or something. "Any idea when she'll be in?"

"Should be anytime now. She told me to be here around nine, so I could get the new visitor settled. You know, get her radiation permit and stuff like that."

"Uh, who's the visitor?"

"It's some woman from Japan," said Barbie. "I don't remember her name, but I guess she's gonna be working with us for a while. She'll take the bench across from me. By the way, Celeste told me you can use Étienne's bench. He's back in France negotiating for his new job and won't be here for the next month."

"Oh, thanks," said Mac. He felt pleased that Celeste had included him in her operation. The new career was taking off.

"Good morning, Barbie, Mac. I'd like you to meet Dr. Hagai from Fukuda." They turned around to see Celeste, accompanied by a stunningly beautiful Japanese woman. Celeste was wearing her usual jeans and blazer. She looked tired. The Japanese woman, dressed in a black, soft cotton tunic with a white T-shirt underneath, looked comparatively elegant and a little fragile.

"Happy to meet you," said Kazuko and shook hands, shyly, with both of them. "I am Kazuko."

"Barbie, I'd like you to show Kazuko around this morning. Get the administrative business sorted out so she can start to work. I'd like to talk to Mac, in my office."

"No prob," said Barbie.

Once in Celeste's office, Mac said, "Dr. Braun, are you sure it's not too much trouble for you to have me in your lab along with this new visitor?"

"Mac," said Celeste, "I thought we'd got beyond this 'Dr. Braun' business. And, no, it's not too much trouble to have you with us. In fact, I was hoping you could help me out with an experiment I started yesterday. I haven't got time to pour a gel this morning. Do you think you can remember how to do it? Then we could prepare the samples together this afternoon."

Mac was thrilled to be of use already. He grinned. "Sure,

Celeste, no prob,'' he said, imitating Barbie.

He looks terrific without his mustache, thought Celeste. Much more kissable. Clark Gable had been replaced by Kevin Costner. In fact, she was reminded of Costner's transformation when he shaves in *Dances with Wolves,* signaling his shift in alliance from the U.S. Army to the Indians. But what was this rubbish? She didn't have the time or inclination to have crushes. She needed Mac's help, and she needed to be professional about it.

Mac stood awkwardly while she was looking at him. He felt thoroughly inspected and quite self-conscious about his bare upper lip. ''I guess I'll go start washing the plates,'' he said.

''No, no. Hang on a second, Mac. There's something else I want to talk to you about.'' She paused, not quite sure how to express her anxiety. She also felt shy about asking for his help. But she was desperate. ''You gave me an idea a couple of weeks ago and I've been thinking about it. Remember our conversation about releasing a mutant virus to make money from selling the cure? Well''—she hesitated and then blurted out in a rush—''there's this company Virotox, owned by that guy Phillipson, who's trying to sell Bazuran to Fukuda. I think they could be planning something like that.''

Mac certainly remembered the conversation. In fact, it seemed to him that it had ignited their recent argument. But Celeste looked so upset, he didn't even consider reminding her. Instead he said, ''What does this have to do with me?''

''Well, I've been trying to figure out what would be the safest way to do something so unbelievably irresponsible as to release a virus intentionally. If you planned to make money from selling a drug to stop its spread, your only chance of the whole thing not getting out of hand would be to use some clever epidemiology. Otherwise, especially with a fatal airborne virus like Eke virus, the project could blow up in your face. You'd have a better chance to control it, though, if you could define the areas of release. This is where you come in.''

Mac looked at Celeste quizzically. He still didn't see what he had to do with it. She continued her line of reasoning. ''One way to disseminate a disease, but still be able to track it, would be to take advantage of some kind of vaccination program. This occurred to me while I was listening to the Monday seminar, given by that guy who traced a *Haemophilus* epidemic to a contamination of whooping cough vaccine. A vaccination program would be a perfect way to infect a specified population. Also, it would be relatively easy to substitute a live virus for the heat-killed or crippled virus that's normally used for vaccination. I know it's a complete long shot, but I was hoping to find out more about the military vaccine trial that your, uh, ex-wife is participating in. Even if this particular trial doesn't have the connection I'm worried about, just knowing how these things are organized might help. After all, since that *Haemophilus* epidemic, the military has been the obligatory testing ground for any new vaccine.''

''You've got a good memory,'' said Mac. ''I didn't expect you to remember the details of my personal life.''

Foolish man, thought Celeste. Any woman, in her right mind, would at least have registered the ex-wife part.

''Unfortunately,'' Mac continued, ''the details aren't any clearer. We're still waiting for the orders about the trial to come through. Apparently there's some holdup in the Pentagon. I'm pretty sure I know how we could get more information, though. Like, maybe where the vaccine is coming from.''

Celeste was pleased to observe that he said "we."

"Martha, that's my ex-wife, is on call Friday night. She handles the emergency vaccination clinic over at Oakland Hospital on the naval base. You know, giving tetanus shots for accidents and adrenaline shots for allergic reactions. I've been there in the evening to pick up Mac, Jr., and it's usually deserted. It'd be pretty easy to sneak a look through the director's office for some clues. Long as a little under-cover work doesn't bother you." Mac's tone was slightly teasing.

"Do you really think we could get away with it?"

"I don't see why not. Martha's a good sport. And there's almost no chance of being found out, unless someone comes into the clinic for an emergency. My guess is we'd be completely safe after about midnight."

Celeste felt an unwanted pang of jealousy at the "good sport" remark. "Why'd you guys split up, anyway? It must be difficult with a kid to think about." She surprised herself with the bold question.

"Julia," said Mac.

"Julia?" Was he going to tell her about some new girl-friend of his?

"Yeah, Julia, her girlfriend."

"Oh," said Celeste, trying not to sound surprised.

"They fell in love while we were separated in Vietnam. Julia was the head nurse for Martha's division. They left each other after the war, when Martha and I resumed our married life in San Francisco. But when Julia was trans-ferred here, a number of years ago now, their relationship started up all over again. Martha suggested she give me my freedom. So we got divorced. We're still good friends, though."

Not knowing what to say, Celeste concentrated on discussing plans for Friday. They would have to go in Mac's truck, since he had clearance to get into the naval base compound. Celeste would ask Kazuko to look after Mac, Jr., at Mac's place. Mac would have to explain the situation to Martha, to get her cooperation, but they agreed not to talk about it otherwise. The conversation then turned to plans for the afternoon's experiment. At eleven, Celeste left Mac to struggle with the gel plates, while she went to a faculty meeting, feeling calmer than she had for days about the Phillipson situation. Now, at least, she had a plan of action.

Friday night seemed ages away. The only way Celeste got through Thursday was by forcing herself to concentrate on science. She held an all-day lab meeting during which three of her postdoctoral fellows and the four graduate students discussed recent progress on their projects. Kazuko and Mac, as new members of the lab, were present and invited to comment. Kazuko's comments were tremendously insightful and helpful. There was no question that Kazuko would be running her own laboratory if she were working in the United States. Mac also made some useful contributions. He operated very strictly on the principles he had read in textbooks and learned in classes. The students and postdocs were a little taken aback at having to justify their lack of rigor in designing experiments. This would undoubtedly have a more profound effect on them than Celeste's routine harping about controls.

Celeste smiled to herself as she thought about this on Friday night, when she and Mac were crossing the Bay Bridge to Oakland in his pickup.

"You're not supposed to be smiling," said Mac. "Remember, you're bleeding to death."

"Don't worry. I can look grim at a moment's notice."

"I'm sure you can."

Celeste's left hand was swathed in a white cloth that she retrieved from her bag of cleaning rags. As they pulled up to the guardhouse at the entrance to the naval compound, she held it against her chest and bent over protectively, as though it were painful. This posture hid her face from full view of the guard's window.

The guardhouse was lit only by the flickering blue light of a television screen, from which it took the guard a full twenty seconds to detach himself. He rose slowly and eased open the window in the side of the hutch, releasing a warm, beery cloud into the foggy night air and into the open window on Mac's side of the pickup. From the smell, Celeste realized their "cover" was hardly necessary. They would have been admitted to the compound dressed in Halloween costumes.

"Reserve Officer Macmillan," said Mac, presenting his ID to the guard, who barely looked at it. "The wife's cut herself with a kitchen knife. Stupid bitch. Need to get to emergency." The guard handed Mac a clipboard to sign and then waved them through, sealing his funk back into the hutch.

"Nice touch, the 'stupid bitch' part," said Celeste.

"Thought you would like it. And really, you better stop grinning. It's possible a patrol car could drive by."

Across the compound the huge hospital loomed in the dark. The Art Deco–style aluminum trim on the doors to the main entrance was dimly illuminated by yellowish light from the lobby behind. Only a few windows were lit on the upper floors, leaving the isolated entrance looking like a deserted diner in an Edward Hopper painting.

Mac drove the truck around to the left side of the building, where the "emergency" entrance was indicated by a backlit bright white sign with red letters. They parked in front of a door to the right of the entrance to the clinic. There were three other cars in the lot. One was Martha's.

In the truck, Mac and Celeste removed their jackets, revealing similar black cotton turtleneck jerseys. Celeste felt a little funny about this get-up, but Mac was pretty insistent on what they should wear. Then Mac called Martha's number on his car phone, and they waited in silence for the door in the wall to crack open. The vaccination cubicle was just down the corridor from the main emergency treatment area, with a separate exit into the parking lot that was only used by the staff. Martha admitted them quickly, and ushered them into the nurses' station, which was sheltered from view of the vaccination area.

Celeste had been curious to see what Martha would look like. What kind of woman had captured the attentions of the youthful Mac and then abandoned him for another woman? She was surprised to see that Martha was a rather short, solidly built, motherly looking woman with a dark complexion, perhaps part Mexican or Native American. Her long black hair, shot with a few silver strands, was braided and wound in a corona around her head. She had a beautiful, warm smile that, after their brief introduction was over, faded into a look of serious competence enhanced by the white nurse's jacket she was wearing over her military shirt and trousers.

"There are no patients around right now, so from that point of view, we're in luck," said Martha. "Ned is the other on-call nurse tonight, and he's manning the front desk. Normally it's just us, but Dr. Samuels is also in. Ever since his divorce, he's been keeping odd hours and shows up almost any time of night to catch up on his case reports.

Unfortunately, his office is on the other side of the hall from the director's. You can hear him talking into the phone recorder when you're upstairs. He's only been in for about twenty minutes, and I imagine he's got a good hour and a half ahead of him. Once he gets started, he just babbles away into the phone, so I think you're pretty safe if you go up now. Otherwise, you could wait till he leaves.''

Mac and Celeste looked at each other. ''I'm inclined to wait,'' said Celeste. ''Won't he see us from his office?''

''Not if you're in the inner office,'' said Martha. ''Both offices have secretaries' desks in the front part that are visible from windows in the hall. The actual offices are through a door behind the secretary. Once you're into the inner office, you'll be hidden from view. The only tricky part will be to avoid being seen going in or out. As long as you can hear Samuels talking, though, you'll know he's tied up on his phone.''

''I think we should do it now,'' said Mac. ''We've left Mac, Jr., with Kazuko and need to get back. I'm sure we can maneuver around Samuels. The longer my truck stays in the parking lot, the more suspicious it will look, since we're presumably here just for stitches and a tetanus shot.''

''You'll be okay,'' said Martha. ''Just put on these white coats, both of you. Then if anyone sees you, you'll at least look official.''

Celeste had no choice. These two seemed almost cavalier about taking risks, and the risks they were taking were at her request. She supposed their attitude evolved in Vietnam. Celeste unwound the white cloth from her hand and stuffed it in the left pocket of the baggy dark trousers she was wearing. From the right pocket, she pulled out two pairs of examination gloves she had brought from the laboratory and handed a pair to Mac. Then she put on the lab coat.

With their black turtlenecks, white coats, and lab gloves, she and Mac looked like evil scientists from a science-fiction movie.

"Ready when you are," Celeste said.

Martha led them up the stairs to the second floor. The wide divided stairwell, with tan lineoleum and institutional light green walls, reminded Celeste of her junior high school. When they turned into the hallway, she almost expected to see it lined with lockers.

Halfway down the darkened corridor, light poured out of the door from Samuels' office. A chair propped open the door to his secretary's area. They could hear him reciting case details into the telephone. Apparently the door to his inner office was open as well.

All three took a deep breath, and Martha set off quickly, with master key in hand, toward the locked door opposite Samuels' office. Her nurse's shoes made no noise on the linoleum. Celeste and Mac, both wearing tennis shoes, followed, equally silent. Within seconds, Martha let them into the secretary's outer office, removed the key from the lock, and handed it to Mac. She turned and walked away quickly without saying anything. Mac motioned for Celeste to get low, below the level of the window in the corridor wall that provided a view of the outer office. He crossed the small room quickly, unlocked the inner office door, and motioned for Celeste to enter ahead of him. He then slipped around the door and clicked it shut behind him.

Celeste's heart was pounding. She was sure Mac could hear it. She could see him by the faint light coming from the sign to the emergency entrance that illuminated the inner office through the drawn blinds. He reached out and put a hand on her shoulder. She could feel its warmth through the lab coat and the cotton jersey.

"Okay?" he whispered.

She nodded brief assent. Celeste reached into her right pocket and pulled out a small flashlight. Without saying anything, she gestured with the light toward the desk, and they both started quietly searching.

The director's desk was quite tidy and had three piles of four to five manila folders each, spaced evenly between empty wire baskets labeled "In" and "Out." A third basket, in front of the "In" basket, contained a single manila folder. The basket was labeled "Reply needed." The director was clearly an efficient man and kept on top of his paperwork.

Celeste and Mac each started on a pile of folders, leafing through the contents, being careful not to change the order. More than half the material in each folder was some kind of government memo, and more than half of those originated in the Office of Biological Defense at the Pentagon. The folders in Celeste's pile were labeled "Protocols," "Personnel," "Congress," and "Oakland Admin." The "Protocols" folder contained a lot of recent memos from the Pentagon about appropriate control populations, but there was nothing pertaining to specific vaccine trials. Celeste caught Mac's eye, and he shook his head. His stack was evidently equally uninformative.

Celeste checked the folder on top of the middle stack. It read "Fredericksburg." Quickly she looked down the stack and noticed "Dallas," "Tacoma," "Atlantic City," and "Oakland." Celeste recognized these cities as being locations with large military hospitals. Gesturing to Mac, she handed him the top two folders, and she started to look in the "Tacoma" file.

There was a single, several-page memo in the file, originating from the office they were standing in. The memo was addressed to the vaccine trial coordinators in the five cities. It was headed with yesterday's date. At the top of the memo was stapled a fax transmission report indicating it had been sent on the day it was written.

The introductory paragraph said that word had been received from the Pentagon that morning, that Code Purple trials would proceed as soon as the vaccines were shipped. July 1 was the target date to begin the nationwide immunization. The Oakland department was coordinating the order, but the vaccines would be shipped directly from the supplier. The memo went on to discuss procedures for selecting the recipient and control populations. Detailed protocols with regard to timing and medical techniques were appended. Nowhere in the entire document was the name of the disease or vaccine mentioned or the name of the supplier. Code Purple was the only reference to a specific plan.

Celeste shone her flashlight on the remaining folders in the stack and noticed that they, too, had lavender/purple labels, on which the trial center location had been typed. Folders "Atlantic City" and "Oakland" contained a copy of the same memo, as did the "Dallas" and "Fredericksburg" folders that Mac was holding. All had been sent by fax yesterday. None of the folders contained anything additional.

Celeste stood for a moment, trying to absorb what they had learned. Trials were to start soon. The supplier was sending the vaccine directly to the centers. But nothing out of the ordinary was indicated, except perhaps the surprising expediency of communicating the orders after the go-ahead had apparently been given. As she pondered, Celeste picked up the last folder they had not yet inspected from the "Reply needed" basket. It had a purple label that read "Monk-

Marley," the name of a well-known vaccine producer and supplier.

The folder contained a single letter, on fax paper, addressed to the Oakland director, dated yesterday. "Sir," it read, "We are extremely surprised at and disappointed with your postponement of the trials of our new measles vaccine. As we discussed, our fiscal planning takes into account the timing of the trials and we had counted on their initiation by the end of this calendar year. It creates enormous problems for us to put the testing off until early next year, as you propose. We urge you to reconsider your scheduling and hope to discuss this with you at your earliest convenience." The letter was signed by the CEO of Monk-Marley Laboratories.

That didn't make sense, thought Celeste. The trials were apparently proceeding, but they canceled the vaccine order. Then she realized: They were going to use a different vaccine from another supplier. This had to be what she was looking for. She handed it to Mac.

While he was reading the memo, she checked the desk drawers and the drawers of the filing cabinets behind him. All locked. No direct clues to the new supplier would be found tonight.

"We're finished," she whispered. Mac nodded. They carefully replaced the folders in their original layout on the desk. Mac quietly opened the door leading to the outer office. The drone of Samuels' case reporting drifted through. Quickly, they locked the inner office door behind them, crossed the outer office, and made it into the hallway.

When they were about halfway down the corridor toward the stairs, they heard the droning stop, then a click indicating closure of Samuels' briefcase. They moved as quickly as possible toward the stairwell door. Celeste reached out to open it and found it locked. Mac searched his pocket for the master key, but it was too late. They heard the door to Samuels' inner office click shut and knew he would step out into the hallway and see them.

Mac grabbed Celeste and pushed her roughly against the door of the stairwell. He clamped his mouth on hers and pressed his body against her. A nasal voice, with a bitter twang, floated toward them.

"Don't you nurses have anything better to do?"

Beyond Mac's shoulder, Celeste could see Samuels turn in the opposite direction, with evident disgust, and stride toward the elevator. They heard the elevator doors open and then bang closed, removing their excuse for remaining in a clinch. Celeste opened her mouth, and their tongues met briefly and electrically.

"Maybe we don't," said Mac as he released her gently. Then he unlocked the stairwell door and they returned to Martha's clinic, with no further encounters.

SIXTEEN

Study Section

The Sunday night after Celeste and Mac made their excursion to Oakland, Phillipson was struggling with hooking up the final tubing connections to the Cell Pharms. These self-contained incubator chambers were designed to culture the carrier cells needed to produce Eke virus for his "vaccine." The cells were derived from human lung tissue, and their growth was maintained in the Cell Pharms by a constant flow through feeder tubes of fresh culture medium, which was essentially their liquid food. It had taken Phillipson three late nights to set up six of these Cell Pharm contraptions in the private lab in his office suite.

Teri had finally left Friday morning. Thus Friday was the first night, since he had paid his motivational visit to the general, that he could begin prep work for the vaccine trials. Thank God the campaign trail was so rigorous. Teri apparently had another fundraiser in Boston on Saturday night and a third one back in Washington on Tuesday.

The whole of Teri's visit, Phillipson had been itching to

get started on the cultures. During the day, he wandered around the Virotox labs, inspecting Cell Pharm setups and memorizing the connections, so he could reproduce them for his own purposes as soon as his evenings were free. Now everything was just about ready for seeding the cell cultures. Once these multiplied inside the Cell Pharms, they would be inoculated with the mutant Eke virus and would provide the perfect hosts for its growth. Speaking of itching, his damned allergies were continuing to act up. It was obvious they were worsening over the past year. Now he was sniffing constantly, and was on a chronic diet of antihistamine. What he couldn't understand was why it didn't even help to be indoors anymore, even though his allergies were primarily to grass and pollen.

Phillipson secured the last plastic tubing connector and went to collect the culture medium from the cold room in the main lab's cell culture support facility. The medium sat in a forty-liter container on a small cart. A white plastic tube emerged from the top of the container, and from it dangled a filter enclosed in clear blue plastic. The pH indicator dye dissolved in the medium gave it a rich red color, but through the opaque walls of the container, it looked pink. Phillipson wheeled his pink baby, with its blue topknot, out of the cold room, down the corridor, and into the back door to his laboratory. The building was completely deserted. The thrill of secrecy and the impending consummation of connecting up the whole apparatus induced a mild feeling of sexual arousal.

Phillipson attached the input line leading to a peristaltic pump to the output filter from the container of culture medium. As liquid was sucked through the filter, it would be resterilized so that what was feeding into the sterile tubing attached to the Cell Pharms would remain uncontaminated.

He checked all the connections, then switched on the pump. It pulsed for about three minutes, feeding medium into six branch lines that led to each of the six Cell Pharms. Filled with the red liquid, the Cell Pharm setup looked like the guts of a giant animal spread out on the white laboratory table. Suddenly the connection to the six-line manifold burst, violently spraying Phillipson and the entire laboratory with red liquid. Luckily there were no cells or virus in the system yet. Phillipson flipped the pump switch to the Off position.

"Bugger," he said aloud.

There must have been back pressure in the main line from a faulty connection. He checked his watch and was reminded of the date. There was no time to piss around. The carrier cells had to be seeded tonight to make enough virus in time for the first vaccine shipment. It was almost midnight, but he would have to call Sofia in on this.

Sofia was the head technician in the tissue culture laboratory. Phillipson had wooed her away from the company that manufactures Cell Pharms with his offer of responsibility and independence, and, of course, a much higher salary. This was the only way in which he wooed her. She was one of the few female employees of Virotox that he never even tried to lure onto the leather couch in his office. The others of this privileged group were either fat, ugly, or ancient. In Sofia's case, it was certainly not her looks. She was a sultry Mediterranean beauty. It was the aura of Catholic piety that she exuded. Until now, he had stopped short at violating sanctity. After all, there were plenty of other fish in the sea. But now, perhaps, he could at least reap the rewards of his "good" behavior. In exchange for letting Sofia maintain her privileged, uncompromised status, he ought to be able to enlist her cooperation and be sure of discretion.

He consulted the personnel files in his secretary's office for Sofia's home phone number. He wondered how many rings it would take to wake her up.

Twenty-four hundred miles east, Celeste lay sleepless in a hotel room in Washington, D.C. She got up to open the window, thinking that the heavy air would have cooled down and might be soothing. It was random luck whether hotel windows would open. But only once, in the Houston Sheraton, had Celeste found the recirculated, refrigerated hotel air preferable to air that could be obtained from outside.

As Celeste crossed the room, a lump of muscle on the right side, at the base of her neck, gave a twinge, contracting into a tangible knot. The trapezoid? Definitely a tension trap. The National Institutes of Health should run a chiropractic clinic or at least pay for a massage. Eighty-two grant proposals must weigh fifty-plus pounds. Celeste considered herself relatively fit, but it was still a lot to carry around as hand luggage. Her more organized colleagues sent the proposals back to Washington to wait for them at the hotel where the review committee met. Celeste used the plane trip to leaf through the proposals, which she wasn't officially required to review. Usually there were a few for which she could provide informal comments.

Celeste had been lying awake worrying about whether she had included a particular detail in one of her grant reviews, in between the many other worries that co-opted her attention recently. As she was already up, she figured she might as well check. Pushing aside an automatic coffeemaker and its brown plastic tray of sugar and supplies, she set up her Powerbook on the laminated table next to the now open window.

Celeste located the grant review file and started to read. The review wasn't half bad, considering that concentration had been virtually impossible. It still was, in fact. She had to read the opening paragraph three times to focus on it. Since Friday night, her mind had been alternately distracted with thoughts of Mac and Phillipson. She was amazed and simultaneously horrified that her hunch about the vaccine trials might be right. Now, here she was, clear across the country, without a clue how to proceed. She still had no proof of what she thought was going on. There was no evidence that the military had switched to Virotox as a new vaccine supplier, only that they had apparently canceled a long-standing order from a more established company. And, if there had been evidence connecting the trials to Virotox, no obvious crime had been committed. Certainly, no legal action was possible. Even if Celeste had tried to make a hypothetical case to the police, to encourage them to investigate Virotox, her one piece of suggestive data had been obtained by inadmissible means.

Celeste's hope lay in a combination of military bureaucracy and virus biology. Granted, the efficiency of issuing the orders about the trials had been surprisingly prompt. But it seemed a safe bet that the presumably substitute vaccines had not been shipped yet. Even if the supplier was geared up for production, the centers would have to arrange the trials first before they called in the order. Particularly if the vaccines contained live virus, each batch would have to be prepared within a week of shipping to ensure infectivity. Celeste figured it would take at least a few days for the immunization center to organize the staff and procedures for the trial. Then there would be a minimal two- to three-day further delay once the vaccine order was called in, to produce the batch for shipping. That was assuming the carrier cell cultures were already grown to capacity. Given the timing, it would be unlikely that anything would be shipped sooner than the end of this week. Study section finished at noon on Wednesday, and Celeste would be back in San Francisco on Wednesday evening. She had to come up with something to do by Thursday. Somehow she'd have to establish the involvement of Virotox, and if necessary, stop the vaccine shipment.

Then there was Mac. Every time she thought of that clinch, she felt a pulse in her groin. Silly woman. His move had been expedient, nothing more. Perhaps they had gotten a little carried away with the excitement of the moment. He had certainly been businesslike for the remainder of the evening.

Celeste would never forget the intensity of the ride back to the city. As soon as they returned to Martha's clinic, she checked that the coast was clear and showed them out the side door. Apparently Dr. Samuels had already left, squealing his tires, moments before. Mac drove sedately out of the hospital compound, and neither of them spoke until he paid the toll to go over the Bay Bridge. Then the speculation started. While they discussed the significance of what they had found, the whole of nighttime San Francisco glittered before them across the water.

Short of a commando raid on Virotox, Mac didn't have any brilliant ideas about what Celeste should do. He was so righteously indignant about Phillipson that Celeste didn't tell him about the suspected murders. She was afraid he might try to take matters into his own hands. The last thing she needed was a renegade Vietnam vet. Her body didn't fully agree on this point, however.

When they arrived at Mac's apartment, at two forty-five in the morning, they found Kazuko and Mac, Jr., playing backgammon. Mac seemed about to scold his son for being up so late, but something stopped him short. The boy explained to them excitedly that he and Kazuko had figured out that she knew a traditional Japanese game that was almost identical to backgammon. They were apparently just completing the U.S.–Japan championship game. Waiting for their charges to finish up, there was no further opportunity for intimacy. Both Mac and Celeste behaved as though the kiss had never happened. As she and Kazuko left, Celeste briefly put her hand on Mac's arm and thanked him for his help. He looked her straight in the eye for a rather long time. She was struck again by how handsome he was without his mustache. "My pleasure," he had said. She hadn't seen him since.

Well, Harry would be joining her tomorrow night, at the hotel, and would presumably provide some temporary physical release from all this tension.

As Celeste had suspected when she finally edited the grant review to her satisfaction, it was pretty tough getting up the following morning for the eight-thirty meeting. Once in the meeting room, the grant reviews got under way with the usual drill. First a meeting date was set for the June session in a year's time. Then the reviewers were reminded of the scoring scale. 1.0–1.5 was Outstanding, 1.5–2.0 Excellent, 2.0–2.5 Very Good, 2.5–3.5 Good, 3.5–5.0 Acceptable. During the two years that Celeste served on the committee, they had so far never "nerfed" a grant—that is, declared it "not recommended for funding." The chair urged them to use the full range and spread out their scores, but the depressing reality was that only grants with 1.2 or lower were being funded. To advocate a grant, you were forced into expanding the lower end of the range. Lastly, they were reminded of conflict-of-interest procedure. You had to leave the room when a grant from your institution was being discussed and, likewise, if it was a grant from a collaborator or a direct competitor. Unfortunately, the ground rules for the latter were rather ill defined, and it was possible to do considerable damage to competitors by damning with faint praise.

The first grants to come up for discussion were the longest-running ones. The applicants were senior investigators, and their labs had become so large and anarchic that they were no longer producing the best science. None of these made it into the funding range. The next set of grants were those that had been resubmitted the most number of times. Some of these had been on the borderline of being funded for the last two resubmissions. These were defended with passionate arguments from the reviewers. Celeste won the argument to reinstate funding for her pet fundless investigator, but she couldn't help feeling she'd shot her wad too soon. It was a Pyrrhic victory anyway. Funding this grant would automatically bump someone else into the resubmission category. Always at about this point, on the first morning, Celeste looked around the room and began to question the efficiency of shipping eighteen scientists from around the country into Washington, three times a year, and asking them to spend two weeks of their time preparing for each meeting to fund eight to ten grants each time. The peer review system was considered the most fair, but funds were so limited that choosing the best 10 percent from the best 25 percent was a crapshoot. Celeste was startled from her existential contemplation by an order to leave the room. Apparently the next grant proposal was from a colleague at BAU.

Celeste stepped out into the lobby of the hotel, closing the double doors of the conference room behind her. She had at least fifteen minutes to amuse herself. First, a necessary trip to the ladies' room. After returning five cups of hotel coffee to the Potomac, Celeste wandered back into the lobby. Some kind soul had left *The Washington Post* on a bench next to the conference room doors. Celeste sat down and began to read about a proposed local development that was threatening to encroach on the Civil War battlefields of Virginia. Her disgust at the chronicity of this issue was interrupted by the arrival of a noisy group, arguing heatedly among themselves. Two of the party had on dark blue suits, in spite of the ninety-five-degree weather outside. Celeste guessed they were Secret Service men. A third man, wearing denim overalls, was carrying a large package wrapped in brown paper, and some folded wooden easels.

The fourth member of the group was an officious-looking young woman with artificially jet-black hair. She was wearing a gray summer suit with a very short skirt and pink blouse and the Filofax she clutched bulged with important-looking scraps of paper. She began to harangue the trainee desk clerk. Her clipped southern accent gave the impression that she was making a conscious effort to control it to sound more educated.

"I want to be sure everything is in order. Last time we had the fundraiser here, the senator was not at all pleased. You all are fortunate to get another chance. Now, Bob here is gonna put up the posters in the lobby today. Then tomorrow, before the event, we got the florist coming to decorate the tables and add some streamers and things to the staircase, leading up to the reception."

The layout of the lobby of this particular Holiday Inn

was unusually ambitious, obviously designed to host political events. It formed an atrium around a "grand staircase" leading to a balconied area in front of the
second-floor reception rooms. One could imagine a guest
of honor addressing a crowd below.

"In the meantime, Randy and Jeff need to check out your
security system," continued the woman.

"Yes, ma'am," the clerk said nervously. "I'll just call
my boss. He's on break right now."

"Well, I haven't got all day. Bob can at least start putting
up the posters."

Bob, on cue, put down his package and set up one of the
easels about ten feet from where Celeste was sitting. From
the brown paper wrapping he withdrew a three-foot-high
cardboard-backed poster of the senator. Celeste immediately recognized the photograph from *Femina*. Across the
bottom the poster said, "Keep Sensible Women in Congress." Below the fashion portrait were three smaller publicity shots of the senator "in action." She was shown
surrounded by inner-city children, addressing a crowd of
inmates at a prison, and speaking at an outdoor rally of
assembled women. Celeste got up from the bench, where
she had been reading the paper, for a closer look. In this
third photo, the senator was wearing an unmistakable black
vinyl raincoat.

Celeste had been right: Phillipson's traveling companion
was a bimbo. But what were *they* doing together? Wasn't
the senator supposed to be involved with General Johnson
at the Pentagon? She and Phillipson had sure looked like
they were headed to the same bedroom in San Francisco.

Celeste stood transfixed in front of the poster. The *Femina* article had unquestionably implied a special relationship
with the general. And his son had certainly confirmed it.

Celeste's luncheon with Ollie suddenly surfaced from her memory. What had he said? That his dad was obsessed with virology lately? Of course, one might expect such an obsession for the head of the biological warfare division. But maybe there was more to it. It was very tenuous, but could this woman be a link between Phillipson and the military?

Ollie had very subtly hinted that he didn't think the senator was as besotted with his father as the general was with her. He was a sweet, sensitive kid. Probably gay, too, disappointing his father on yet another score. Maybe he would be sufficiently inspired by his Oxford experience to rebel and pursue his studies of the Greek classics for a higher degree. After all, he had mentioned other siblings who could inherit the family mantle. Kukla and Fran, the other two puppets, so to speak. Puppets. Holy shit! Didn't one of the Virotox backers have something about puppets in the name?

"Celeste," said a man's voice. The door to the conference room had opened without her noticing, and a fellow committee member was peering out into the lobby. "We're ready for the next one."

The committee plowed through ten more grant proposals before the lunch break. Celeste had to force herself to concentrate, not think about the telephone call she needed to make as soon as they finished. She knew Harry was leaving his office sometime in the afternoon, to have dinner with his mother in New Jersey and pick up his thesis on the way to Washington. She had to catch him before he left. Surely one of his colleagues at the financial desk of the *New York Times* should be able to tap into some computer file that would reveal the names behind the investment firms on her Virotox list. She was kicking herself for not thinking of this before.

•   •   •

The "dinky" train, as it is known, travels the spur line from
Princeton Junction to Princeton. After the twelve-minute
vibrational experience, Harry felt his stomach needed settling. He decided to walk to his mother's house from
Princeton Station, through the campus. Commencement had
taken place a couple of weeks earlier and left the campus
in its quiet summer mode. In the late-afternoon overcast,
the large-leaved trees looked almost black. The peacefulness of his hometown soothed Harry's raw New York
nerves. They were extra raw after an all-day editors' meeting from which he had to rush straight to Penn Station,
without even stopping to collect his messages.

He found his mother exactly as he expected, as she had
been since he could remember. She was sitting at the
kitchen table with a cup of coffee and the *New York Times*
spread in front of her. Her long brown hair was barely
streaked with gray, belying her age. It hung in a French
braid, a soft thick rope, down her back. As soon as Harry
walked in, she shook a cigarette out of the pack lying next
to her coffee cup, lit up, and inhaled deeply. Harry could
smell the sharp sulfur of the match over the rich, comforting smell of whatever his mother had in the oven for their
supper. By the kitchen clock, it was 5:00 P.M. They would
eat at five-thirty, as they had always done when Harry and
his brother were growing up and their father was alive.

Harry kissed his mother's cheek gently. "Finish the paper yet?" She read the entire *New York Times* every day
and was one of the best-informed people Harry knew. As
an editor, he rarely had time to read anything but his section.

"Not quite, dear," she said, removing her reading
glasses. The world went through its frenzied and violent

business outside his mother's kitchen. In the cool kitchen, she sat in cynical judgment. No wonder that kitchen and her company were a focal point for his high-school friends. They had sat for hours talking with her, soaking up her wisdom, while she smoked her way through packs of Tareytons.

After supper, Harry and his mother went down to the basement to look for his thesis. The strong musty smell, mixed with the sharp scent of mothballs and cedar chips, again transported Harry back to his childhood. He used to hold his breath whenever he was asked to fetch anything "down cellar." The walls of the cellar were lined with unfinished wooden bookshelves, housing years of accumulation. One wall was filled with dusty colored glass vases and pitchers, a round-edged toaster, and other superfluous household items. The adjacent wall displayed Harry's father's collection of rocks and minerals. Harry had contributed substantially to this collection, with specimens he and his father collected from abandoned mines in New Hampshire and Maine during summer vacations. The other walls were entirely filled with books, overflow from the book-lined walls of the living room, study, and bedrooms upstairs. Harry started to look for the thesis in what appeared to be a more recent section, containing some paperback books.

"Oh, no, dear," said his mother. She gestured toward a pile of cardboard boxes next to the dusty relics of his father's woodworking shop. "Your things from graduate school are still in those boxes. These are your college books."

Harry moved over to the boxes. They were stamped with the logos of a variety of different scientific supply companies. The second one he opened contained his thesis, lying on top of some vintage scientific textbooks.

"Here it is. The masterpiece," said Harry.

"Now, Harry. You really should've let me keep that on the shelves upstairs. It is your thesis, after all."

"I don't think it belongs with Dad's and Lew's theses, Mother," said Harry. "They published. Mine is just a daily diary of events in the Stanley laboratory. Anyway, I need to take it with me now. It may be useful after all, to one of my friends."

"Oh, I'm so glad you reminded me. I keep forgetting to tell you that your piece on Jane Stanley's testimonial dinner was terrific. Extremely thoughtful, and timely. It's a shame what's happening to her with that congressional investigation. Surely they could find someone more appropriate to pick on."

"No question about that," said Harry. "Jane is the absolute last person on earth to have done anything for personal financial gain. It's almost as though that senator, what's-her-name, has some ax to grind."

"Teresita Jiminez, dear. The senator from Massachusetts."

After a long discussion about the growing number of conservative women in Congress, Harry finally left the house on Vandeventer Avenue to catch his train. At least, his mother had observed, gender was no longer a political issue.

SEVENTEEN

Rough Reception

Harry thought ironically of his mother's parting remark as he walked by the "Keep Sensible Women in Congress" poster on the way into the bar in the lobby of the Friendship Heights Holiday Inn.

Celeste was waiting for him, nursing a Sam Adams lager and chatting with the bartender. She had long since been abandoned by her colleagues. After their traditional Monday evening committee expedition for dinner, most of them went back to their rooms to call their families. A few die-hards had joined Celeste for a nightcap, but after one drink they, too, retired. It was a pleasant relief to talk to the bartender about how the early baseball season was shaping up.

"Just in time for last call," the bartender said to Harry, who walked in and pecked Celeste on the cheek. "I figured the little lady was waiting for someone. My bad luck, to be right." After serving Harry a double Johnnie Walker

Black Label, straight up, he discreetly went down to the other end of the bar.

"Did you get it?" asked Celeste.

"Okay, greedy guts. It's right here." Harry dug around in his oversized leather satchel and pulled out his thesis.

"No. I mean the KFO Puppet investors."

"The what?"

"Didn't you get my message?"

"No, darling, you're lucky I'm even here. I barely made the train to Princeton, out of the editors' meeting."

"Damn," said Celeste. She had to think how to explain things to Harry. She took a deep breath and launched into it. "I think I could be onto a major story for you. Possible abuse of military authority for personal gain. Possible threat of a fatal epidemic. Before I can be sure, I need your help in getting some information. But"—she hesitated, in response to his rising eyebrows—"I'd better start at the beginning."

She told him her suspicions about the Virotox scam and the Fukuda murders and her theory about Phillipson releasing the mutant virus through a military vaccine trial. She also explained the possible reprieve of Harry's Ph.D. work and the need to consult his thesis. It was a huge relief to unburden herself to someone she trusted so much that she didn't have to hide anything. Winding up, she said, "I'm convinced there may a connection between General Johnson and Virotox. First of all, he and Phillipson appear to be sharing the same woman. Whether Johnson knows it, I'm not sure, but I doubt it. Certainly the article about her in *Femina* didn't mention it. Second, there's a pretty eclectic list of investors in Virotox. One is called KFO Puppet Productions. I think there's a possibility that Johnson is the backer of KFO, in which case he would have a vested interest in the success of Virotox.''

Harry's eyes widened as Celeste spilled out her story. Naturally, the whole business about his thesis shocked and infuriated him. He'd always resented Phillipson. Now he was experiencing unqualified hatred. But these feelings had to be put on hold while he dealt with the crisis at hand. He didn't need his reporter's intuition to tell him that what Celeste was suggesting would be a huge scandal, perhaps another Watergate, if it broke. First he needed to get the facts straight.

''Two questions,'' said Harry, quite seriously. ''Since when did you start using *Femina* as resource material? And what the hell do puppets have to do with a general in the Pentagon?'' Celeste told him about her encounter with Ollie. She ignored the question about *Femina*.

''Jesus.'' Harry shook his head in amazement. ''If you're right about KFO Productions and Johnson is behind Virotox, then we are talking major-league government corruption here, as well as potential criminal genocide, on top of cold-blooded murder. Comparatively, Watergate is a silly prank.'' Harry thought for a minute. ''With something of this magnitude, you've gotta be damn sure of your ground before you blow it open. The first thing we need to do is check out your hunch about the puppets. I think I know exactly who might be able to get us that information.''

''That's great,'' said Celeste, her confidence growing enormously. ''Who is it? Someone at the *Times* financial bureau?''

''Well, actually, I had in mind cashing in a different debt. A couple of years ago I wrote a story about the rise of the monoclonal antibody biotech company Abgen. I just made an honest assessment of where I thought they had done a better job than most of their competitors, which was why they were so successful. It turns out that they were about to go public, and my article was responsible for making a few investors quite wealthy. Ever since then, the broker who was selling the stock on Wall Street has wanted to return the favor, inadvertent though it was. I'm sure I could ask him to investigate the money behind KFO.''

''That sounds perfect. We can fax him the list right now, from the modem in my Powerbook.''

Upstairs in Celeste's hotel room, they quickly composed their request and transmitted the fax. Then she flopped down on one of the beds and started to look through Harry's thesis, searching in the Table of Contents for the chapter on Bazuran. Her body looked tense through the soft knit outfit draped around her. Harry started to massage the muscles at the base of her neck, loosening the knots. His hands moved slowly down her back, kneading the muscles surrounding her spine. Then he spread her legs gently, massaging all the while, and reaching toward her front, started to knead the soft mound between them. In the early hours of Tuesday morning, Harry got what he had come for and Celeste finally fell into a deep, satisfied sleep.

The next morning, Celeste left Harry in bed and descended to the complimentary breakfast buffet to fuel up for another long morning of haggling over limited grant funds. At breakfast she finally had a chance to look carefully at Harry's thesis. Sure enough, the gel photograph was there. It looked close enough to the data that she and Mac had developed last week that it could have been a duplicate experiment. Here, at last, was definitive proof that Harry had already discovered the effects of Bazuran on a mutant Eke virus strain. Given what Celeste now knew about Phillipson, she had no doubt that he had suspected the potential value of the result and switched the strains that Harry was working with. Whether Phillipson was aware at the time that the mutant strain was resistant to Protex, they would never know. But the idea that the viral protease had mutated was proposed in the Discussion section of the chapter on Bazuran in Harry's thesis.

Celeste's further speculation about the motivation behind Phillipson's destruction of Harry's scientific career was postponed until the study section committee broke for lunch. As Celeste rode the elevator up to the hotel room, she wondered if what she had told Harry about his thesis work would restore his confidence in himself. The entire time she had known him, he had been an apologetic and cynical character, in spite of the fact that he became such a successful reporter once he left the lab. Taking a philosophical view, maybe Phillipson's foul play had pushed Harry in the right direction for his talent anyway. Nonetheless, Harry must have some desire for revenge, which would be a helpful boost to "the good fight" at this point in time.

When Celeste got to the room, Harry was still asleep, and the fax icon was blinking on Celeste's Powerbook. She anxiously clicked open the "Received" folder.

"Dear Harry," she read. "Glad to finally do *you* a favor. Below please find the investor info you requested." Celeste scanned down the page. "KFO Puppet Productions, Inc.: Solely owned and operated by Ralph O. Johnson III. Investment portfolio includes mainly shares in Fukuda Ltd. and Virotox, Inc. Holds 25 percent of Virotox, Inc. total shares."

Harry got out of bed, pulled on his underpants, and stood at Celeste's side. She could feel the sleepy warmth of his body while he read over her shoulder.

"That explains the vendetta against Jane," said Harry.

The apparently irrelevant remark brought Celeste back to reality with some annoyance. "What does that have to do with the price of eggs?" she asked. It was her favorite expression for indicating when she thought someone was totally off track.

"Well, if Virotox is going to market Bazuran through Fukuda, then it would be in their interest to disprove the Stanley theory, or I should say the Stanley-Freeman theory, of toxin inefficacy. I gather from what you said based on the *Femina* article, General Johnson has a lot of influence with the senator who's spearheading the CSI campaign against Stanley. In fact, she's also opposing the Biodiversity Treaty, which would probably invalidate the patent on Bazuran. Though I suppose I ought to be pleased about that. Since it appears the patent, if it's granted, would actually belong to me."

Celeste realized that Harry was absolutely right about Jiminez. Not only was she bedding the embodiment of evil, she was also using her influence in Congress to carry out his plans. Stimulated by her rage, Celeste suddenly had a brilliant idea.

"Maybe we can't yet do anything about the virus release," she said to Harry, "but I think we can do something about Jiminez. Ten to one, the general shows up at the fundraiser tonight. I think you and I should have a little chat with him." She explained her plan to Harry before she returned to the committee meeting.

That afternoon the study section meeting was at its most intense. Knowing where three-quarters of the grants stood in the lineup made it harder to argue scores for the remaining quarter. In addition, they were pressed for time, since it looked as though they could finish by the end of the day, allowing the committee members to catch late-night flights back to their loved ones. Celeste was amused by this rushing back to the nest. Her colleagues behaved like they were getting out of school early. Unfortunately, the last flight to San Francisco left Dulles at 6:00 P.M., so Celeste had spent a number of evenings on her own in Washington. Occasionally she resented the abandonment by her colleagues. But usually she was happy to stick with her original flight reservation and enjoy a morning at the Smithsonian. And tonight her freedom would make it easier to put her plan into action.

The fundraising reception was in full swing by the time Celeste and Harry got there. It was easy to spot General Johnson. He was in full regalia, with a huge array of ribbons and medals pinned to his expansive green front. To Celeste he looked like an overgrown Boy Scout. Celeste was also dressed for battle. After the study section ended, she rushed down to the cluster of boutiques near the Friendship Heights metro stop and picked up a tight, short, poppy-red dress with a low-cut front. She didn't usually travel with appropriate gear for a Washington society party. Luckily, she had a passable pair of high-heeled black sandals with her. These, along with black fishnet stockings, the new dress, and twice as much makeup as she would normally wear, allowed her to blend in easily with the crowd of aspiring bimbos. Harry could barely take his eyes off her. She had never looked like this in the lab. The ubiquitous reporter, he was able to get away with his corduroy jacket and knit tie as long as he sported a Press pass.

Celeste waited for the general to turn away from the cash bar at the fundraiser with his umpteenth double bourbon. He was already looking suitably unsteady.

"You must be General Johnson," gushed Celeste.

He appraised her appreciatively. "Call me Buck, honey."

"Well, I'm thrilled to meet you after hearing so much about you from your son."

"You know Frank?"

"No, actually. I met Ollie in Oxford. We happened to be using the same library facility. I was doing some research there a couple of weeks ago. He and I got to chatting and from what he was saying, it sounds like you know more about my field of science than anyone else in the government."

The general knew he was being admired. In fact, it was pleasant to have a little attention to himself, since Teresita had been in the limelight all evening. But he wasn't quite sure what this was all about. The puzzlement showed on his face.

"I'm sorry. I should have introduced myself. I'm Celeste Braun, a virologist at BAU."

"Did you say 'virologist,' dear? I've never seen one as good-lookin' as you."

"Why, thanks, General," said Celeste, flirting with her eyes. "But I am a card-carrying union member." Celeste handed him one of the business cards she used for her trips to Japan, with her name and position in English on the front and Japanese on the back.

While the general was inspecting the card, she motioned for Harry to join them. "General, I'd like to introduce you to someone else who's been admiring your career and wants to meet you. This is my friend Harry Freeman, the science editor for the *New York Times*."

"Pleased ta meet ya," said the general obligingly, inspecting a second card, offered him by Harry.

"The pleasure's mine, General. I've been wanting to

schedule an interview with you for a long time. I've been planning an article on the future of germ warfare, and I think an interview with you could be a major focus of the piece. After all, you're our country's expert.''

The general glowed from the combination of flattery and bourbon.

''In fact, I don't see why we couldn't start tonight,'' suggested Harry. ''Maybe just sketch out the topics for some initial interview sessions. If you can slip away for a few minutes, we could sit downstairs at the bar, where it's a little quieter.''

The thought of another bourbon, in a more civilized setting, appealed to the general. He glanced across the room at Teresita holding court. ''I think I can spare you all a few minutes,'' he said. ''Looks like there's still a lot of fund-raising to be done.''

Harry and Celeste escorted the general to the darkest corner of the bar on the ground floor and set him up with another double. He was going to need it.

They were followed by two Secret Service men, who hovered nearby as they were settling in. The general shooed them away.

''It's okay, boys. These guys are gonna make me famous,'' he said jauntily. The boys in blue skulked off to barstools at the far end of the bar, out of earshot but in full view.

''Actually, General Johnson,'' said Celeste, ''Harry and I would like to do you a different kind of favor. It has to do with your girlfriend upstairs.''

The general was a little confused by the change of subject. But, of course, he was always willing to discuss Teresita, even if it did divert attention from himself. ''Nice piece of . . . uh, work, ain't she, boy?'' he addressed Harry.

"Same league as the little lady here." He indicated Celeste.

"We thought you might want to know that Senator Jiminez has been seen out and about in San Francisco with Simon Phillipson," Celeste continued sweetly.

The general forgot to pretend not to know who Phillipson was. "That's all right," he said. "I introduced them."

"Well, it sure looks like they appreciated it," said Celeste, raising her eyebrows in a knowing way.

"Cunt," muttered the general. It wasn't clear if he meant Teri or Celeste.

"We've also been wondering whether she has anything to do with your financial interest in Virotox," said Harry pleasantly. "You know, it doesn't look so good if your girlfriend is pushing government policies to protect your investments. But, it would certainly interest the readership of the *New York Times*."

Even in his inebriated state, the general realized the shit was hitting the fan. Years of dissimulation had taught him survival tactics, and he marshaled his defense. So what if it put Teresita at risk? She was evidently cheating on him anyway.

"Jesus, that case about Standish, or Stanley, whatever the hell's her name, is a complete fabrication anyway. Health, Incorporated, put a lot of money into Teri's campaign if she promised to pursue it."

"Oh, that's very interesting," said Harry. "I don't suppose you would agree to be an anonymous source for *that* piece of information?"

"Depends what's on offer," slurred the general.

"I think I could overlook writing about your interests in Virotox," said Harry. "After all, exposing corruption of a woman senator, especially a finger-pointing one, will make a much more interesting story."

The general shook his head. "I knew it wouldn't last," he muttered to himself. "We don't need the two-timin' bitch anymore anyway."

"Great, General. It's a deal, then," said Harry, extending his hand.

"Get away from me," snarled the general. Then he slumped down in his chair, with his eyes closed.

Celeste took the opportunity to retrieve hers and Harry's business cards from where the general had laid them on the table. "I guess we're done with the interview," she said to Harry and stood up. "Should we signal the escort service?"

But they didn't have to. The bodyguards were already making their way over from their lair.

"Shall I tell the bellman to call the military limo?" Harry asked them. "It looks like you guys've got your hands full." Indeed, large though the men were, it would be a struggle to get the general upright.

"Uh, yeah," grunted one of them. "Thanks, pal."

Celeste ordered a double of her own and sat down at the bar to wait for Harry.

Thursday morning Simon Phillipson swabbed the metal surface of the biohazard containment cabinet in his private laboratory, latched the glass window at the front, and flipped on the ultraviolet light. The bluish tint coming through the window made his face as gray as his hair. He was burning the candle at both ends, but it was worth it. The Cell Pharms were happily humming away since he brought Sofia onto the job. It had been easy to get her under his thumb. He hadn't even had to threaten her. She was glad to work overtime for "the good of the company." Phillipson was now contemplating the possibility of getting her under another part of his anatomy.

It was 6:00 A.M., and he had been at work since midnight, inoculating two more Cell Pharms with the second batch of Eke virus. He needed to get some sleep before he harvested the first batch later in the afternoon. So far, things were on schedule. The first shipment would be out the door by late tomorrow.

Phillipson shut the door of the laboratory behind him and entered the back room of his office suite. He unfolded the leather couch into a bed. It was already made up and looked wonderfully inviting. But first he had to leave a note for Madeline, his secretary. He didn't want to be disturbed until two. Also, he really ought to take a shower to wash off any lab residue before turning in.

In the outer office, Phillipson bent over Madeline's desk. He left a note specifying when he wanted to be awakened and listed what he wanted delivered for lunch. The sound of soft knocking on the glass window facing onto the corridor startled him. He was pretty jumpy these days. Sofia was standing out in the hallway, looking absolutely angelic and virginal in a fresh white lab coat. He opened the door to her.

"You're here awfully early," he said suspiciously.

"Oh, sometimes I don't sleep very well, Dr. Phillipson. Then I like to come into the lab and get things going before everyone else gets here," she explained. "I saw your car in the parking lot and was wondering if everything was working okay."

"That's very thoughtful of you," said Phillipson, softening. She looked extremely appealing, even in his exhausted state. "Maybe there is something you can do for me. Why don't you wait here a few minutes while I check on the apparatus. I'll be right back."

Phillipson checked on his apparatus in the shower. He

would have to play this one slowly and hope it would co-operate. It was a long time since he had seduced a virgin.

Two hours later, Sofia inspected the Cell Pharms, on her way out of the private laboratory. Her groin still throbbed beautifully. She may have lost her place in heaven, but what Dr. Phillipson had just introduced her to seemed like a terrific substitute. She would do anything for that man.

For Phillipson, the experience had only been so-so. He'd forgotten how clueless virgins are when it comes to a partner's needs. In any case, she seemed to enjoy it. He'd certainly made all the right moves, figuring it would be a good idea to get her hooked on the activity. It would undoubtedly give him more leverage later, if he needed it. With a feeling of accomplishment, Phillipson promptly fell into a sound sleep until Madeline phoned him on his private line, exactly at two.

"Luncheon is served," she said. "Shall I bring it in to you?"

"Yes, please," said Phillipson. "I'm still in the back room."

If Madeline noticed that the sheets were more rumpled than usual and the heavy smell of sex that hung over the room, she certainly didn't let on. She wheeled in Phillipson's lunch on a cart, with today's *New York Times* folded at the side of the tray. Before her husband relocated to California, Madeline worked as a private secretary to the owner of a gentlemen's club in London. She understood a gentleman's needs.

"I'll need pickup and delivery from the linen service this afternoon, Madeline."

"I'll call right away, Dr. Phillipson."

As soon as Madeline left, Phillipson unloaded the tray onto a small dining table that looked out over the landfill.

He took a bite of crab omelette. It was still hot, and creamy. The Dine, One, One delivery service from top restaurants in the neighborhood had improved Phillipson's life significantly. Feeling pretty pleased with himself, he opened the *New York Times* and scanned the headlines.

It wasn't uncommon for him to see Teri's photo on the front page. She was a favorite, photogenic subject for the media. So he wasn't disturbed in the least, until he read the caption.

"Science-watchdog senator implicated in drug company scandal. Details, page 10." In a panic, he flipped to page 10 and read how Jiminez was allegedly being paid off, through campaign support from Health, Inc., to initiate investigative proceedings against Jane Stanley. Phillipson's sense of well-being evaporated rather quickly. That was the story that he and Johnson agreed to use if the connection between Virotox and Johnson was ever discovered. It was, of course, a death warrant for Teri's reelection prospects. But he and Johnson didn't need her anymore, since Fukuda had already signed on the dotted line.

Phillipson was more concerned with the implication that someone knew about the general's investments. He looked at the byline: Harry Freeman. He should have guessed. That meddling fool. Well, he had outsmarted him once, and could easily do it again. It would just be helpful to know what had led him to poke around in the general's business.

It was far too risky to call the Pentagon. Phillipson would have to wait until evening, when he could call the general's private line at home, from a phone booth. Meanwhile, he needed to finish his lunch and get the second set of virus cultures inoculated.

EIGHTEEN

Antigenic Stimulation

Celeste stood up from the desk in her office and stretched into a facsimile of the yoga tree pose without standing on one leg. There was one more book to consult before her lecture notes were complete. She had been putting it off, since it required going to the campus library across the street, fifteen floors down and two elevator rides away. The lecture wasn't until 5:00 P.M., when afternoon rounds for the new residents finished.

Celeste's lethargy was due to the fact that she and Kazuko had spent most of the night going through Phillipson's thesis. The copy from the Bodleian had arrived while Celeste was in Washington. Kazuko noticed it sitting on her desk, but wouldn't open it, of course. The only liberty she took was to bring it home to Celeste's apartment, so that Celeste could open it as soon as she returned. The chapter on alcohol-activated toxins told them everything they wanted to know.

Certain hydrophobic plant derivatives, which included

Dunga toxin, were highly toxic only under special circumstances. Normally the plants that contained them could be eaten with no consequence because the toxin would not dissolve in stomach acid. But exposure of the toxin to heat and alcohol caused a chemical modification that altered the solubility properties of the toxin. A minute quantity administered in a warm alcoholic drink was fatal. The toxin blocked nerve connections. Thus early stages of toxicity resembled drunkenness, and poisoning was rarely suspected as a cause of death.

Celeste and Kazuko realized that hot sake was perfect for activation of Dunga toxin. Once activated by chemical modification, the Dunga toxin in the blood would be slightly different from the original toxin. This explained why Celeste and Kazuko had been unable to see an exact match between the HPLC data from Minoru's blood and Phillipson's data on Dunga toxin that Celeste had brought from Oxford.

Kazuko was anxious to notify Toshimi of their findings. They had accumulated all the data needed for the Japanese authorities to prosecute Phillipson on two murder charges. Celeste tried to explain to Kazuko the possible consequences of putting Phillipson under pressure. He had the perfect blackmail weapon. He could threaten Fukuda with implication in a scheme to release the mutant virus to keep them quiet about the murders. She pleaded with Kazuko to give her a few more days to establish whether Virotox was providing virus for the vaccine trials.

Kazuko was as skeptical as Toshimi had been. Their Japanese sense of honor made it impossible for them to conceive of how devious Phillipson might be. But in deference to her protectress, Kazuko agreed to compromise. Anyway, both of them realized that if Celeste couldn't make any headway by Monday, then it was probably too late, and the mutant virus would be disseminated. Under those circumstances, accusing Phillipson of murder would be their only hope of arresting further spread of the virus.

Capitulating on both sides, Celeste and Kazuko agreed to complete the document summarizing their findings that Celeste had drafted on the night Kazuko arrived. They would send it to Toshimi at Fukuda by Federal Express on Friday. He wouldn't receive it until Monday, but Kazuko felt safer that the information would be on its way, in case anything happened to her or Celeste.

Given the time constraints, the pressure on Celeste was unbearable. It was imperative to figure out a way to infiltrate Virotox and look for evidence that they were supplying the vaccine trial centers. Celeste cursed her teaching obligation, not for the first time that day. She hadn't realized that the resident training program had already started, until she looked at her calendar during the plane trip home from Washington. She had forgotten that she was supposed to lecture this year on molecular mechanisms of allergy, to replace a colleague on sabbatical leave. It was time for that trip to the library.

The new library, completed three years earlier, was an attractive improvement over the old one. But to Celeste it was a monument to the city's factionalism. The library filled the last square foot of usable construction space on the BAU campus, as mandated by an unalterable agreement between the local neighborhood and the university. Celeste considered the neighborhood's stubbornness regarding the space limitation totally unfair, seeing as BAU was one of the city's biggest employers and its largest care center for AIDS patients. As it was, new programs were stifled for lack of space, and the spaciousness of the library seemed extravagant to Celeste as she sought out Rathbone's *Principles of Allergic Reactions*. She hadn't reviewed the detailed literature on allergy since the last time her colleague went on sabbatical.

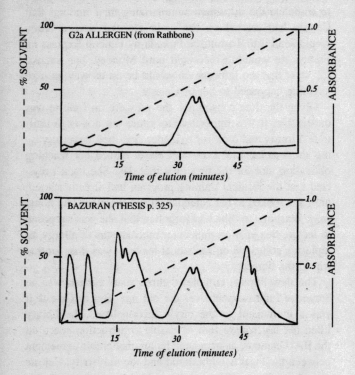

Celeste discovered that a year ago, when the most recent edition of Rathbone had gone to press, surprisingly few allergy antigens or "allergens" had been analyzed in molecular detail. These included the cuticle protein of the house dust mite, two ragweed pollen proteins, and protein G2a, common to several species of grass. Rathbone reproduced an HPLC analysis of each of the four allergens. A month earlier, Celeste wouldn't have even bothered looking at the HPLC data, but she had been staring at so many similar analyses from Phillipson's thesis that she automatically took them in.

Then Celeste did a double take. The G2a allergen had a familiar-looking peak in the HPLC data. During her scrutiny of the Phillipson data, which was practically etched on her memory, Celeste had noticed that several of the toxin preparations, including Bazuran, had a similar peak at the same position. She had presumed it was a residual contaminant from the toxic plant. Celeste now understood her assumption had been correct. The plants from which some of the toxins were isolated had grasslike leaves and would share molecular properties with grass.

Celeste's mind began to churn. If the Bazuran preparations contained a protein like G2a, then patients treated with Bazuran against the mutant Eke virus strain would also be exposed to the G2a protein. It would cause serious trouble for individuals allergic to grass, a relatively common allergy.

Then Celeste recalled that the proposed administration of Bazuran was to dose it through an inhaler. It was well established that inhalation of allergen proteins tends to stimulate an allergic response. So delivery of Bazuran, even to a nonallergic patient population, would, in the long term, promote allergy development. Over time, patients would no longer be able to tolerate Bazuran because of its contamination with trace amounts of the G2a-like allergen.

Celeste suddenly realized she must have seen evidence of this when she met Phillipson in the allergy clinic. Wasn't he suffering from increased severity of grass allergy? It was likely due to constant low-level exposure to G2a-like protein in the toxins he was purifying in the laboratory.

Bad science is unmistakable, and Phillipson had done the worst. Furthermore, the consequences of his particular brand of bad science would be horrifying. Celeste's discovery of the G2a contaminant revealed that Phillipson's miracle cure would be a bust. He intended to spread a new fatal disease and then to make money by selling a cure that most people would have an allergic reaction against. Celeste now understood that it was not only prophylactic but also essential to stop release of the mutant virus. The mutant was resistant to Protex, and Bazuran was effectively useless. Release of the mutant Eke virus would be a guaranteed global death warrant.

Anxious to compare the HPLC data from Rathbone with Phillipson's thesis and thereby confirm her theory, Celeste bypassed the line at the copy machines and checked the book out of the library using her faculty identification card. There was no one waiting at the checkout desk, as copy mania had rendered this procedure almost obsolete. Her efficiency was thwarted, however, when she joined the crowd waiting for the elevators on the ground floor of her laboratory building across the street. The illuminated panel indicating where the elevators were located revealed that two were on nine and going up; one was blinking at seven, indicating it was out of commission; and the fourth was inching down from thirteen. The air was thick with impatience, which Celeste ignored by lapsing into elevator-waiting mode, a mental exercise perfected during the thousands of elevator rides that punctuated her academic career at BAU.

Celeste's thoughts inevitably returned to Phillipson. This

revelation of hers indisputably introduced a monkey wrench into his works. It completely invalidated the marketability of Bazuran and made his plan for release and cure of the mutant virus inoperable. Celeste assumed he would have to listen to reason once she explained the scientific flaw to him. The direct approach seemed almost too simple. But it was an undeniable fact that he would be in jeopardy from his own mutant virus, since he wouldn't be able to tolerate treatment with Bazuran. Celeste convinced herself that it would be worth taking the risk of direct confrontation.

She checked her watch: It was 3:55 P.M., 8:55 A.M. tomorrow in Osaka. She would call Toshimi and get him to provide an excuse for her to make an appointment with Phillipson. He could explain she was Fukuda's local consultant and needed to ask him a few questions about the Bazuran project. Somehow she would figure out how she could also have a look around for evidence of the trial shipments, once she got to Virotox headquarters. In case Phillipson wouldn't cooperate, they would need hard evidence of his intentions.

Celeste dialed Osaka as soon as she got back to her office. Fortunately, Toshimi was in. She didn't have enough time to explain everything in detail, but he agreed to send a fax to Phillipson, requesting that he see Celeste as soon as possible. It would be too late to catch Phillipson's secretary after the lecture tonight, so Celeste pressed Toshimi to send the fax immediately. She asked Toshimi to send the fax to her at the same time, so that she would know when the entrée was established and she could call Phillipson's office to make an appointment. Then she plugged her Powerbook into the phone line to wait for her cue.

While Celeste was waiting, she flipped through her notes for the upcoming lecture. She had decided not to use the slides her colleague left behind from his lecture on the same topic last year. She found that the process of writing on the blackboard slowed her down to the speed of comprehension of the group to whom she was lecturing. Celeste began to think through how she planned to diagram a few of the more complicated points. And when she next checked her watch, she realized she had only ten minutes left before she had to head down to the lecture hall. Thank God the fax icon on her Powerbook was blinking. She tapped into the message that Toshimi had sent Phillipson moments before.

"Dear Dr. Phillipson," she read. "At Fukuda we now suspect a problem about the Bazuran project. We need you to discuss, as soon as possible, with our local consultant, Dr. Celeste Braun from Dept. of Microbiology, Bay Area University. Dr. Braun will call to make her appointment. We appreciate your cooperation."

Celeste called information for South San Francisco, got the Virotox switchboard number, dialed, and asked for Phillipson's office. His British secretary answered the phone. "Dr. Phillipson's line, Madeline speaking."

"This is Dr. Braun calling from BAU. My colleagues at Fukuda have asked me to make an appointment to discuss some urgent matters with Dr. Phillipson. I was hoping to see him sometime tomorrow."

"Ah, yes. We just received a fax to that effect from Dr. Matsumoto. I haven't yet had time to consult with Dr. Phillipson about it, but I'm sure he'll be happy to see you."

I don't know about that, thought Celeste.

"Let me just check his schedule for tomorrow," said Madeline. Her British pronunciation of the word "schedule" gave Celeste an idea. This woman sounded like the type who would, retaining her native habits, religiously break for coffee at eleven and for tea at four, no matter how long she had lived abroad.

"Noon would suit me perfectly," suggested Celeste, "if he's free at that time."

"He certainly appears to be free at that time," said Madeline. "I'll check with him before I leave, and have him leave a message of confirmation for you tonight."

"Thanks very much," said Celeste and gave Madeline her home phone number.

Celeste hung up, grabbed her notes, and raced down twelve flights of stairs to the lecture hall on the third floor. The elevators could not be relied on to get her to the podium on time, even though BAU lectures never began until ten past the scheduled hour.

Madeline put the cover on her typewriter. Surprisingly often, she was called on to hand-type letters for which Dr. Phillipson did not want a computer record. In preparation for leaving, she straightened her skirt, put on her suit jacket, and buzzed Phillipson in the laboratory.

"What is it? I'm in the middle of something." He sounded harassed.

"I'm leaving now, Dr. Phillipson," said Madeline calmly. "You've got an urgent fax from Fukuda, and I've taken care of the request. I'll leave the details in a folder on my desk. Have a good evening."

"Cheers," said Phillipson, and hung up.

An hour later he transferred the last of the harvested Eke virus into the saline solution for shipping. Carefully he distributed 5-milliliter portions into the vaccine bottles and sealed the tops with a rubber stopper. Each stoppered bottle was then capped with an aluminum seal. The expanding home brewing industry had revolutionized small-scale vaccine production, developing cheap and reliable machines for safe bottling. Last, Phillipson filled in the numeral "1" in the space after "Lot Number" on a hundred printed labels, and stuck these labels onto his handiwork. He left the bottles in cardboard trays in his lab refrigerator for overnight storage. They would be packed up in the morning and shipped out by early afternoon.

Phillipson washed his hands and went through his own office to Madeline's outer office. He picked up the folder on Madeline's desk and read the fax message from Toshimi. At the bottom Madeline had typed, "Appointment scheduled with Dr. Braun for 12 noon, tomorrow, Friday. Call to confirm."

I wonder what this is all about? thought Phillipson. His feeling of uneasiness reminded him that he had to call the general. First he needed to confirm the appointment with Celeste Braun. It would be interesting to see her in action. He dialed the number at the bottom of the fax and reached an answering machine message. "This is Celeste speaking. You may leave a message at the sound of the tone."

"Simon Phillipson here. I'll be delighted to see you at noon on Friday. Perhaps I could interest you in lunch after our official meeting. No need to respond. Just let my secretary know if you'll be dining with me, when you arrive. Till tomorrow, then," said Phillipson to the answering machine.

He locked the offices and headed out to his BMW. Time for a little spin, in search of a phone booth.

The bank of phones in the Serramonte shopping mall were adjacent to the McDonald's. Phillipson hadn't realized that 6:00 P.M. was the rush hour for the mall. He was held up for several minutes in the complete standstill of traffic merging off Route 280 into the mall. The cars on either side of him were driven by people in their office clothes, apparently headed for an evening's recreation. A good number of these cars pulled into the parking area near TGI Friday's, which advertised a happy hour from 4:00 P.M. to 7:00 P.M. with "Free snax, Mon–Fri."

From the telephone booth, Phillipson could see that the McDonald's crowd was younger. Pimply youths with backward baseball caps and baggy shorts lined up for their culinary treats, alongside frenzied mothers trying to control small children. Phillipson fed change into the telephone and dialed the general's home phone in Virginia. He identified himself with the usual code name.

The general sounded slightly drunk. "I've told you, boy, that I would mightily prefer if you didn't call me here at home."

"I realize that, sir," said Phillipson with exaggerated respect. "But I believe we need to talk."

"I dare say," said the general with a sigh. "What's your number?" Phillipson gave him the number of one of the phones in TGI Friday's that he hadn't used recently. Then he heard the general hang up. Now the general would drive to his nearest public phone and dial Phillipson at precisely five minutes past the next hour. One thing that worried Phillipson was that the general's usual choice of public phone was in his local bar, only fifteen minutes from his home. That would give him twenty minutes to down a couple of doubles before he called Phillipson back. Phillipson hoped he would still be coherent.

With half an hour to kill, Phillipson crossed the Serramonte mall at a leisurely pace, heading for TGI Friday's. He did a little window-shopping. There wasn't a single store that wasn't part of a chain. Even Tracy's Trousseau, where he used to outfit various mistresses rather fetchingly, had lapsed into selling inexpensive mass-produced lingerie. Phillipson considered this cheap and nasty and was disgusted.

The scene in TGI Friday's was exactly as Phillipson expected. By now, ties were loosened and carefully applied lipstick was smudged. Once in a while Phillipson came here, trawling for sex-starved secretaries. But his early morning with Sofia had left him reasonably sated for the moment. He was considerably relieved that he didn't have to deal with the meat market tonight. He ordered a pint of Bass ale and sat down at the end of the bar near the telephones. At 7:05 P.M. he picked up the second phone from the end after one ring.

"I read the story in the *New York Times*," said Phillipson. "What did she do to you?"

"Cheated on me with you, you prick," said the general. He had definitely had a few.

"Rather harsh treatment for a little dallying, I'd say."

"I was put up to it. That nosy reporter and his girlfriend found out about my shares. Threatened me with exposure."

"Jesus Christ. Who's the girlfriend?"

"Some sexy-looking virologist from out near you."

"That wouldn't be Celeste Braun, would it?"

"Uh, yeah. I think that's the name. I can't seem to find her card."

"How much do they know? No, wait—don't say. I think we better play Twenty Questions. Is it the bread box they're on to, or is it bigger than the bread box?"

"I don't know what the fuck you're talking about."

God, the general was useless. This is the last time I'll throw my lot in with the military, thought Phillipson. It probably wasn't a coincidence that Celeste Braun had an appointment to see him tomorrow. But it was certainly convenient. His methods for finding out how much people knew, and for keeping them quiet, were extremely effective.

"Don't worry about a thing, old chap," Phillipson reassured the general. "I've got everything under control."

"Well, I fucking well hope so, boy." He slammed down the receiver.

Stupid, blustering idiot, thought Phillipson. He downed the rest of his pint and left the bar. He was already considering possibilities for coercion and, if necessary, elimination. It would be almost too easy if Celeste Braun accepted his invitation to lunch.

Celeste was exhausted at the end of her lecture. A performing artist is allowed to get up in front of an audience and play a rehearsed piece, regardless of the audience response. But an academic lecturer has to gauge every sentence to see if contact is being made, and make ad hoc modifications accordingly. In her stressed-out state, Celeste felt drained by the intense concentration required.

But Mac's presence in the front row of the lecture hall helped keep her energy level high during the lecture. It was the first glimpse she'd had of him since the Oakland trip. She had expected him in the lab during the day and was disappointed that he did not appear. So when he greeted her with a grin as she hurried up to the podium, she felt a surge of pleasure that he would bother to show up.

Now he was standing in front of her, smiling, as though he were equally glad to see her. "Welcome back, Professor," he said. "Sorry I didn't make it to the lab today. Mac, Jr., picked up some bug, and Martha was in the clinic. Glad I made the lecture, though. Good trip?"

"It was okay. I'm relieved to be back. But this was the

last thing I needed to worry about,'' said Celeste, gesturing toward the scribbles she had made on the blackboard. As she spoke, she barely knew what she was saying. She felt a new warmth emanating from Mac's look and became shy.

''Well, you did a good job,'' said Mac. ''But I'd like to clear up a couple of things you mentioned. Think we could talk about it over a beer?'' He smiled.

''I'd love to.'' Celeste was falling fast. But she checked herself, anxious to get home to hear from Phillipson and to sort out her strategy for their upcoming confrontation. Under the circumstances, though, it wouldn't be too bold to invite Mac home with her instead, would it? So she took the plunge, and Mac seemed happy enough with her counterinvitation to come back to her place for a ''picnic supper,'' since she was ''fading from jet lag.''

Celeste, driving the wombat, led Mac in his pickup through the city streets. The awareness of him following her felt as though they were performing an intricate dance and heightened the delicious tension of anticipating further intimacy.

Celeste's apartment was not at all as Mac had imagined. They had the place to themselves, as Kazuko was still at the lab. Mac had expected a harsh modern interior and was pleasantly surprised by the comfortable eclecticism of the academic clutter. He was particularly impressed by the bathroom, where he was trying to piss away some nervousness. The shelves above the large, deep tub were lined with a variety of bath gels, salts, and bubble bath. Next to the sink was an old-fashioned cake stand piled high with glycerin soaps in different colors, and huge, fluffy towels hung along the wall. Mac got the feeling that this was the center of Celeste's private female universe.

Mac's request to use the bathroom as soon as they arrived gave Celeste the chance to listen to her phone messages in privacy. As soon as she heard Mac peeing, she turned on the answering machine. The indicator light said there were two messages. She hoped one of them was from Phillipson.

"Hello, dear. It's Mom. Dad and I were wondering how you were and whether you're coming up to New York, when you have to go to Washington this month. Give us a call, if it's not too late when you get in. Or call me at work tomorrow morning. 'Bye now." Whoops! Why did they always remember about her trips to the East Coast, when she decided not to visit them? She'd have some explaining to do.

The answering machine whirred, beeped, and Phillipson's clipped accent emerged just as Mac stepped out of the bathroom.

They stood in the hallway, listening to the message together.

"So, you're going down there tomorrow. You should have told me," said Mac.

Celeste was slightly irritated by his proprietary attitude. "Well, I wasn't sure it was still on until I heard this message just now. I'm hoping to have a look around for more evidence about the vaccine trials while I'm there."

"Do you think you should go alone?"

"I don't see how I could take anyone with me. I managed to get an appointment through my connections as a consultant for Fukuda."

"At least you should take some protection."

"What could possibly happen?" Celeste laughed. "You expect me to be taken prisoner? It's only a biotech company, after all. There's no way Phillipson could have any idea what I'm there for. Anyway, I think I've figured out how to stop him. Let me get us something to eat and I'll explain it to you." She left him in the living room and then went into the kitchen to open a bottle of wine and raid the refrigerator.

Over a glass of cabernet and nibbling on olives, bread, and cheese, Celeste explained her discovery to Mac. "You see, Phillipson's made a major scientific flaw. It turns out that this fancy antiviral drug of his is contaminated with an antigen that's common to many plant species related to grass. As you know, anyone who's allergic to grass would react strongly to the antigen, even at very low levels. To make it even worse, he plans to administer the drug by inhalation. That would ensure anaphylaxis for anyone with allergies, and it would tend to induce allergies in most patients, eventually rendering the drug completely useless for anyone."

"Sounds like lousy science to me," reflected Mac.

"No kidding. Worthy of an outright criminal. Kind of serves him right for stealing from Harry in the first place."

"So what're you gonna do about it?"

"Well, the guy is at least smart enough to understand the mistake he's made, when I explain it to him. Obviously I won't reveal our suspicions about his plans to release the virus. I'll just tell him that Fukuda is concerned that Bazuran won't work as a drug because of its allergenic properties. Then he'll realize he can't release the mutant virus. He, himself, would actually be highly at risk, if he went through with his scheme now."

Mac was skeptical. "I'm not sure he's the kind of guy who will listen to reason. He might still turn the situation to his advantage and use his position to blackmail Fukuda."

"I don't agree. He wouldn't threaten to release a virus that would put his own life in jeopardy."

"You're entitled to your own opinion, but I'd be very careful if I were you. Have you got any kind of weapon?"

"Get serious, Mac. I'm not going on military reconnaissance."

Before Mac could reply, they heard Kazuko's key in the lock.

"Well, I better be going," said Mac. "You've got a big day tomorrow." He stood up, greeted Kazuko briefly, and headed for the door. Celeste followed him, to see him out. She wished things between them weren't so unresolved.

"Mac," she said tentatively.

"Yeah."

"I appreciate your concern. I'll be okay. Don't worry."

"I guess you should be able to take care of yourself by now, Professor," he said, smiling at her. "I'd just like to see you again, that's all."

Celeste didn't sleep very well. Mac's flirtatious but ominous remark kept running through her mind. The threatening feeling she experienced during wakeful interludes was interrupted with strange nightmares. Right before her alarm went off, she experienced a complete rerun, in dream form, of the lecture on allergies she had given that afternoon. She woke up thinking about allergy medication and suddenly realized that while she was asleep, her mind had worked out what she needed to do to protect herself.

Celeste searched in the back of her bathroom cupboard. It had to be in there somewhere. When Dr. Sandoval prescribed the cromolyn sodium last year, Celeste thought it sounded useful at the time. But, in fact, she never remembered to use it, even though she had lectured about it since. Basically, it was a prophylactic. The patient had to remember to inhale the drug before being exposed to something that would trigger an allergic response. The drug actually paralyzed mast cells and prevented them from releasing histamine, blocking the final phase of the allergic reaction. Dr. Sandoval suggested it would be useful for Celeste to use cromolyn if she was visiting friends with pet cats.

It wasn't exactly a pet cat that Celeste was planning to confront. She found the little green-and-white atomizer-inhaler behind a dispenser of hair mousse that she had used once and then abandoned. Celeste tucked the inhaler with its cromolyn sodium into her fanny pack, along with a plastic Ziploc bag. Then she drove over to Golden Gate Park, to go jogging. She didn't take the usual route around Stowe Lake this morning. Instead, her run led her to the grassy fields near the grazing buffalo herd. A mile into the run, Celeste stopped, took a deep hit of cromolyn sodium from the atomizer, and harvested her weapon. Mac would have his armed commando raid after all.

NINETEEN

Eke Evidence

At ten o'clock Friday morning, Sofia packed the ninety-sixth bottle of Lot Number 1 into the eighth styrofoam box. Each box contained a dozen bottles nestled into ice, surrounded by cold packs. Two boxes were addressed to each vaccination center, enough to start trials with 120 military volunteers at each of the four sites. When Lot Number 2 was ready Saturday afternoon, it would be hand-delivered to Oakland, the fifth site. By a week from Monday, 600 recruits would be in the infectious stage, with apparently a bad cold. They would be capable of spreading the virus to anyone within coughing range. Epidemiological studies indicate that modern abandonment of the handerkerchief has made this mechanism of virus transmission highly efficient, especially in an environment of recirculating air, such as an office building or an airplane. Phillipson estimated that each recruit would minimally infect twenty bystanders, bringing the number of carriers to at least twelve thousand by two weeks from Monday. For Eke virus, the time from the bad-cold stage to development of more serious symptoms is about three weeks. Then there is a three-week window in which treatment can be effective. The first recruits could be diagnosed and clamoring for Bazuran by the beginning of August. The exponential spread during that month, by each subsequently contaminated person, should boost the numbers into the millions by September. Of course, a few might succumb to the mutant virus before the diagnosis of disease and supply of Bazuran could reach an equilibrium. This might reduce the numbers slightly at the initial stages, but Phillipson wasn't too worried about it. After all, several thousand dead wouldn't make a big dent in the millions they expected to be buying Bazuran.

The only remaining detail was to test the efficacy of Lot Number 1. Because of the instability of the virus preparation, the lot had to be shipped before its potency could be assessed. Phillipson didn't expect any problem with the harvest. All the test preparations had given good yields. But at this stage, it would also be useful to test the virus in a human volunteer, so that doses of Bazuran could be worked out. Phillipson had a pretty good idea of how to scale up from earlier experiments infecting animals, but confirmation of his predictions would be helpful for manufacturing plans. He opened the bottom drawer of his desk, where files were supposed to be kept. Behind a few hanging files was a cardboard box marked "BAZURAN. Development Prototype—Not for Sale." The box held a half-dozen prototype dose dispensers containing Bazuran, which the Virotox development lab had produced earlier in the week. Phillipson removed one for inspection. After many discussions of design efficiency to maximize drug delivery, the development lab had been able to make appropriate modifications to the spray mechanism of a handy small atomizer, similar to an asthma inhaler. Each spritz delivered a 10-milligram dose that could be absorbed immediately into the nasopharyngeal mucosal tissue, where the virus multiplied most rapidly. The residual drug that found its way into the circulation would be sufficient to inhibit the slower replication of any virus that had begun to infiltrate other tissues of the body. Phillipson was pleased with the strategy and looked forward to testing it.

Sofia knocked twice on the door connecting Phillipson's private lab to his inner office and let herself in. Phillipson quickly kicked the file drawer shut and dropped the dispenser he had been examining into the top drawer of his desk. It wasn't time yet to give her the Bazuran. Sofia was carrying a container full of ice, with the four extra vials of virus from Lot Number 1, that were not packed up for shipping. She glowed with the frequent sexual stimulation that had become part of her life in the past few days. Phillipson congratulated himself on his technique for drawing her into the project. There was no question she would trust his judgment in selecting her as the human volunteer for testing the virus and drug dosage. But he wanted to pick the right moment to discuss it with her.

Phillipson took the ice bucket from Sofia and put the vials of Eke virus in the small refrigerator he kept stocked with beer, champagne, mixers, and mineral water. He instructed Sofia to bring him two syringes and two 25-gauge needles from the lab, and then to take a shower in his private bathroom. Meanwhile, he unfolded the leather couch. After all, he had almost two hours to kill before Dr. Braun was expected, and he needed to exercise his persuasive techniques on Sofia. His guinea pig would be inoculated in due course.

Just before 11:00 A.M., Celeste drove the wombat into

the parking lot signposted for Virotox. It took her a few minutes to locate the main entrance. Virotox occupied one of four identical buildings with ocher-colored cement walls, and red-tiled roofs. According to the sign outside the central walkway, the other buildings housed two computer companies and a law firm. Celeste's circuit of the parking lot revealed that the Virotox shipping dock was on the right side of the building relative to the main entrance. She parked in one of the designated visitors' spaces in front of the complex, as close to the shipping dock as possible.

The fog was just lifting. It was still cool, and there was a sickly-sweet smell in the air that made Celeste think of the compost heap in her grandfather's garden. She recalled a news story about the open-air concert arena that had been built on the landfill just to the south of the Virotox complex. Apparently smoking had to be banned because the air became combustible after a hot day.

Just inside the tinted glass doors emblazoned with the Virotox, Inc., logo was a uniformed security guard, with a gun in a leather holster slung at his thick waist. He was perched on a tiny stool and sat awkwardly behind the high reception desk. His badge indicated his name was Tony. He looked like a recent retiree from a troupe of Mafia bodyguards. Tony gave Celeste an appreciative once-over.

"What's the company, sweetheart?"

"I beg your pardon," said Celeste. Then she realized that he had taken her for a company sales rep. Her automatic reaction was to be annoyed at this sexist assumption. But in her "consultant's" skirt and jacket, carrying a briefcase, she looked more like someone who wanted to sell something than a visiting scientist.

"I'm Dr. Braun from BAU. I have an appointment with Dr. Phillipson at eleven o'clock," she lied.

"Goin' to the top, are we?" The guard still hadn't figured out that Celeste was not a sales rep. "I'll hafta call upstairs."

Celeste held her breath while he contacted the switchboard. If she was right, the British secretary would be on break for her eleven-o'clock cup of coffee, and no one would be able to confirm that she had arrived an hour early. If Celeste was wrong, she could always plead crossed signals.

The guard put down the receiver. "No answer right now. Sit over there and I'll try again in a few minutes." He gestured toward the front corner of the lobby, in full view of his perch, where a couch and two armchairs upholstered in industrial plaid wool were grouped around a blond wood coffee table. The table held a white ceramic vase with fake sprays of autumn leaves and several copies of the Virotox, Inc., annual report.

"Uh, would you mind if I used the ladies' room while I'm waiting?"

"No problem, honey. Down that hallway on your left."

Celeste walked past the guard, into the hallway on the left, noisily opened the door to the ladies' room, and let it fall shut. She remained out in the hall, hidden from view of the guard's desk. Then she sneaked quietly back to the point at which she could see the back of the guard's head. She needed to get across the lobby, into the hallway on the opposite side, to have a look at the shipping area. She would have to wait until the next visitor arrived and the guard was temporarily distracted. It had to be soon, to give her time for reconnaissance before the guard remembered her existence.

Within a minute, the building doors opened. A stocky man wearing a short-sleeved blue shirt with a button-down collar backed into the lobby. He dragged a large, black leather tool kit on wheels across the threshold. Celeste recognized him as the same centrifuge repair man who serviced BAU. He wasn't a particularly chatty fellow, so her crossing would have to be quick. As soon as the guard lifted the receiver to contact the repairman's destination, she walked as calmly as possible across the back of the lobby. From the shelter of the opposite hallway, she looked back. Her little trek had gone unremarked. Now she had to hustle to find the room leading onto the shipping dock.

The hallway was lined with dark wooden doors. Plaques on the doors to her left indicated that Celeste was passing the offices of Human Resources, GMP Regulations, and Patent Licensing. To the right, a door was propped open slightly. Through the crack Celeste could see a small conference room with books and journals lining shelves on the walls. There was a meeting in progress. Celeste slowed down so her movement would not attract attention. The library-conference room was only dimly illuminated, and the audience appeared to be mesmerized by the colored slides being projected on a screen at the front of the room.

The corridor ended in a T-junction. Considering the location of the shipping dock, the shipping room was probably to the left. Just as Celeste was about to turn, a door about halfway down the corridor opened. A young woman dressed in dark green work pants and work shirt, and wearing a baseball cap and a beeper, backed out into the hall. She was pulling a cartful of boxes that appeared to contain lab supplies. She turned the cart into the hallway and wheeled it toward the far end of the building.

Celeste waited at the T-junction, peering around the corner until the woman with the cart maneuvered it through a distant doorway. Celeste kept glancing nervously behind her, but the hallway remained deserted. The door to the room where the woman disappeared clicked shut, and Celeste walked quickly to the door the woman had come out from, assuming it had to be the shipping room, and entered. The lights were off, but Celeste could see by the light cast through the sliding glass doors of a huge illuminated refrigerator case at the far end of the room. The room was crammed full with irregular piles of boxes that seemed to be sorted for delivery to the labs. Celeste followed the maze of open space around the piles and made her way over to the refrigerator. Through the glass doors she could see that the case was empty except for four sets of two boxes each. On the side of the first pair of boxes she read, "U.S. Army Hospital, Tacoma, WA." The second set was likewise addressed, but to Dallas, TX. The third was destined for Atlantic City and the fourth to Fredericksburg.

Here it was at last, the evidence that Celeste was looking for. Her heart, which was already beating pretty fast, went into overdrive. She slid open the door of the refrigerator and easily located the latch for propping it open. It was just a larger version of the refrigerator case in her own laboratory. To get a photographic record, she needed the door open to reduce the glare. Then she opened her briefcase and pulled out the camera. Ever since she had replaced her manual 35mm camera with this automatic model, she felt like she was cheating each time she took a photograph. Her Japanese colleagues called these "idiot" cameras, or the equivalent in Japanese. But she could always count on the photographs being in focus and appropriately illuminated. Now she was grateful for this assurance.

The camera indicated that it would flash when she pressed the shutter button. Fortunately, nobody was in the room. She took a couple of shots, making sure that the

focus window was locked onto the writing on the boxes.
She stepped back to take a third shot, in case the focus was
better from farther away. Just as the flash ignited, the door
to the shipping room opened, and the light was switched
on.

"Hey, what's goin' on here?" said a woman's voice. It
was the shipping clerk, returning for another load of boxes.

Celeste quickly dropped the camera into her briefcase
and clicked it shut. Perhaps the woman hadn't distinguished
the flash from turning on the room lights. Grabbing her
briefcase, Celeste tried to make her way past the piles of
boxes to the shipping platform. She figured she should be
able to get out to the parking lot from there and get to her
car. There were fewer piles of boxes in the way of the clerk
than between Celeste and the platform, so the clerk got to
the platform before Celeste, blocking her escape. Celeste
turned around to go back out the door to the corridor.

"You'll never make it, babe," said the woman. "I've
already buzzed security."

As she spoke, the door from the corridor opened and
Tony from the front desk appeared, holding his gun.

"I thought you was kinda too long in the john." He
walked over to Celeste, pointing the gun at her. When he
reached her, he twisted her arm roughly behind her back
into a half nelson. Celeste was familiar with the gesture as
one her little brother used to practice on her. "Now, you'll
get your appointment with the boss, sweetheart," he said.
His breath smelled of stale cigars.

Celeste's brain raced. Then she started to cough and
wheeze, pretending she was having trouble breathing.
"Asthma," she whispered hoarsely to the guard. "Inhaler.
My purse."

The guard still held on to Celeste's arm with one hand

and clutched the gun with the other. He gestured to the shipping clerk with his head. "Look in her purse," he said gruffly. "See what she's talkin' about." The clerk walked over to Celeste and unzipped the handbag hanging from Celeste's shoulder. Celeste's free hand was clenched around her briefcase.

"See if she's clean, while you're at it," growled the guard.

The plastic dispenser for cromolyn sodium lay on top of the clutter embedded in Celeste's purse.

"This it?" asked the shipping clerk.

Celeste nodded. The clerk handed the dispenser to Celeste. Celeste set down the briefcase and, taking the inhaler, breathed a substantial hit that would have protected her against an army of pet cats. The clerk meanwhile dug around in the bottom of the handbag, while it was still hanging from Celeste's shoulder. Then she unsnapped the briefcase Celeste had set down on the floor. Besides the camera there was only a sealed manila envelope inside. It was too flat and light to contain a firearm. The clerk clicked the briefcase shut, and set it back at Celeste's feet. Then she expertly ran her hands up and down Celeste's body.

"She's clean," said the clerk.

Celeste replaced the cromolyn sodium in her purse. As she bent down to pick up the briefcase, she rolled the combination lock a couple of notches. She didn't want anyone else opening it without her permission.

Back at Celeste's laboratory, Mac had been pacing restlessly all morning.

"Mac, shall we go to get coffee?" asked Kazuko in her office lady mode.

"Good idea, Kaz. Better put your jacket on." In that part

of the city the fog was still swirling until at least noon.

Kazuko and Mac descended to the open-air student union café on Olympus Avenue. A line of at least twenty people snaked around the plastic tables and chairs where the clientele, shivering in white lab coats, were nursing frothy cups of double latte and mocha concoctions. A glance beyond the counter at the head of the line revealed that the café was short-staffed, as usual. They decided to walk down to the Humbuggery Bakery on Washington Street.

Mac and Kazuko were both uneasy about Celeste, but didn't talk about it until they were seated in front of steaming cups of cappuccino in the Humbuggery. Newspapers hanging from wooden holders provided a protective paper curtain around their table, nestled against the wall. Most of the other patrons were writing or reading in solitude.

Mac looked at his watch. It was eleven-thirty. "Her appointment with Phillipson is at twelve. She's probably on the way."

"How far is it?" asked Kazuko.

"I dunno, about thirty minutes from where Celeste lives, and about the same from here."

"I suspect she return about two o'clock, then," said Kazuko.

"Well she might stay and have lunch with him."

"No," said Kazuko abruptly. Mac was taken aback by the vehemence with which she spoke the word. "She would not be that foolish."

Mac was puzzled. "What do you mean?"

"You do not know?"

"Don't think so."

"That man, Phillipson," Kazuko said with loathing. "He murder with toxin. He kill my husband. We have evidence.'' Her hate for Phillipson radiated forcefully from her almond-shaped eyes.

''Jeezus,'' said Mac. ''I was totally clueless when I heard him invite her for lunch.''

''When?''

''She got the phone message last night, before you came home.''

''This is dangerous,'' said Kazuko. ''Celeste must be careful.''

''I knew I shouldn't have let her go alone.'' Mac rose abruptly from the table, leaving his cappuccino untouched. ''I'm going out there right away.''

Kazuko was too astonished to say anything. Did all American men behave like John Wayne? Until now she had assumed it was an exaggerated stereotype.

Mac hurried out of the café and ran the three and a half blocks to where his truck was parked in Golden Gate Park. If he stepped on it, he could be at Virotox before the presumably poisoned lunch was served.

Kazuko had no appetite to finish her drink, either. She slowly climbed back up the hill to wait. There had been too many losses recently. When she returned to the lab, Kazuko put the Federal Express package, with the HPLC data from Phillipson's thesis, in the mail to Toshimi.

TWENTY

Anaphylaxis

The guard arrived at Madeline's office, pushing Celeste ahead of him by leverage of her twisted arm. Madeline buzzed the inner office. "The security breach is here, Dr. Phillipson."

Phillipson emerged from his office. He smiled. "Dr. Braun, you're a bit early for your appointment. I should really make you wait, but under the circumstances, I suppose I can see you now." To the guard he said, "You can let go of her now, Tony. I'm sure I can handle her."

"After you," said Phillipson. He gestured for Celeste to precede him into his office. Inside, he shut the door and stood in front of it. "Please sit down, Celeste. You don't mind if I call you Celeste, do you? We *have* been introduced before."

"Yes, we have," said Celeste.

"Can I offer you a drink, perhaps?" Phillipson continued his overly polite tone.

"No, thanks," said Celeste in the same manner.

"Well, I could use a drink," said Phillipson. "If you'll excuse me for a moment."

He left Celeste sitting in a wooden chair, opposite his desk, while he went into the back room of his office suite. The room still smelled of sex, and the convertible couch was a tumble of sheets and shed clothing. He had quickly ejected Sofia when security called, and evidently she was now walking around the labs missing her undergarments. Phillipson opened the small refrigerator by the door to his private lab and poured himself a glass of mineral water. From the top of the refrigerator he picked up one of the syringes that Sofia had left behind. He attached a needle and filled the syringe from an unlabeled amber-colored test tube, stoppered with a rubber gasket that was easily pierced by the needle. Then he replaced the cap on the needle and slipped the loaded syringe into the pen pocket inside his tweed jacket. He'd need this alternative if Celeste continued to refuse refreshment.

Phillipson returned to his outer office, carrying a glass of mineral water, and sat behind his desk. "Now suppose you tell me what you're doing poking around in my shipping room. Is that what Fukuda sent you for?" he said to Celeste.

"They sent me to tell you about a problem with Bazuran that I discovered."

"It's a little late for that now; they've already signed the contract for the rights to Bazuran. Now, you haven't answered my question."

Celeste tried to quell her rising panic. It threatened her ability to think clearly and Phillipson didn't give the impression that he was going to be patient. She needed to sidetrack him onto the scientific issue, away from the break-in. "If there's a major problem with whether the drug will actually work, which there seems to be, then Fukuda could take legal action,'' she said, trying to bait him.

"Oh, it'll work, all right. Stanley's theory is totally passé. In fact, she didn't even see the data disqualifying it, when they were right under her nose."

"You mean Harry Freeman's data?"

"That's right," said Phillipson.

"You mean the mutant strain he characterized and you stole from him?" In spite of her mounting fear, Celeste was irritated by Phillipson's condescension.

"Can I help it if he lost the mutant strain and let it overgrow with wild-type?" Phillipson said smoothly.

"Well, you might succeed in rewriting the history of Bazuran, but you can't do anything about its allergenic properties."

"Please, madam, explain yourself." Phillipson's formality was getting colder.

Celeste took a deep breath, as if starting a lecture. She was a hell of a lot more nervous than she'd ever been on the podium. "I don't suppose you know about G2a, the major grass allergen. Well, Bazuran and all derivatives from related plants are contaminated with a G2a-like protein. Anyone with grass allergies will react to these compounds—in fact, not be able to tolerate them, even at subtoxic doses. Furthermore, inhalation of Bazuran will stimulate an allergic response in those who are not allergic in the first place. Respiratory intake is widely accepted to be a major route for triggering allergies."

Phillipson realized immediately that she was right. Here was the explanation for his own increasing allergies. But this wasn't an irrevocable problem. "Very clever, Dr. Braun. You may be right. But so what? It should only be a matter of weeks before we can figure out a method for

further purification and removal of the contaminating allergen.''

"No," said Celeste. "The allergic response is exquisitely
sensitive. You'll never be able to purify the toxin sufficiently.''

Phillipson was at a loss for only a few seconds. He
needed to find out if Celeste suspected his plans for release
of the mutant virus. She was too damned smart for her own
good. "Fukuda wasn't planning to market Bazuran anyway," said Phillipson. "They just bought the rights as a
safety measure, once I showed them that Eke virus could
become resistant to Protex. They would never actually have
to produce the drug, so it doesn't matter whether it will
work.''

"An accidental, on-purpose release of the mutant might
have been an appealing strategy to make them and you a
lot of money," said Celeste, taking a foolish gamble. "Appealing, of course, if you didn't know that Bazuran was
useless.''

The bloody bitch. She must have been searching for
proof of her suspicions in the shipping room. But if she
was searching, then she didn't actually have proof, meaning
there was still a chance for damage control. With everything so perfectly in place, there was no way Phillipson
was going to halt the trials now. It would take months and
millions of dollars before Fukuda realized that Bazuran
didn't work. Phillipson could then claim the problem was
due to a defect in their production. It would be pretty easy
to fabricate some better-looking HPLC data from the Virotox batches of Bazuran, to use as evidence of Fukuda's
incompetence. Easy as long as Celeste wasn't around to
advise them.

She had provoked him long enough.

Phillipson walked around to the front of his desk where Celeste was sitting, pulled the syringe out of his pocket, and uncapped the needle.

Celeste's blood froze. Mac had been right.

"Bazuran may be useless as a drug when inhaled at sub-toxic doses," said Phillipson. "But it's still a lethal toxin if injected at high concentration into the blood. The beauty of your death by Bazuran is that no one will know you didn't have an unfortunate accident visiting the Virotox production facility. I'd like you to open your briefcase now and hand over the camera."

Celeste needed a second to think how she was going to make the right moves. She was no longer frightened. She was enraged. She picked up the briefcase and placed it on her lap, glaring at Phillipson with the defiant look she gave offensive challengers at a scientific conference.

"Don't be so incensed, my dear. Security warned me about the camera before they brought you upstairs," said Phillipson.

Celeste fumbled with the combination lock. The needle was getting awfully close.

Suddenly the door to Phillipson's office flew open. Mac stood on the threshold, brandishing a gun. In his blue jeans, flannel shirt, and corduroy jacket he looked like a cowboy who had lost his hat.

'Steady, partner," said Phillipson calmly. "You wouldn't want to be responsible for the death of a famous scientist, would you? I suggest you drop the gun."

Mac stared open-mouthed. *He* was supposed to be doing the threatening. He lowered the gun.

"That's right," said Phillipson, as though he were talking to a child. "Now place it over there, on my desk."

The extra few seconds were all Celeste needed. The

briefcase on her lap clicked open. She tore into the manila envelope and grabbed a handful of the grass she had picked in Golden Gate Park that morning. She ground the green wad into Phillipson's face.

Instantaneously he started to sneeze. The syringe moved wildly with his spasm and flew out of his hand. Celeste pushed the briefcase from her lap and rolled off the chair onto the floor to get out of the way.

Mac picked up the gun from Phillipson's desk and pointed it at the wheezing Phillipson, who had collapsed onto the chair vacated by Celeste. Then, keeping the gun trained on Phillipson, Mac went over to Celeste and helped her up from the floor.

"We've got to stop the shipments," said Celeste. "Call that secretary in here."

Mac backed up toward the office door and stood in view of the secretary he had intimidated a few moments before. Madeline could see he was pointing his gun into the interior of the office and rightly assumed it was aimed at Phillipson.

"Ma'am," said Mac, "Dr. Phillipson needs your help. Please come in here."

Madeline obliged. A strange scene confronted her. Phillipson was sprawled in the wooden chair he usually reserved for visitors. He looked extremely pale and was breathing too hard to speak. Once in a while Madeline had seen him like that when he returned from jogging. Usually he headed straight for the asthma inhaler in his desk. Dr. Braun was bending toward the carpet in front of Dr. Phillipson. She picked up a camera off the floor, put it in an open briefcase that was also lying on the carpet, and shut the case. Then she stood up, picked up the case, and turned to address Madeline.

"Call the shipping department downstairs and tell them

that Dr. Phillipson wants to cancel the pickup for the outgoing shipment to the U.S. army hospitals,'' instructed Celeste. ''I'll be taking it back to my laboratory for testing, in Mr. Macmillan's truck.'' She gestured toward Mac. ''He'll pick it up at the dock. The truck has his name on the side.''

''Yes, certainly,'' said Madeline. She walked over to Phillipson's desk, never taking her eyes off Mac and the gun. She picked up the receiver and pressed zero. ''Get me the shipping department, please.'' She stood silent for a few moments. ''This is Madeline Trotter here, calling from Dr. Phillipson's office. I've been asked to cancel the shipment to the army hospitals. Dr. Braun will be taking it back to BAU instead. You have permission to load it into Macmillan's truck.'' She paused, listening to the response on the other end, then replied, ''Yes, that's right, Macmillan. That will be all for now, thank you.'' Madeline hung up before any further questions could be asked.

Well done, Madeline, thought Celeste. A perfect secretary gets all the details right.

''Now, we'd like an escort out of the building to avoid any further trouble with security,'' said Celeste to Madeline.

''What about Dr. Phillipson?'' asked Madeline. ''Shouldn't we call an ambulance?'' Phillipson was still audibly hyperventilating and appeared incapable of moving, even if a gun hadn't been trained on him.

''He'll be okay,'' said Celeste. ''He's had a severe allergic reaction, but his breathing should stabilize in about twenty minutes. He should be able to move in about thirty minutes, without any need for medical attention. Meanwhile, he's sufficiently out of it that we needn't worry about his further interference.'' She turned to Mac. ''You two walk ahead of me, and keep the gun discreet.'' She hustled Mac and Madeline ahead of her, out of the office.

Celeste glanced back triumphantly at the gasping Phillipson as she pulled the door shut behind her.

As soon as he heard the door to the outer office click, Phillipson raised himself gingerly from the slouch he had collapsed into. He was so loaded with antihistamine that he was recovering more rapidly than Celeste had predicted, though it was still incredibly difficult to breathe. If he could just get over to his desk, he could get a hit from his asthma inhaler and the constrictions would relax. Then he could call Tony before that interfering bitch managed to take off with all his ''vaccine.'' Well, even if she did, he still had another batch of virus to be harvested this afternoon. It would only delay things by a few days.

Phillipson had to catch his breath again, just from the exertion of sitting up. Then slowly he rose and made his way over to the desk, resting and breathing hard after every step. His nasal passages were completely stopped up and he felt as though a heavy weight lay on his chest, so his lungs couldn't expand. By the time he reached the desk, he was dizzy and light-headed. He eased the top drawer open and fell back into the soft, upholstered desk chair. He rested for a minute with his eyes closed, while his hand felt around in the open drawer for the asthma inhaler. Ah, he felt the familiar shape of relief. Raising the inhaler to his mouth, he spritzed twice and inhaled deeply. Seconds later, a shuddering spasm closed off his throat and he began to choke violently. As he fought the inevitable losing battle for air, the inhaler dropped to the floor and lay on its side, exposing the Virotox logo. He realized it was not steroids that he had just snorted, but a double hit of the subtoxic dose of Bazuran meant to cure Eke virus. Subtoxic, as Celeste had just explained, only for those with no previous allergies to grass.

Smiling a smile of frozen courtesy, Madeline ushered her visitors past Tony and out the front door of the Virotox building. Tony, who privately thought she was a stuck-up hag, saw nothing unusual in her expression. Nor was he surprised when she rushed past him without saying anything on her way back upstairs. She rarely had the time of day for him. But he knew the boss appreciated her skills as much as his, so he tolerated her snobbism for Phillipson's sake. He assumed that Phillipson must have set the two visitors straight, or they wouldn't have had the royal escort treatment.

During the seemingly endless descent from the executive suite, Madeline had debated her subsequent course of action. She knew Dr. Braun should be stopped, but she was also worried about Phillipson. She didn't trust that woman's judgment. She decided she first needed to get Phillipson's inhaler to him. Then they could call the police to stop Macmillan's truck, leaving with the shipment.

Madeline knew exactly where the inhaler was. When she opened the door to the inner office and saw the top drawer of the desk sticking out toward the desk chair, she was overwhelmed by relief. Phillipson had moved into his proper seat behind the desk and had his back to her.

Madeline entered the room, saying, "Well, Dr. Phillipson, shall I call the police, or have you already done so?" He didn't answer. Then she saw the body in the chair. The face was violet and the eyes protruded from their sockets, as though he were performing a mime of being strangled. His hands were covered with blood. They were apparently cut while scrabbling at the metal edges of the desk drawer, which were also covered with blood. His chest was not moving. Madeline picked up the receiver and dialed 911.

Six hours later, Celeste was driving the MGB, fast, down Route 1 heading south. Mac was in the passenger seat, and the heater was on full blast. Their bodies felt cozy and their faces tingled from the sharp breeze. At every curve of the road, the Pacific Ocean stretched in front of them, punctuated by stone pillars and arches that glowed rustily in the setting sun. The coast was usually blanketed in fog this late in June, but this evening was one of those rare occasions when a west wind blows in to remind San Franciscans that Earth is not the only planet in the universe.

It had been Mac's suggestion to drive down the coast. They had done everything necessary to tie up the loose ends of their lunchtime adventure and were still high on adrenaline. The virus shipment was safely locked up in the strictest, Level 4, biohazard facility on the BAU campus. Kazuko was in there, busily inoculating cell cultures to obtain the final proof that the vials of putative vaccine contained live, mutant virus. While Mac took the film from Celeste's camera to the one-hour processing studio and waited for prints, Celeste had phoned Harry. She provided the few final details he needed to finish off the exposé of General Johnson. When Mac returned from the photo shop, they sent off a set of prints to Harry by Federal Express. The gesture was anticlimactic, and they continued to burn with energy.

Moving south, Route 1 straightened out into long, smooth curves, rising to the top of the coastal cliffs and then plunging down to sea level. At the bottom of each descent, the breeze from the ocean projected a sharp, kelpy smell inland. Dramatic rock formations gave way to crescent-shaped beaches nestled into protective cliffs and then to cultivated fields sloping gently toward the sea. This agricultural segment reminded Celeste of the pastures atop the cliffs on the southern coast of England. She was soothed and calmed by this thought and by the now crepuscular purple of the sky.

Both Celeste and Mac were wearing sunglasses that reflected the view in front of them, so neither could tell what the other was thinking. They hadn't spoken since leaving the last traffic light in Half Moon Bay. Both were mesmerized by the view, the wind, and the aftermath of their ordeal together. Celeste broke the silence.

"What made you follow me to Virotox, anyway?"

"Kazuko gave me the scoop on Phillipson. About him poisoning her husband. After I heard that, there was no way I was gonna let you deal with that bastard unarmed."

"Well, luckily I *was* armed, thanks to you."

Mac grinned and shook his head. He still couldn't believe she considered a handful of grass an adequate weapon. But he had to admit, the woman knew enough science to be sure it would be.

"Damn smart cookie," was all he said.

"How'd you get upstairs, past that thug of a security guard? I'm sure he would have enjoyed a shoot-out."

"I only wave guns at people weaker than myself. Anyway, it wasn't loaded. I haven't had ammunition since I went civilian."

It was Celeste's turn for admiration.

Mac continued, "I just gave the guard my nursery card and told him I had an indoor plant scheme we were selling. I said it was a special deal that was for consideration by the CEO only. Luckily, Phillipson's secretary agreed to talk to me about it. I didn't take out the gun until I got to her office. You know the rest.''

Celeste was distracted for a few minutes, following the signs directing the car past Santa Cruz and onto the next stretch of coastal road.

''Where are we headed, anyway?'' she asked.

''Well, I haven't been down here since I was a kid. We used to swim at the town beach in Portofino. My parents liked it 'cause there was a bar they used to dance at. Mo's or Larry's or something like that. My sister and I used to fall asleep in the car after pigging out on fish fry. They would have a few dances and then drive us back to the peninsula.''

''I guess that's history. No one would leave two sleeping kids alone in a parking lot these days,'' remarked Celeste, as they passed a sign for the Portofino exit in two miles. ''Well, shall we check it out? Suddenly I'm starving.'' Celeste realized she hadn't eaten since breakfast, and the thought of a fish dinner got her stomach interested.

The exit ramp for Portofino delivered them into a typical California housing tract of asphalt and dusty bougainvillea, not exactly the pleasant seaside town Celeste had been expecting. The car climbed steadily upward through this uninspiring neighborhood, and at the top of the hill bumped over a set of railroad tracks, causing the nose of the MGB to point abruptly down toward sea. Before them lay Portofino Bay, glassy and serene, interrupted only by a rickety wooden pier extending out from the semicircle of the town beach. On either side of them now, as they descended toward the bay, were white stucco buildings with irregular tiled roofs. A profusion of colorful flowers burst aromatically over the walls of enclosed gardens. Crossing the tracks had transported Mac and Celeste into the past.

At the bottom of the hill they turned right onto Main Street. It looked exactly as Mac remembered, except the Spanish-style buildings now housed galleries and New Age boutiques instead of tackle stores and surf shops. On autopilot, he directed Celeste onto the street that led to the pier. There was still a restaurant on the side of the hill with a view overlooking the bay.

Over a meal of fragrant calamari, washed down with Sauvignon blanc, they watched the moon rise over the water, and a tremendous calm enveloped them both. By the time they finished dinner and walked down the hill to be drawn into The Fog Bank by a plaintive saxophone, Mac and Celeste felt they were playing out a script.

The striped awning outside The Fog Bank was new and flashy. Inside it was still the Larry's Bar of old. There was a framed black-and-white photograph of Larry and the band at the entrance, but Mac didn't need to see it to recognize the place. The same chrome stools covered in red leather stretched along the familiar mirror-backed bar. Off to the side was a raised disc jockey's platform formed from red, yellow, and blue molded plastic. This structure had fascinated Mac as a child and was not easily forgotten.

The disc jockey's platform was in the dark tonight, in deference to the five-man band that had inherited the mantle from Larry, complete with red jackets and pompadour hairstyles. They were playing serious jazz, and the crowd was there to hear them. In some establishments, Celeste and Mac might have felt out of place, she in her professional consultant's outfit and he resembling the Marlboro man. But here, tattooed surfers in long Bermuda shorts danced by themselves, and a group of women in aerobic gear were dancing with each other. They were mingling with couples in their fifties and sixties, who had danced to this music all their lives. They all joked with the razor-shorn chubby Chicana who was tending bar. Anyone who was enjoying the jazz was welcomed, and it was impossible not to get caught up in that timeless mood.

Mac drew Celeste out onto the dance floor. His mother had taught him to dance to this music, and he directed Celeste with a light touch at the small of her back. At junior-high dancing lessons, Celeste had never learned jazz steps, but she relaxed into him and was swept away. The band played "Stardust," then "As Time Goes By," and Mac led Celeste through the music.

The moon was high in the black sky when the band quit for the evening. Its reflection in the ocean was joined by the light from a green-and-yellow neon palm tree flashing next to the blue letters of the Beachcomber Motel. Celeste and Mac stood on the beach for a few minutes, watching the waves break. In red letters, below the palm tree, the Beachcomber Motel claimed vacancy. It was clearly too late to drive back to San Francisco.

Celeste and Debbie were savoring their last afternoon at the Millstone Wildlife Refuge in the Bitterroot Valley, winding up a long weekend of blissful relaxation. Celeste had been in a vulnerable mood, the day after Mac left San Francisco for graduate school, when Debbie had phoned out of the blue with her invitation to Montana. Debbie had made all the arrangements, including complimentary airline tickets, and then been stood up at the last minute by her latest excuse for a boyfriend. Celeste was grateful for the chance to get away from the prospect of missing Mac too much. She blushed pleasurably every time she thought of their last week together, in and out of bed. At least there was the promise of seeing him during her next trip to Washington for the study section meeting. Mac had enrolled in the Ph.D. program at the National Institutes of Health in Bethesda, since Martha and Julia were posted to Walter Reed Hospital when the vaccine trials were canceled.

Debbie wanted to do some more catching up on her chronic sleep deficit. So Celeste put on her bathing suit under her shorts, grabbed her backpack and set off on a bicycle for a solitary trip to the swimming hole. It was about a mile from their lodgings, where the Bitterroot River ran through the northern part of the refuge. The unpaved road up to the northern property paralleled the river valley and carried Celeste through shorn fields, with freshly mown hay baled into enormous green rolls. To the left were the jagged Bitterroot Mountains on the Idaho border, and to the right the smooth Sapphire Mountains created a gentler horizon.

Celeste stowed her bicycle at the northern property gate and set off on foot for the river's edge. The track was deeply rutted, overgrown with weeds, and lined with huge, velvet-topped bulrushes. In two places, the track was submerged under irrigation ditches, bordered by blue forget-me-nots. Celeste particularly liked wading through these submerged sections in her sneakers. Just before reaching the river, Celeste went through a second gate, which she considered the gate to her personal heaven.

A few days earlier, when Celeste first saw the Bitterroot, she was smitten. From her childhood she was familiar with the freshwater lakes of New England and the Atlantic Ocean. But she was introduced to the Western River as an adult, and it struck a deeper chord. It was cold and swift and chose its own direction, throwing up random piles of whitish rocks along the banks and making islands in the middle.

The islands were the territory of the persnickety killdeer. These decorated birds, with their neat black-and-white collars, always objected when Celeste took a dip in the swimming hole. Afloat, Celeste couldn't reach the bottom, and although it was only about ten feet square, she could swim for a long time, by facing the current. There was something magical about swimming hard and remaining in the same place.

After swimming, Celeste clambered up the smooth, round rocks at the pool's edge, feeling just for a moment that her feet would never take hold. She sat down on the bank to dry off in the sun, breathing hard from her exertions and from the cold temperature of the water. From her pack, she withdrew the scientific journal she had intended to read all weekend. Here in the Bitterroot sunshine, she could think positively about the world to which she was returning. She was going back refreshed and ready.

She turned to the news section and began to read.

The National Institutes of Health announced this week that the directorship, which has been vacant since E. Howard Farmer, M.D., returned to Chicago last year, has been filled. Jane Stanley, M.D., recently retired from the Dept. of Microbiology at Harvard University, has accepted the position. Dr. Stanley was the top-choice candidate for the vacancy a year ago but had withdrawn her name when she was accused of mismanagement of biotechnology funds by the Committee on Scientific Integrity. The accusation was subsequently found to be fraudulent. Senator Teresita Jiminez of Massachusetts, who spearheaded the investigation of Dr. Stanley, is expected to lose her seat to her Democratic challenger, Hannah Rennick, in the fall elections.

A sharp splash in the pool startled Celeste from her reading. She looked up to see ripples spreading from where a trout had snapped a grasshopper, then turned her attention back to the journal.

The indictment of General Ralph O. Johnson III for criminal abuse of military programs was made public by the Pentagon earlier this week. The court-martial is scheduled for next month. The indictment followed substantiation of an article in the *New York Times* alleging the general's involvement in a scheme to use military vaccination trials to release a strain of mutant Eke virus that is resistant to the commonly used drug Protex. The scheme was perpetrated by the late Dr. Simon Phillipson, CEO of Virotox, Inc., who planned to market an alternate therapy against the mutant virus. The incident was uncovered by Dr. Celeste Braun of Bay Area University and revealed through investigative reporting by the *New York Times* science editor, Dr. Harry Freeman, who has been nominated for a Pulitzer Prize.

The dark shadow of a circling osprey fell across the page. Without looking up, Celeste could tell its identity by the raucous cry of its offspring waiting for food in the scraggly nest high above the pool. She continued reading.

Dr. Toshimi Matsumoto, the vice president for research of Fukuda Pharmaceuticals Ltd., announced last week in Osaka that Japanese authorities have concluded that the two Fukuda employees who died last month were murdered. The victims were Dr. Minoru Yamaguchi, director, and Dr. Akira Hagai, virology laboratory chief, of the Biotechnology Division of Fukuda Pharmaceuticals Ltd. in Sapporo. Dr. Matsumoto also announced that the Sapporo Division directorship will be filled by Dr. Kazuko Hagai, the widow of one of the murder victims. In accepting this appointment, Dr. Hagai will become the highest-ranking woman in the Japanese biotechnology industry.

Celeste was now completely dried off by the sun, and closed the journal issue with a warm sense of accomplishment. She was overwhelmed by a feeling of resolution that was very close to the thrill of suddenly seeing the significance of a set of data from an experiment in the lab. Good science was good science, and its application had good consequences. Celeste stood up on the rocky beach and stretched in satisfaction. Then she folded her towel and bent down to return it to the backpack for the cycle back to the refuge. She tucked the journal next to it, and something on the cover caught her eye. She hadn't noticed it before, but her secretary had stamped the issue with the stamp the students had given Celeste for her birthday in November. Dr. Celeste Braun, P.I., was emblazoned across the top in purple ink. Celeste smiled at the double entendre.